STAY FREE

By John Hilla

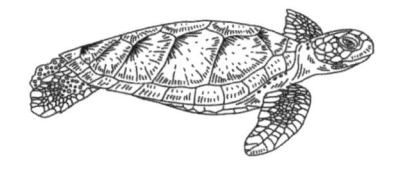

MersinBeat

Copyright © 2021 John Hilla

All Rights Reserved

The characters and events portrayed in this book are fictitious. Any similarity to real persons, living or dead, is coincidental and not intended by the author.

No part of this book may be reproduced, or stored in a retrieval system, or transmitted in any form or by any means, electronic, mechanical, photocopying, recording, or otherwise, without express written permission of the publisher.

first american edition

ISBN-13: 978-0-578-85311-6

MersinBeat
19500 Middlebelt No. 223E
Livonia, MI 48152
mersinbeat.com

Printed in the United States of America

For Mom.

For Tony.

For Arya.

"... in the absence of an outer life, incidents are created by the inner life, too."

- MARCEL PROUST

1.

They say your life flashes before your eyes at the moment of death, but, in my case, it happened regularly, no moment of death required. Only, the life that flashed before me was not my own. It was the life of an obscure Russian revolutionary named Aleksandr Anosov who had, as far as anyone knew, died in an uprising against the Bolsheviks in 1922.

As before, it happened one morning in August while I was edging my front lawn in a hurry before the afternoon heat would make the job impossible. I trimmed the left side of the walkway up to my porch, and the facts of Anosov's life reeled past me like film footage. It felt wrong that these were not the facts of my own life. It felt wrong to me that lawn-edging was my life. Anosov's biography rolled through my mind in a newsreel tone slightly more vibrant than sepia, and that old data, buried deep within in me since childhood, was more real to me than the drying brown grass that my humming blade spat across the concrete.

I had inhaled Anosov's story since the age of

twelve, reading one of my mother's old college history course texts, and had exhaled them since: Anosov's mother thrusting him into the midwife's arms, peering up over her distended belly, her breath dying on her lips, as she glimpsed her son for the first and last time. Anosov growing hard under the rule of his widowed father, an illiterate ex-monk, who believed scholarship and labor secondary to obeisance to God's will—and his own. Anosov struggling against his father's wish to place him into a monastery, his escape, his flight across Russia to the tutoring position in Petrograd and the arms of Lyudmila, the woman who would introduce him to Trotsky. That fatal handshake! The lectures to the tradesmen! The encounter with Rasputin! The midnight ride to Moscow to retrieve Lyudmila from prison. The Revolution ... His disenchantment with the Bolsheviks ... The uprising in Tambov province, and his final, fruitless attempt to escape. Abandoned by Lyudmila, forgotten by everyone ... The cell in the dark reaches of the building that would become Lubyanka Prison under Stalin, and the firing squad.

 I saw it all, and I remembered how Anosov's story had so affected me in my youth. We were connected, I liked to think, our histories intertwined through the past forty years of my life. It all came flooding back: youth, misery, deception, history, listlessness, friendship, love, ambition, desolation. That was the sum of it. The sum of me. And Anosov. But there was nothing that could be said about me that wasn't better framed in terms of the life of Aleksandr Anosov.

 There was no mistaking me for a Russian revolutionary. Unemployed for nearly three years, I edged and mowed and raked the lawn or heaved snow from untraveled sidewalks and kept the house as dust-free as human habitation could allow while Karen, my wife, managed the expenses from her more-than-full-time gig with one of the larger law firms in Detroit. I no longer had any idea where the battlefield lay. Anosov's example had not encouraged me to any martial action in quite a long time.

For reasons unknown, this knowledge chafed in my pocket like a walnut shell that morning.

It could have been the heat. The humidity of August in the historical swampland of southeastern Michigan often sank me in muddy minefields of thought.

When I was finished with the lawn, that day, my forehead beading, on my way indoors for the balance of the day, I squeaked open the mailbox beside the front door to check for the previous day's mail. Or the previous week's, who could say? I slipped my hand inside and plucked out a single postcard that I presumed, upon first contact, to be a dentist's advertisement or one of the regularly hand-delivered realtor pleas for a quick phone-call to discuss the rising value of our oversized home that received from local realtors from time to time.

Instead, it was a lurid picture postcard sporting, on one side, a color photo of a mouth-wide-open, shouting punk rocker guy in leather motorcycle jacket, red flannel shirt tied around his waist, and twenty-four inch green mohawk haircut aiming a British flip-off—two fingers up—at the camera. Red block letters overlaying the photo read, "If Punk's Dead, Then Why Am I Still Alive?" The other side of the card was blank: no message, no return address.

Funny that a postcard would echo the very thought I'd only just entertained I the throes of lawn maintenance.

Of course, it was from Hugo, my oldest friend, who would, wherever he was, not fail to divine that, on a certain August morning, I would require a good slap in the face. No return address or signature was necessary.

A message would have been nice, though.

It had been how long now? His last visit had been sometime after my lay-off from the Troy Public Library, and he had entertained my kvetching about the ugliness of local millage votes and inadequate city services funding for exactly nine minutes before dragging me downtown to see some random band play at The Old Miami. Awful band, good night. Just what I had needed in the moment, though, as I recalled, Karen had wanted to talk me into some part-time job as a law librarian at her firm when he'd banged on the door, spoiling the conversational moment. Hugo's presence never thrilled her.

Had it been two years, really? Yes, and where had he been?

I was no revolutionary, maybe, but Hugo was, sort of. Or an itinerant bum, I wasn't totally clear on the distinction.

At an earlier stage, I'd been on one side of the line with him, or I at least liked to think so. As a kid, I perpetually thought of myself as a thorn in the side of *somebody*, even if I couldn't always identify the body. Maybe I was some level of revolutionary in that I bothered to think about politics at all during the reign of Ronald Reagan, when Citibank and Walt Disney were busy constructing the inescapable marketing and propaganda engines that had kids captured from birth nowadays.

Probably I thought that just because I listened to punk rock and glowered a lot in the hallway at school. I spiked my hair (Hugo used industrial glue in his!) and wore Sex Pistols t-shirts and wraparound shades from the Incognito store in Royal Oak and presumed that to be a form of action. I complained a lot. About everything. All the time. Once in a while, I mouthed off to a teacher and landed myself in detention after school.

Hardly Anosov-level stuff.

The complaining that Hugo and I did over our bologna sandwiches and foil-wrapped pizza in the school cafeteria about Reagan, shitty pop music, jocks we hated, and the general state of things was revolutionary to us. At that time, little words made a big difference, and clothing really did say nearly everything that there was to say about a person in high-school. Uniforms may not have been mandatory in our school, but there were uniforms up and down the hallways of the place regardless. The football players had their jerseys; Hugo and I had our t-shirts, leather jackets and trench-coats, and boots; the kids who just wanted to get by and move on to college slinked around in neatly tucked button-down shirts and navy blue khakis.

Any real difference in the way that Hugo and I lived our lives from other teenagers of the time—watching television, eating potato chips, stealing beers from somebody or other's parents, seeing concerts, mooning over girls, worrying about acne, swearing over bad die-rolls during games of *Risk*—was immaterial. To us.

These days, there were few parallels between myself at that age and myself at forty. For Hugo, it was a different story. There were easy parallels there, and I relied still on him to remind me that we had had something at that time that did draw some sort of meandering dotted line between the two of us and likes of Aleksandr Anosov. I needed Hugo for that, whether I actually saw him every two days or every two years. He was my totem, the spirit of something that I wafted past at some point without noticing.

Still, revolutions have been waged by seventeen year-olds. Anosov couldn't have been much older than that in 1917, after all. Those upraised two fingers on Hugo's postcard still said something, Hugo had picked out that postcard for that reason. I knew, and, wherever he was, he knew it. Times change, true, and kids age out of putting glue into their hair, but, once in a while, it was useful to be reminded that things don't need to change quite as much as they might.

I folded the postcard into the pocket of my cargo shorts and retreated inside into the air-conditioning, in search of lemonade, which Aleksandr Anosov would surely also have enjoyed.

2.

The next morning, I stared at my wife Karen in bed beside me before her cell phone alarm propelled her into her daily flurry. She was sound asleep, her back to me, her hips and legs raising the sheet like a snow-bank, her brunette hair—finally graying here and there—spilling across the linen. Her breathing was rough, a semi-snore, like the jagged sound of a lumberjack at work some distance away. She even slept at a distance from me these days. If I stretched my arm out full-length, I would be able to shake her awake—but that was it. I considered rolling closer to lay my hand on her hip but decided that I had better not. Her irritated "What??" hung in the air over me night and day as it was. Karen was not a cuddler; she was more like a barricade. There was nothing to do when I awoke before her alarm except to lay back and stare at the hanging light fixture and attic crawl-space hatch over my head.

When the alarm finally did ring, it felt like an hour had passed. She struggled out of bed without turning or greeting me, her slip riding up past her broadening thigh as she stood to reveal the elastic waist-band of the sort of white, baggy panties she tended to wear when she was having her period. I had no idea whether this was the case or not, however. It was something to add to the list of things I no longer needed to be informed of on a daily or weekly or even monthly basis. She scratched at her freckled shoulder and then hobbled out into the hallway, toward the bathroom. Her backside swayed a bit more than it once had under new weight that I had not noticed before, but, before I could consider whether it was a turn-on or a turn-off, she was out of sight, running water behind closed doors.

  Post-shower, Karen was more animated over her plate of honeyed toast, catching me up on the latest at her office. The small television on the kitchen counter near the toaster and electric tea kettle relayed the latest criminal misdeeds, local weather and traffic, and prospects for the evening's Tigers game behind us, the usual backdrop to our conversations.

  Forty had been good to Karen, for the most part.

  When we sat together, like this, chewing over the daily grind, I could lean back and appreciate that my wife was aging better than I was. A little less definition to her jaw-line and collar-bones, maybe, but her skin wasn't wrinkled parchment like so many in our age-group, at least to the extent that I ever interacted with anyone else any longer and could compare. She didn't look forty. She didn't look twenty anymore, either, but, particularly in comparison with the other female lawyers in her firm, some younger than Karen, there was no question that she was aging well. Her hazel eyes still popped against her dark hair, and her lips still pursed when she was speaking with intensity, as she now was. I had always loved that.

The furrowed brow and the pursed lips and the passionate diatribes. The centers of Karen's gravity where I was concerned, the reason she'd drawn me into her magnetosphere in college without even meaning to. The reason I'd tossed my leather motorcycle jacket into a box and forgotten about it.

As for me, my gut strained the wherewithal of my sweatpants, and the effort of buttering the toast had winded me. God only knew what Karen saw when she looked at me.

"Beth just keeps asking me to do more and more," Karen said, slicing her toast diagonally. "She's taking her sick-leave for at least three months, and I'm just supposed to pick up all of the slack, just because everyone else in the department has been laid off."

"Fired," I said.

"Whatever. They pare our practice area down to nothing but try to hang onto the clients. They won't let me hire an associate or two to do the grunt-work. God knows there are plenty of law students milling around needing jobs."

"Are there?"

"Thousands. The ABA keep accrediting new law schools and churning out new graduates. I have a job for one of them, at least, if Jim and Angus would loosen the purse strings."

"If they aimed to do that, they wouldn't have laid everyone else off to begin with, right?"

"Too true."

"So quit," I shrugged, already knowing the response.

"Get a job, and I'll think about it," she said, not raising her eyes to look at me. She bit into her toast and leaned back on her chair, looking over her shoulder at the television.

That was the response. It wasn't incorrect, but it was the usual termination point of any conversation that meandered toward money or career. Most of them did end up in one of those two places at some point—but this wasn't unique to Karen. I had come to realize that lawyers always ended up talking about one of those two things. I'd ended up in the company of enough lawyers following her through her career path to realize that very few of them actually liked their jobs, though almost none of them would ever admit that. Or stop doing them. Far fewer of them earned a great deal of money than was commonly believed, furthermore. Karen loved to use the example of one of her clients who shoveled snow for a living who earned more money than she did.

"If I had to do it all over again," she enjoyed saying, pretending to be joking, "I would become a plumber."

That didn't stop her from bringing up my employment status every five minutes, however.

Further, no one who knew her could see her standing hip-deep in a septic tank. Still, she was the sort of person who would not have considered becoming a plumber, not really, not ever. She was the sort of person who became a lawyer. When I had first met her, she had been an English major who claimed to harbor an ambition of teaching German literature at the college level. It had been years, now, since she'd last mentioned Günter Grass or Heinrich Boll.

She ate her toast, and I listened to the weather. Hot and dry again, meaning I'd have to turn on the sprinkler and water the lawn, lest it brown further. I hated wasting water, as it seemed obvious to me that we were, as a planet, running out of this fairly valuable commodity pretty quickly. When I ran the sprinkler, I tended to sit on the front porch and watch it scatter this precious recourse all over the place, thinking of those residents of remote villages in Africa who had to walk for miles with clay jugs on their heads to retrieve just enough potable water for the day's use from well. How could I care whether a decorative lawn that served no purpose turned brown or not thinking of such things? I did not, but it was a fact that Karen did.

"I don't want to have the worst lawn on the block," she insisted, standing her ground, when I brought the nonsensicality of this practice up.

Who was she competing with? Nobody cared. Not one of our neighbors had ever complained when we let the lawn grow or when it dried up in the summers. Their lawns did, too. That was summer for you. That was nature.

After she'd left for work, apparently not to return until much later at night due to the increased workload, I watered the lawn anyway, predicting the response if I did not with some practiced level of accuracy and not wanting to hear it—later, much later, or ever.

It did me no good.

She arrived home from work later that evening already irritated with me and ate leftovers alone at the kitchen table even though I'd set her a place in the dining room. Afterward, she went straight to bed, leaving me the dishes to tidy up.

The next morning, it was more of the same, and then off to another extended work-day, followed by a repeat dining style with only a few cursory words. I asked her what the matter was, and she only smiled as if I ought to know better than to ask.

For the next few days, this seemed to be the new arrangement between us, and I acclimated myself to it as best I could. Silence filled the house and blanketed the furniture, covering the books on the shelves that had passed from my hand to hers, the vase on the windowsill given to us by her Uncle Bill, the framed photograph of Millie, our first and only cat—now deceased—on the wall. All of the things that surrounded me all day long, the things she was able to avoid and ignore by escaping this house she had wanted so badly to buy for the better part of her waking day, struck me as carefully arranged relics of what we'd been like together at the time we'd obtained each and every one of those objects. Each of them reminded me of how much I missed her, by which I meant that girl I'd met in college. I missed her the way a paleontologist misses the presence of extinct animals.

I didn't bother fighting it, feeling the hand of fate and time in it all. I imagined myself as an ashen silhouette excavated from the ruins of Pompeii, struck suddenly, unable to react, mineralized in a single moment that had long since passed. I wafted rather than walked around my house, the way I had in high-school, before I met Hugo, when I didn't particularly feel a part of anything going on around me. As I had in every high-school class except for history, I stared out of the windows, squinting into the sun outside. Nothing was any more significant than Karen and I allowed it to be, but I lent that silence she was carrying around the greatest importance. I hoped Karen was suffering as I was, but she wasn't around the house enough in those weeks for me to take a guess at it.

I couldn't help but think, again, of Anosov, rotting away in his cellar prison before his execution. Not that I had any intention of exaggerating my petty marital hardships into anything so dramatic. Indeed, Anosov's own suffering was not, in the end, particularly important in an historical sense. He lived his entire life in the footnotes of other, more significant lives, dodging the real scope of history, party always to incidental events but never personally offering any final resolution to the conflicts in which he participated. Anosov, my hero, only stood tall enough to peer out from the pages of books briefly, to wave his flag and shout and fire his pistol and make love to his woman before disappearing forever. It was probably the nature of this peripheral existence that attracted me to him; I imagined that I lived a similar life, lacking only his revolutionary context to score a few footnotes of my own. But that was the essential dream of every history buff: to become a part of what it was we studied. In fact, the proclivity of people like myself, rank amateurs without a single scholarly publication anywhere, to think of ourselves as "historians" rather than "history buffs" was rather astounding. There was hubris involved in this particular scholarly affectation, but I'd reconciled myself to it. Others that I occasionally met or chatted with via the internet had not. They took themselves very seriously, as well as what they considered to be their particular areas of expertise. Military history buffs were the worst, and a great many of them tended to be right-wing white power types.

   I tried to avoid doing it as much as possible, but it happened every now and again anyway. I had only the same Bachelor of Arts in history degree that fifty thousand other customer service representatives and hotel desk clerks across America had, but here I was, lolling about my living-room, comparing myself to Anosov. My MLS, my library science Master's degree, had landed me a job after college, eventually, not the history BA at all. Even in the midst of my misery, the self-importance I ascribed to myself by way of that BA made me laugh. History buffs like myself were generally happiest only when arguing over Facebook about whether Jeb Stuart was personally responsible for the Confederacy's defeat at Gettysburg or not. I preferred to think that my fascination with Russian history had more to do with my political preferences than the fact that I don't get out of the house much, but there it was. We must treat ourselves honestly first if we are to recognize truth in any form. If I had one redeeming characteristic, I thought, it was that I was more or less honest with myself about my failings, if not with Karen or anyone else, to whom I would never admit any of this.

Anosov probably never had the spare time necessary to engage such mental masturbation. Not even in prison, I imagined, would he have bothered to over-think his place in the universe to such a moronic extent. Pyetrovicz, in his one decent book, *Footprints of the Tsar*, described Anosov as being a literate man despite his rural background, with a habit of journal-keeping, though no such writings had ever surfaced and most of Pyetrovicz's other assertions had been thoroughly disproved. Anosov was a man of action, not of introspection, quite the opposite of myself.

I wouldn't have lasted long in Anosov's shoes, but, for his part, he would certainly have handled Karen's silence with stoic ambivalence. He would have leaned against a grimy wall or lounged on his moldy straw cot, smoking, debating horseflesh with his guards, waiting without thinking, without concentration, without self-examination, doing nothing but exhibiting the sort of composure that only fictional characters—and historical figures who had become works of fiction through the constant reiteration of the facts of their lives at the hands of historians—could. If Anosov weren't long dead, I could never expect such cool heroism from him, but what we expect from our heroes is really what we expect from ourselves.

When Karen passed through the room without acknowledging that I was in it or didn't bother to come home until I was too tired to make a big deal out of it, I wanted something heroic from myself, but, fictionalized or otherwise, I was, as always, no Anosov.

After she retired on the night of the postcard, I sat in the living-room, in the dark, drinking another glass of wine and staring out through the open window, the temperature having finally sunk enough to shut the a/c off for the evening. The cool breeze flowing in and telling me that some much needed rain might be on its way was a refreshing counterbalance to the heat of the wine inside me. Cicadas played their sitars out in the trees and nearly succeeded in drowning out the omnipresent sound of traffic from busy Woodward Avenue, Detroit's main drag-strip artery, just three or four blocks away.

I liked the moments of solitude I had in the evenings, after Karen and I had finished with each other, much more than the longer moments of solitude I had through the days. Things seemed properly still and quiet at night, whereas the general fact of daylight always implied that I ought to be doing something less tranquil. I finished my wine and stared across the yard at a lit window in the house behind ours. Someone moved inside, wiping a hazy silhouette across the closed blinds. The cicadas quieted, and a truck's brakes squealed somewhere over the trees. I was drowsy, but I didn't want to sleep, or even enter the bedroom, because that's where Karen was. She had spoken much, coming home from work, simply acknowledging that I'd done a serviceable job with the lawn-edging and then had taken her dinner alone to the remote end of our longish dining room table so that she might continue pouring over some deep pile of printed legal cases in preparation for a brief she muttered simply having to have done the following morning.

In college, her hardness had smelled like simple self-assuredness. It was one of the first things that had attracted me to her. I'd never cared for the squeaky girls in high-school, the ones who skipped around in cheerleader outfits (not that they took any interest in me, either). I had always preferred the bookworm type, the ones who no one else paid enough attention to, and I especially liked the bookworm girls who didn't care whether anyone paid attention to them or not. I liked straight hair, short or long; I liked eyeglasses, disheveled clothes, and skin as pale as moth's wings. I liked any attitude bitchy enough to fall under the umbrella of *punk rock*, regardless of any actual musical taste or fashion sense involved. When I spotted Karen in the student union my first year at college, she cut a swathe through everyone around her without saying or doing anything. She walked toward the Little Caesar's Pizza counter in the union's food court as if she were the only one in the building, the other students mysteriously parting like tall grass to let her through. Struck, I stepped after her and ordered some pizza that I didn't even want and, while we waited for our orders, I said hello and asked her whether she lived in my dorm. She arched an eyebrow at me, rolled her eyes at the band-stickers on the beat-up leather motorcycle jacket I was wearing and asked, "So what suburb did you crawl out of?"

  I laughed, and her scowl broke down into an overdrawn grin, and I invited her out to see a hardcore band from Detroit at a hole-in-the-wall club off-campus. She said no, and, summoning some resolve I hadn't known I had, I insisted that she'd have a good time. That got her: my one, brief spinal exhibition. Later that night, after the show, we talked until nearly dawn, wandering around campus, flipping snowballs at each other in the empty fountain in front of the Liberal Arts building. The rest was history. And history was exactly what that time felt like to me now: an episode from the distant past described only in crude stone carvings, subject to much scholarly debate.

I refilled my glass and walked out into the backyard to finish it off in my favorite lawn chair. I sat down and looked up, hoping to draw some comfort from the galactic wheel, but there was no moon, no stars. These were the suburbs, after all. No starlight penetrated Detroit's light-polluted parasol. I stared upward into a grimy, glowing haze and raised a silent toast to Lyudmila, who had at least helped Aleksandr Anosov to become a great man before abandoning him. I ground the balls of my feet into the dry grass and remembered a night before Karen and I were married, when we drove to a private lake in the wealthy suburbs further to the north to skinny-dip.

In someone's backyard, under the dark tent of a willow tree, we stripped down to our underwear. Shivering and glancing back at the single lit window in the large house across the lawn, Karen hugged her arms across her breasts, and I tugged them away to kiss her goose-pimpled flesh. She scooted away, out from beneath the tree, and, sticking her tongue out at me, slipped into the water. I watched her white panties pass beneath the dark surface, vanishing toward the center of the lake with a seal's eloquence. Her voice and splash echoed across the backs of the houses when she surfaced, but she dove under again with a mermaid's flip of her legs, not caring if anyone heard. When I caught sight of her next, her panties were gone, and she was pure porcelain. She sprang up again, a few feet further out, arms raised over her head, a come hither glint in her eyes. I leaped out from beneath the tree, more self-conscious than I'd predicted, and hurled myself into the water. My lungs seized in the subarctic water, and I choked to the surface. Karen bobbed over and wrapped her thighs around my waist, holding me until I warmed.

The memory burned through me with the wine. I overturned my glass onto the lawn and looked downward from the sky at our house. On the upper floor, the light clicked off in our bedroom window and, left alone in the best darkness the neighborhood could offer, I inhaled, hoping to fill myself with the scent of lilacs or forsythia or anything natural from the hedges and shrubbery surrounding the yard, but there was only the smell of the ragweed growing along the freeway, not so far away.

3.

    I sat on my porch with a can of beer later one evening watching my divorced neighbor, Ellen, unloading groceries from the back of her old Toyota Matrix in a pair of shorts that would've looked great on a woman half her age but which looked spectacular on her mature curves. I thought about offering to help her, but the distance across my yard to her driveway seemed vast and my legs seemed pleased with their current state of limpness. She had a teenage son, Leonard. Where was he to help his mom? She waved at me before hefting the last couple of her plastic shopping bags slamming shut her hatchback. I waved my beer can back at her, feeling for all the world in the process like some hick sitting outside a mobile home. She struggled with her front door a bit, then unlocked and kicked it open and was inside.
    The sight of her legs and shorts stirred me, for the first time in days, and, for a moment, I thought about Karen and her "time of the month" panties and wheth-

er sex was even a remote possibility. She was working late again, had a trial coming up in the morning on a real estate dispute that she had thought would settle out but then hadn't, leaving her to run around prepping at the last minute. Or so she'd informed me in a short afternoon telephone conversation in which she'd relayed that information and then hung up without waiting for much of a response. No, there would be no sex when she came home, probably much later, nor would there me in the following days if she didn't win her trial. She would spend that time fuming that the loss had been the fault of some new associate hired only because he or she had made law review at Wayne State University and not because they actually had two brain cells to rub together. I drank my beer and tried not to think of Ellen and what she might look like out of those shorts.

    The air was warm and thick in a way that I didn't enjoy, but the irregular breezes were worthwhile. I leaned back against the floor of the porch and shook off the idea that somewhere, Karen was looking as hard at some other guy as I had been looking at Ellen.

    Anyway, with Ellen out of sight, I looked up and down the street instead. My line of vision was obscured by the tall, old oak trees standing in front of every other house, but I didn't see any of my other neighbors out of doors. My other neighbor, Ron, an architect who designed the interior spaces of retail stores of all things, was rarely to be seen other than coming and going from his car. Like myself, he was not the sort of guy who fixed his own brakes or purchased elaborate grills and barbeque accoutrements. I liked him for that, for not putting me to shame, but, otherwise, he didn't seem to have a lot to say when we bumped into each other and I expected that he would say the same. His house was beautiful, though, a big Cape Cod with an even larger porch than mine. His wife I had not caught sight of in a long while, and I presumed that a divorce had quietly occurred. Even her car, which was the basis upon which I really knew most of my neighbors when it came down to it, was rarely to be seen in the driveway or parked on the street outside. When I'd mentioned this to Karen, she had simply shrugged. Neighborly goings-on were beneath her notice.

Across the street lived an elderly couple who had moved in at the time of the original passing of the guard, in the late 1960s and early 1970s, when the original residents of the Royal Oak area who had moved in after it was incorporated into a city in the 1920s, were initially dying off or selling out in order to retire elsewhere. The neighborhood had been a bit more exciting then, they'd told me, when a large number of families had all moved in almost simultaneously with small or newborn children, the men largely auto workers who departed each morning with their lunch-pails, leaving their wives to form klatches for coffee, baby-sitting, Mah Jongg, and whatever else they needed from each other. There had been parties, there had been affairs, people were a little crazier, to hear it told. Beer was drunk, pot was smoked, kids grew up and went to the same high-school together, and, now, most of those folks were gone, too.

My neighbors, Tom and Lil, enjoyed bending my ear with stories of people leaping from roofs to swimming pools and lightning strikes and car accidents between teenage boys and dogs that had run freely from house to house to house knowing they would be fed at each stop. Tom viewed me with suspicion, too, I think, given that I was home all of the time and hadn't managed to find a job in a while, but unemployment was an understandable state of affairs for an old auto worker like him. Beyond Tom and Lil and Ellen and Ron, my neighborly knowledge was quite thin. I hardly ran up and down the street with plates of brownies, although Lil and her old friends may have done just that once upon a time.

My street was a street of cordial but distant neighbors, really. Carefully distant, waving and nodding as required, but no more than did transient neighbors in an apartment complex where there is no particular reason to get to know anyone. Given the foreclosure crisis and the state of the mortgage industry, it was nearly the same with homeowners now. Beyond, that, though, there was television and the internet and Facebook and every reason in the world to hurry home and shut the door behind you without speaking to anyone for more than couple of seconds. We had too much entertainment at our fingertips, worked too many long hours, had too much to do to reach out from isolation to the people living twenty-five feet away. I could drool after Ellen's ass all day long—not to mention her chest—but, in fact, we'd almost never spoken at length despite many years of close proximity and a major effort would have to be made for me to act on any impulse and get close enough to her to find out if anything could come of it—even if I weren't a married man not inclined to undertake the bother and hassle of cheating.

It was so much the stuff of daily life to me at this point. I didn't give it that much thought, generally, except when Hugo rumbled through from time-to-time, accusing me of various socio-political crimes. The suburbs were some level of Hell, or at least Purgatory, for him. Hugo's castigation of my life was simply rooted in his own upbringing, clearly. He was a kid in one of those suburban houses in the 1970s, watching his mother have the ladies over for cake and strange lemon drinks that left them giggling and whispering words like "diaphragm" at each other. His parents were a version of Tom and Lil. Hugo had treated them badly, always talking back with utter, snide bile to even the simplest statement by his very patient father, never agreeing with anything that they said or suggested, no matter how benign. He saw his home and neighborhood and school as a cage and his parents as blue-suited guards who always had nightsticks concealed behind their backs. I thought they were nice; they gave me cookies. Hugo was given too much and was an only child, and, even back then, when I knew as much as a snail about people and why they did what they did, I thought it showed. Hugo now accused me of having voluntarily locked myself into a cage. I didn't always disagree, but there was irony involved, for sure.

There was also the possible truth of what exactly it was that he was doing out there in the wide, free world that kept him holding me at arm's length a bit. I suspected but did not know for certain that he was involved in some level of criminal activity and that he simply didn't tell me anything about it for my own good. I liked that idea, actually, as it allowed me to continue to hold my old friend up to a noble ideal of self-sacrifice and consideration for my best interests. Probably, the first half was true but not the second half. Certainly, Karen did not buy that when I proposed the theory to her. To the contrary, she contacted the state police one time to ascertain whether there were any warrants out for him and seemed disappointed when it turned out that there weren't.

A girl walking a dog on the sidewalk approached from the direction of Ron's house. She was dressed in a black sweatsuit that looked uncomfortably warm for the temperature and humidity and stared at me with wide, alarmed eyes beneath a shock of bleached, messy hair as she closed in and slowly passed. Her little white dog, some kind of Scottie or terrier, had dirt all over his paws and fur and struggled and strained at the leash as if it were its first time being walked on one.

"How's it going?" I said to her, and her eyes simply widened. She opened her mouth momentarily as if to reply but then clamped it shut again and hurried on past Ellen's house and out of sight up the street, between the oak trees.

Wandering meth-head with unfortunate dog: another hole in Hugo's conception of 21st Century suburbia. There were more starving people in suburban neighborhoods than in urban neighborhoods, I'd recently read. When Capitalism fell apart, it fell apart everywhere, not just in inner cities. I could see it starting to do that now. In college, I tended to argue with the campus Marxists handing out pamphlets despite the fact that, ideologically, I pretty much agreed with them across the board. Americans were not living like serfs in Tsarist Russia in 1917. Things were not uncomfortable enough for the man on the street to make any kind of unrest seem likely in the late 1980s and early 1990s, as much as Ronald Reagan and the George Bushes seemed to me to represent an alarm of some sort that ought to be sounded.

I felt that dispute bending further these days, as it was clear to me now that the moneyed interests in the US had successfully managed to consolidate their hold on our political system and divert the majority amount of the wealth generated by our huge country to themselves. Elections seemed ever more pointless given the lack of a real opposition political party, and, during the past election, I had been tempted for the first time in my life to simply not bother to vote at all. To help sweep in America's first African American president, I had gone ahead and done so, but, as I'd feared when listening to his lofty but essentially vacuous campaign speeches prior to the election, he had proven himself to be utterly milquetoast and co-opted, a weak president who had only acted vigorously since his election when it came to the matter of installing Wall Street's finest blue bloods into his Cabinet.

More campus Marxists were perhaps needed in the vicinity of Royal Oak.

In the suburbs, the so-called Tea Party festered, clinging to small collections of shotguns and home weaponry as a hopeful bulwark against what they saw as governmental tyranny despite the fact that the government's primary role in what was going on, as far as I could tell, was simply to bend over and spread itself open. The confused tension between bumper stickers on the backs of battered Ford F-150s parked in suburban driveways in the areas northward of Detroit was telling: "I Love Capitalism!" sat next to "I Love the Constitution!" next to "I Love My Country But Fear My Government!"

People didn't know what the hell they were talking about, but they were talking. The problem that I saw with a potential revolution now was that it would not, if it ever occurred, be fueled by well-educated college campus Marxists in expensive leather jackets but by morons with shotguns. I did not own a shotgun; I would not fare well in this revolution. However, the dysfunction of the US government was walking us, certainly, down a road toward something unpleasant, and I did not see any possibility at this point of a quick remedy. It was perhaps time for an Anosov of some sort, or several, to inject some kind of useful ideology into people's general discontent.

About the time that I considered that possibility while watching the twitchy dog-walker, I realized that I'd run out of beer. I walked into the house to get another one, decided to sit and check my email quickly, then idly started a computer game in which I was required to re-fight the Revolutionary War in a tightly compressed timeframe, and that was the end of that.

When Karen came home, much later, she was, as I had predicted, not in the mood for much of anything, including conversation. I had fallen asleep reading in bed but opened my eyes as she quietly entered the room and undressed. As she unbuttoned her blouse, she turned and saw me awake and watching and then turned back around to finish removing her clothes. I held my breath without meaning to when she unfastened her bra, catching myself hoping that she would turn around suddenly and fling herself bare-breasted on top of me, but she only pulled on an oversized t-shirt instead. The shirt fell down nearly to her knees, and she shimmied out of her pants under the cover of its hem. Even the backs of her calves were inviting, although she sported a large bruise on one of them.

"What happened to your leg?" I asked her. "Did you fall?"

"It's nothing," she sighed. "I whacked it."

She left the room for a long while to wash up in the bathroom across the hall outside, then shuffled back in and slid into bed beside me.

"Ready for tomorrow?" I asked her.

"Not really," she said. "Can you turn that light out? I need to sleep like now."

I clicked off my nightstand reading lamp and listened to her fall quickly into light snoring. I was now wide awake and staring at the ceiling again, trying to ignore the mysterious hard-on I'd developed looking at Karen's bruised calf.

4.

After Karen fell completely asleep, I stepped outside onto the porch to get some air. Thick haloes of moths and June bugs undulated around the streetlights, so I reached back inside to click my own porch light off. As soon as the light snapped out, someone hissed from around the corner of the house.

"Ivan!"

I jumped but saw nothing, first looking in the direction of Ellen's house, then the other way, and then back at my front door.

"Ivan!" the voice hissed again. "Ivan!"

I reeled back and froze as a figure slid out from beneath the short trellis leaning against the side of the porch and moved toward me. A man crept forward onto the sidewalk, and I tripped back toward my door, panicking.

"Relax!" the man said. "It's me!"

He edged a little closer, stepping up onto my walkway, emerging from the shadows.

"*Hugo?*" I gasped, my heart pounding.

He held his hand out.

"Dude," he laughed. "Jesus Christ. Do not audition for the next *Batman* movie. You will not get the part."

He strode forward and stepped up onto the porch, clomping across the wooden floor in his customary motorcycle boots.

I squinted, doing my best to assimilate his sudden presence. Something was wrong with his hunched posture. It was not his usual hangdog slouching; it was more of a deliberate crouch, as if he planned to run across enemy lines under heavy fire. His eyes, when he got close enough to let me see them, darted between me and the space behind me, as if he expected someone else to be standing there at any moment. When I loosened up and allowed him to wrap his big hand around mine, only then did he feel three-dimensional as he pumped my fist with the same pointlessly crushing grip he'd offered me years ago in school, as he claimed the empty desk beside mine in Honors English class.

"What in the world are you doing here?" I whispered at him, now more terrified that we would wake Karen up.

"Passing through," he said. "Just passing through, as usual."

His voice sounded like a can of marbles.

"You were passing through my trellis?" I said.

"Something like that."

He shifted his weight from one foot to the other, his joints creaking as if he'd been packed into a crate for several hours, and then removed his hand from mine to jam it into the pocket of his leather jacket. His haircut hadn't changed since the last—or first—time I'd seen him, his dirty water blonde spikes standing like a moonlit cornfield under the electric light. His eyes darted again, and he took a step or two further onto the porch, closer to the wall of the house.

I saw immediately that this was and also was not the old Hugo. It was the same body wearing the same clothes, but, before, that body would been kicking cans and rocks into the street or tearing branches from my shrubbery rather than standing still for one second. It would not be furtive and uneasy. In worse light, I might not have recognized him at all without that damn jacket that had to be hot as hell in this season. The leather dulled, worn beyond any hope for hipness, parts of old stickers and bits of slogans and band names hand-painted with white-out still half-legible in places, indistinguishable in others, there was less leather than graffiti to the thing. It was the billboard with which Hugo had identified himself since high-school, probably an odd thing for a grown man to be wearing but uniquely his and unmistakable for that. He himself was even less legible, though, as he scanned his peripheral vision while doing his best to appear relaxed. He slumped darker space along the wall of the house as I stepped closer to him, his eyes fixed upon me as I moved toward him in the pleading but still threatening manner of a junkie asking for spare change on a street-corner. The twitchy woman walking her dirty terrier earlier came to mind.

"It's good to see you again," he whispered, his usual jocularity gone.

"Sure," I said, "but why the surprise?"

"Can we go inside?" he asked.

"Yeah," I said, "but let's keep it down. Karen is sleeping."

"You got it," he said, stepping in as I held the door for him.

He and Karen had hated each other from the

first, ever since he'd called her a pretentious Yoko Ono—whatever that meant—within seconds of my introducing them. Karen's reaction was as expected, and their relationship had never improved. At the time, I was fine with that. I had a girl on my arm, and that meant more to me than Hugo's approval. When she migrated to my bed, the deal was done. Hugo exited college without graduating at some vague point and our trilateral arrangement had not evolved much since.

"It's been a while," I said, following him into the foyer and shutting the door behind us.

He walked into the living room and unfolded himself onto the sofa, sighing and rubbing his hands together.

"Mind if I take these off?" he asked, cocking his chin at his boots.

"I insist, in fact. Karen would go haywire if she saw you walking around in here with those."

A fragment of his old "I told you so" smirk gathered on his lips but then dissipated into a long, relieved exhalation as he kicked the noxious boots off and flexed his toes inside a pair of dirty-looking tube socks.

"Want something to drink?"

"Man, I'd love that," he said.

I fetched two bottles of beer from the kitchen refrigerator, opening over the sink, and carrying his to him on the couch. He took a long, grateful swallow of it and then leaned back into the couch, closing his eyes as if he were ready for a long winter's nap right there on the spot. I cleared my throat, and he perked back up enough to drink half of the bottle empty in another couple of swallows but didn't say anything else. He cradled the bottle between his knees and looked over everything in the house but me, as if he were casing the joint.

"So, let me guess," I said, "the story begins in an

aristocratic Russian household. Napoleon's troops are only miles from the estate …"

"You're half-right," he laughed.

"Which half?"

"I was only miles from your estate."

"Does that make you Napoleon, then?"

"A lot of things make me Napoleon."

He cracked his knuckles. They were chapped red and knotted.

"Still got your wit in fine, working order, I see."

"It's the only part of me that hasn't atrophied," he said, swallowing the last of his beer. "Can I have another one of these?"

"That's the end of it, sorry," I said. "Wasn't expecting company tonight."

"That's okay," he said. "My fault. If I'd known I was headed this way, I definitely would've let you know."

"Well, you know. *Mi casa, su casa*," I said, stifling a yawn.

"I'm keeping you up," he said.

"I haven't been sleeping at all lately, anyway," I said.

"Too many feathers in your pillow?"

I didn't respond. He wanted to lead me into the same swamp of a conversation we had every other time we saw each other, which essentially involved him railing against me for being married to Karen and living in a house. He was never trying to badger me, I realized, just encouraging me in his own tactless manner to change. It was never enough for Hugo to harbor an opinion; he wouldn't rest until the entire world agreed with him. Or at least me.

He searched his pockets and handed me a wilted, folded piece of cardboard: another postcard, now ruined. The writing was smeared, spattered with water in several places, but the photo side was intact. It was a black and white snapshot of Steve Martin in 1940s suit and hat, holding a gun. Hugo's handwritten message on the flipside had read "Death or Glory!"

"I don't get it," I said.

"It's from *Dead Men Don't Wear Plaid.*"

"So? What does the back mean?"

He waved me off.

"Who knows why anyone writes anything on postcards?" he said. "It's just a postcard that says 'Hi, Ivan, having fun, wish you were here,' same as every other postcard. You got my last one, right? I didn't write anything on that one at all … Actions speak louder than words, right? People can send postcards with nothing written on them at all, and the message is still loud and clear. It was enough that I mailed it."

"But you didn't mail this one."

"No, but you get my point, right?"

"Uh-huh."

I set the postcard on the coffee table beside me.

"Aren't you going to hang it on your refrigerator?" he asked. "Isn't that what people do with postcards?"

"I don't know," I said. "What would you do with a postcard?"

"I don't get postcards, and I don't have a refrigerator."

He leaned over, dropping his head onto the arm of the sofa.

"Goddamn, I'm tired," he said, cracking his knuckles again.

"So, tell me, really," I said, trying again, "what brings you here?"

"Meeting someone," he yawned. "Really. I was in the neighborhood."

"This neighborhood? That's convenient."

"It is, isn't it?"

He sat back up and smiled, casting another glance around the room.

"You need a place to crash for the night?" I asked him.

"Would Karen mind?" he asked.

"Yes," I said.

"Is that a problem?"

I thought about it for a while. Yes, considering all that was or wasn't going with my marriage, it could be a problem. Regardless, I wasn't going to say no.

"I'll get you a blanket," I said. "Something in a nice sack-cloth, perhaps?"

"Cotton will be fine. I prefer Egyptian or Turkish. Only the finest. Got a pillow, too?"

I retrieved a blanket from the hall linen closet and threw it over him. He withdrew beneath it, turtle-like.

"Who were you meeting?" I asked him, but he pretended to be asleep.

His pale cheeks reddened as he warmed and fell asleep. For a moment, he looked like himself again—the strong, youthful Hugo—and this whole meeting seemed like just another sleep-over, like so many we'd had in high-school. Back then, we'd have stayed up all night playing records and defacing the photos of people we didn't like in our yearbooks. Now, he was unconscious before we'd even gotten down to some serious casual small-talk, and I was worried about whether my wife would approve. He turned over. The back of his head, I now saw, was knotted, matted, and greasy. It was the head of a homeless man dozing in the public library. It was not a teenager's head. The back of his neck was covered with tiny scratches, as if he'd been ducking through pine needles. No, there was no use in pretending: something had changed. For the worse.

I thought about Hugo's other postcard, the one he did mail, still folded up in my shorts pocket, now crumpled in the laundry bin. He did think he was the living paragon of punk. The card wasn't a random joke selection, for sure. That was up for debate, but Hugo had been a bit more Anosov than I, though he could have cared less who Anosov was. My feeling that this was true had more to do with what he'd done and where he'd been in the last couple of decades, as near as I or anyone could determine those things.

Where had my old friend been? I usually didn't know. I had no idea where he was now. He avoided social media and made no particular point of keeping in touch, not even with me. Or particularly not with me. I felt that kept me at arm's length, and not just because of Karen's open dislike for him. It had something to do with my domestication, I was pretty sure. When I did speak to him, he was dodgy about where he was and what he had been doing to get by; he preferred to ask me questions about my life and then challenging me on the answers with questions such as "Are you really satisfied with that?"

Now, crumpled on my sofa, it was difficult to see my school friend at all. His good looks had receded, and he was just a skeleton, his own and mine.

In the morning, I hurried downstairs when Karen's alarm went off to wake and prepare Hugo for her. However, when I descended into the sitting-room, I found the blanket I'd given him folded neatly on the end of the sofa, with the pillow balanced on top of it. A white envelope with my name scrawled on it in black ball-point lay beside the bedding. Hugo was gone. I ripped the envelope open to find a short note and a smaller sealed envelope inside. The second envelope was unaddressed, but the note wasn't.

Ivan,

If you get this before Karen, I wasn't here and your marriage is safe! Please give this envelope to Francine when she stops by.

I held the second envelope to the light to ensure that it wasn't empty, a joke, and I saw that it wasn't. I didn't know who Francine was, but I brought the envelope up to my study and slid it between the pages of my paperback copy of Bruce Lincoln's *Red Victory* along with the note on my bookshelf. I evened the book's spine with the others beside it. If Karen had missed Hugo's visit, I agreed with Hugo and couldn't see any reason why she ought to know about it now.

I'd learned long ago not to overreact to Hugo's little mysteries, and I did my best to file this one away with a dozen others I'd long since forgotten about. He loved innuendo, and he loved to tease and flirt. As intensely as he lived the rest of his life, it was sometimes hard to take him seriously. It amused him to mislead and deceive, and the diet of red herrings he'd fed me for years had inured me to the implications of this note—that someone named Francine might come to my house to retrieve it. I made coffee and breakfast for my wife, wished her good luck with her trial, took a shower, grabbed a book off of my shelf to re-read, and then forgot about all of them.

5.

On the second morning of Karen's trial, I was assigned the task of gathering some things she had left behind in her rush to get out of the door to hurry over to her before the action started. I scooped up scattered papers and files from the desk in the corner of our bedroom and managed to locate her briefcase on the kitchen table to stuff them into. I hoped that I might spend the day in court with her, catching her in action. She wouldn't appreciate my spectating, likely, but it had been a very long time since I'd had the opportunity to do that.

It sounded like fun, even though Karen did not exactly litigate the sort of stuff that made headlines. Often this meant that she did not litigate cases that anyone who wasn't a lawyer involved in these particular issues would find entertaining or even understand. In fact, Karen always said that one of the biggest problems with our jury system was the difficulty in the need to educate the required jury of peers," meaning a jury comprised of local car mechanics and ice cream vendors, on the subtleties and nuances of anti-trust or mergers and acquisitions issues. What did regular people know about SEC regulations? It boiled down to courtroom histrionics, she said, as there was no way to teach anything substantial about anything complicated to a jury in a very short amount of time.

Her usual rant on this subject sometime included additional components involving the deficient public school system and the basic intellectual capacities of people who chose professions in the trades that I found that view to be borderline offensive, but even I had to admit that it was, statistically speaking, more true than not in the US, where our patchwork, state-by-state educational system—one of many sad side-effects of our Federalist system—had left the U.S. generally mediocre on nearly any global scale. Still, slagging off tradespeople—many of whom were fellow history buffs of my acquaintance—irked me.

In any case, the trial would probably be boring, when push came to shove. I would look bored, and Karen would notice me and become nervous and agitated. She would try her best to ignore me, but it wouldn't work. At some point, I would leave, and then that would irritate her even more. No, prior audiences had not gone over well. I might or might not bring it up this time.

I drank a second cup of coffee and looked the briefcase over. It was brand new, but I had no idea when she'd purchased it. It was beautiful, with a dark brown leather exterior that retained the texture and smell of flesh when I leaned into it and took a deep whiff, with a gold combination lock engraved with her initials. It was unlocked, so I flipped it open to find a scattered mess of file-folders, post-it notes, and business cards inside, all weighed down by her ponderous daily planner.

I picked the spiral-bound book up and scanned

a few pages. The notes inside were incomprehensible, a weird runic language constructed entirely of dates and initials. She appeared to be booked solid for months, with scarcely a moment to herself in any of the next several days. Her life was divvied into time-slots that belonged to other people. I tossed in the papers and file from the upstairs desk and felt sorry for her.

What sort of life was it that my wife was living? I couldn't think of anything worse than being a lawyer. I'd never told her that, but it was true. She filled her date books up with meetings and filings and research and court-dates, all of which probably did the world more harm than good on balance—although, to be fair, people in other professions weren't constantly required to justify the rightness or wrongness of what they did on a daily basis. Only politicians and lawyers endured that obligation.

Once upon a time, Karen had thought that, in specializing in mergers and acquisitions, she'd end up meeting all sorts of interesting people through that pursuit—politicians, corporate leaders, mover and shakers of various stripes. This was Detroit, though, not Washington, DC or Silicon Valley. She hadn't gone to the right law school in the right part of the country to end up with those sorts of clients. She only met the same khaki-panted and blue button-down-shirted dweebs that she met at the local supermarket. She threw herself into it anyway, though, because that was the professional thing to do and because she didn't know how to not go full-bore at something. She probably looked at her booked schedule with absolute delight.

For myself, I slammed the briefcase shut, feeling pleased with myself for not having such a date-book to live by, never mind that I avoided it only by way of living off of my wife's largesse. If I had one talent in life, it was letting that little fact slide past my attention. Thus, she was indeed right in bringing it up when the subject couldn't be ignored.

Why didn't I just get a job? It wasn't impossible to find one with an MLS degree. Why didn't I just do it?

It was easier to turn my nose up at Karen's planner than to answer those questions.

I waited in the lobby of Karen's office with her briefcase, clothes, and other necessities piled in my lap, staring alternatively at the burgundy carpet and at the picture of the sexy model on the cover of the *Marie Claire* magazine that the receptionist was holding upright in front of her. When Karen finally pushed open the interior glass doors leading back into labyrinth of the suite, shushing at me around her cell-phone, I took one last long glance at the model on the magazine cover before tumbling after her, just to hang onto the image of something pleasant before giving it all up for the next several minutes. She led me down the hall to her office, still talking on the phone, where she pointed at a chair in the corner and turned her back to me as she spoke. I complied, sitting down, the magazine model sucking in one, deep, expansive breath in my mind.

"Yes, I know," she said into her phone and sliding behind her desk. "$20,000 is all they're offering at the moment. We haven't uncovered any real proof of anything from the discovery materials, so they're just trying to make us go away, that's pretty much it. It's your decision, though. We'll proceed however you want. I'm just here to tell you what your options are …"

She was animated as she spoke, nodding and shaking her head as if this person on the other end of the line could actually see her. Her hands were all over the desk, flipping papers, moving objects from one side to another, straightening her chair, retrieving a pen from a drawer, replacing it. When I'd been employed, I had never put this much motion into an entire work-week. I placed the briefcase on the edge of her desk before she asked for it, careful not to disturb her personal whirlwind.

"No, no. They've already said that they don't want to go to trial. Not in so many words, but that was the gist of it. Yes, I recommend you accept. It's a P.R. thing for them. I don't think we can expect a significantly higher payout without a lot more man hours and much bigger bill for you. Okay? It's your call. You have to approve it or reject it, not me. Okay, then."

She clicked the phone off and tossed it into her flooded in-box.

"Sorry," she said. "He called just when Marsha buzzed me that you were in the lobby."

"That's okay," I said. "I was enjoying the carpet out there."

She was already leafing through another pile of papers, flipping the corners up with her thumb. She looked harried and angry and again reminded me of my last boss. I felt like apologizing for something, but I couldn't think of anything in particular that I'd done wrong. Her hair was a mess, half-tumbling from a plastic clip dangling from the back of her head, and her shirt was untucked. Something like spaghetti sauce stained her collar. Her eyes were dark, hollow from sleeplessness. I kept my mouth shut and remained still, uptight and uncomfortable in the chair, essentially simply waiting for her to dismiss me.

While she fidgeted, I inspected the room. It was arrowhead-shaped, wedged uncomfortably in a corner of the triangular building. A rubber plant grew from a plastic pot beside, and a Wonder Woman calendar turned to the wrong month hung on the wall. A low, metal bookshelf stuffed with books on civil procedure, the Michigan court rules, and the Federal Rules of Evidence ran along the well beneath a tall window, which saved the room from feeling like the hall closet of a very dull packrat. Through the tinted glass, the sky was muted. An airplane stitched a contrail between clouds that looked like mile-wide fists. I walked over and pressed my face to the glass to get a better view, and noted, several floors below, a Volkswagen driving around and around in the mostly empty parking-lot. Something metallic glinted in a window in the next wing, and I squinted at it, but it didn't reappear. Under the low hum of the air ventilation system, I became aware of the sound of my own breathing. I turned away from the window in time to watch two women gliding shoulder-to-shoulder past the office doorway like pieces of newspaper being blown down the street.

"Jesus. It's always like this here, isn't it?" I said.

Karen looked up from her shuffling.

"Like what?"

"Like a morgue. Or a morgue museum, even. You're the only thing moving here."

"That's why I get the big bucks."

"You get big bucks?"

"Bigger than some."

"Ah."

She retrieved a sheet of paper with a brown coffee mug ring in the center of it from within her stack and held it up against the fluorescent ceiling light.

"Here it is," she muttered to herself.

Reaching across the desk, she pulled the briefcase toward her, upsetting everything else beneath it. She flipped it open and stuck the coffee-stained paper inside and then spun the combination lock on the case, sealing it.

"Are those the clothes you brought?" she asked, glaring at the bundle remaining in my lap. "I really wanted the blue suit."

"Well, you should have told me that," I said.

"I thought I did."

"No."

"Oh. Well. This will be fine, I suppose," she sighed, taking the bundle from me. Shut the door, will you?"

I did so, and she began to unbutton her blouse. I quickly moved to shut her door, but she waved me off.

"Don't worry about it," she said. "Nobody's here today."

It seemed to me that there were plenty enough, so I shut the door anyway and stood with my back against its small window. She pulled her stained blouse off and tossed it onto the floor, and her skirt followed. Before she had time to don the new clothes, her phone rang again, and she picked it up without regard to her state of undress.

"Again? No, throw him into my voicemail, please. I just got off the phone with him."

She hung up and shoved her chair back from her desk in frustration and squeezed her eyes shut as she caromed against the wall. Her face reddened and her chest flushed around her flesh-colored bra. Her breathing was heavy, and I wished that her mood matched her clothes. Instead, she glared at me, misreading my gaping as impatience rather than lust. She frowned, stood, and turned her back to me as she pulled on the change of clothes I'd brought her. I imagined walking over and sliding my hand into her panties but, of course, did not. She dressed quickly without speaking and then browsed through the rest of the stuff I'd brought from home, double-checking to see if I'd forgotten anything. I continued to prop the door shut, wanting more and more to walk through it with every passing second.

"Great, great," she finally said, completing her inventory. "You got it all."

"I'm qualified for some jobs at least."

"I guess," she muttered.

"Need a cheering section in court today?" I offered.

"Nah, you'd be bored stiff," she said, inspecting her makeup with a tiny mirror from her purse. "No need to waste your time watching me have a stroke."

"Alright," I shrugged. "Want anything special for dinner?"

"Whatever," she said again, glancing up at me finally. "But don't wait for me if you get hungry. Who knows when I'll be home? This will go till whenever, then I'll have to catch up all the work I'm not getting done being in court before I can cut out. What a waste of time. I hate trial days."

"Me, too," I said, meaning it.

She flashed me a business-like smile and tossed a fat file from her desk into the brief case. I stepped toward her and tried to give her a kiss, but she ducked me accidentally, reaching down to fiddle with the strap on her shoe. I didn't try again. She tucked her case under her arm and pushed past me out of the door.

"Got to run," she said over her shoulder. "Thanks again."

"You didn't thank me a first time," I called after her, through her doorway.

She stopped and looked at her watch and frowned.

"Well, consider yourself thanked twice, anyway. I'll see you at home."

She blew me a kiss and dashed into the hallway, out toward the lobby. I tried to imagine some way in which a blown kiss was better than an actual one, but nothing came to mind. I circled her desk instead and flipped the Wonder Woman calendar to the proper month and then moseyed out, back through the glass doors and the lobby, whistling as loudly as I could to ward off the miasma of the place.

In the car, I gripped the hot vinyl of my sunbaked steering wheel and stared out through the windshield at the door of Karen's office building. I wanted to march back in, find her, and tell her that she needed to knock all this shit off, by which I meant everything and anything that could even loosely be defined as shit. I wanted to get down on my knees and confess my frustration, to let slip the extent to which the silence at home had been getting to me. I wanted to surrender to defeat in whatever battle it was we were fighting, ask her for her terms, agree to them, and to sign a treaty in blood if necessary, calling an immediate armistice. I wanted her to thank me for bringing her clothes and briefcase with even a modicum of civility. I wanted her to take the day and drive out to Stony Creek Metro Park with me, to eat crackers and cheese on an old blanket beside the lake, surrounded by the petrified shit of Canadian geese.

Instead, I felt like I had visited the office for a job interview and had been cruelly rejected. "There is no job," Karen had seemed to say. "And, if there was, we'd hardly hire the likes of *you!*" Booted out through the glass door, given no more consideration than an encyclopedia salesman.

I let go of the steering wheel. My palms were sticky and smelled like the new leather of Karen's briefcase. I opened the window, then fired up the engine and let it run, waiting to drive until the air-conditioner warmed up. The smell of baking bread from a nearby bakery flooded the interior of the car and reminded me of the doughy biscuits that my mother made from instant Jiffy-Mix when I was a kid. Leaning back in my seat, I bathed in the memory of the taste of those biscuits, slathered with melted margarine and cinnamon, and recalled the flowered shelf-paper my mother used as a tablecloth on our wobbly-legged kitchen table. I remembered tracing smiley-faces in the layer of cinnamon left on the table from the bread and my mother singing "Luck, Be a Lady Tonight" at the stove, and, once, a grackle landing in a messy flutter on the window-sill beside me, every color of the spectrum reflected in its shiny, black feathers. I wished badly that I had one of those biscuits with a tall glass of milk to wash down the past thirty years with.

Alas, my mother was gone, and so was the utility of wishful thinking. Nostalgia was always a calming mantra for me, however. It flattened and smoothed my irritation. I rolled up the windows, turned the air-conditioner up full-blast, and resolved to give Karen whatever space she needed. Forgetting about the office and my dented pride, I pulled the car out of the parking-lot and into the street. There was no wound that couldn't be healed between us as long as one of us was willing to bend, even if it had to be me. Every time.

6.

    I sat down in the chair by the window at nearly midnight that evening and stared out into the yard. Our big tree swayed a bit in an unseasonably hard wind, creaking like some old-fashioned, crackpot flying machine—part bicycle, part glider, part apple-juicer. The small, yellow moon was caught up in its leaves. The summer had overstepped its apex. Soon, that moon would be orange and much larger, and the yard would be filled with snow—which I would be obliged to shovel immediately in the morning lest I suffer the wrath of our very delicate local mailman, who left snide notes instead of mail when required to walk through anything more than a half inch deep to get to our porch. The lawn was a dark, square shadow now, though, boxed in by the houses around it and the overarching canopy of the tree. It looked like spilt ink.

    Hours earlier, I'd set aside my plan to drink a lot of beer before Karen's arrival, recognizing that I was already waxing poetic to a nearly terminal level and that she was apparently not coming home anytime soon. Instead, I sat and watched the yard until all of its details fell away, leaving only an empty, uncluttered space. It was beautiful like that. I fell asleep at odd intervals as I waited, waking with a start and a shortness of breath each time, surprised each time to be waking alone in a chair. I had always hated Karen's late nights. Not out of jealousy or suspicion but due to the cavernous sense of foreboding that I encountered when alone in the house at night. It was the largest place I'd ever lived, a cathedral compared with the flats I'd grown up in, and, late at night, it was not an easy place. Too many shadows creased the walls, and there were too many entry-points.

After sundown, the neighborhood felt like Dresden, or another of the bombed-out European cities after World War II. I felt like I could wander for miles alone, with nothing more remaining to do than to scavenge and remember. It reminded me that the only reason for me to be in this place, at this time, was Karen, and I felt marooned when she failed to appear by nightfall. However, was that really the only reason? I didn't really miss relocating every time the rent was raised by some all-powerful landlord, which was the pattern of my childhood. I did love having a room upstairs just for my books to live in.

However, it was convenient to pretend that this was not the case, when the hour drew long.

Finally, though, Karen made it home. She opened and slammed the front door shut, snapping me upright just as the digital clock on the cable box flashed 1:00 a.m. She walked into the room and tossed her coat and purse onto the wing-chair in the corner.

"Hey," I mumbled.

"What are you doing down here?" she sighed.

"I fell asleep waiting for you."

"Why?"

She kicked her shoes off and sat down on the far end of the sofa, rubbing her toes on the carpet.

"How did it go? Did you win?" I asked, rather than answering.

"I'm beat," she yawned.

"Sorry I asked."

"I'll bet."

"We didn't finish," she said. "We're continued. Barely got through their cross-exam before it got to be dinner-time, so the judge cut us off."

"So where've you been?"

"Office," she yawned again, rubbing her eyes. "Prepping for Phase Two, next week. They had some new stuff in there we weren't ready for. Actually, it's lucky the clock ran out so that we can scramble and respond properly now."

"That's good," I said, "I guess."

She leaned back, relaxed her shoulders, and collapsed into the sofa cushions. Her chest rose and fell at a pace even with the creaking of the tree outside.

"Want some quiche?" I asked her. "I ate most of it, but there's still some left."

"No. I need to sleep, that's all."

"Less work for me."

Somehow, in the process of waiting, dozing off, waiting, watching, and waiting, I had imagined a more romantic homecoming, springing instantly from my resolution in her office parking lot to be less ponderous for her. I recognized that the disappointment I felt was a form of self-involvement that needed to be beheaded.

"Well, glad you're home. I'm going to hit the sack," I said. "G'night."

I stood and made for the stairs. On my way past

her, she reached out and touched the inside of my wrist with her forefinger. I looked down at her, but she kept her chin fixed on the ceiling. Her eyes were closed. I took another step, and she allowed her hand to fall slowly across mine. Our palms pressed and passed; our fingers interlaced for just a moment. Another step away, I paused again, but she remained still.

"You coming, then?" I asked her.

She stayed where she was, following me up only later. When she slipped under the covers with me, I turned onto my side and mumbled as if she were disturbing a powerful sleep, but she unraveled the blankets from my ankles and rolled herself into them. She wrapped her arms around my shoulders and hung across me like a cape, her hands roaming over my neck and shoulders, across my chest and belly, and along my arm. She stopped moving when her fingertips touched mine again and grappled my hands, grazing my earlobe with her lips.

"Are you dreaming or something?" I asked.

"Yeah," she said, kissing me once more before lying still. "I must be."

In the morning, Karen arose earlier than me and opened all of the windows. The already warm breeze rolled through the bedroom and disturbed me awake the same way a fly landing on my cheek might have. The out-of-place exterior sounds of a dog barking and truck brakes squealing pulled me the rest of the way out of sleep.

"Get up!" Karen yelled, peeking in and clapping.

I didn't move at first and just listened as she stomped back down into the kitchen and banged pans and silverware and slammed the refrigerator door. These were typically the sort of sounds my mother had made on Sunday mornings and not the sort of sounds Karen generated, on any day. When she'd flooded the house with the smell of frying pancakes, I figured out that she wasn't going into work, or not yet, and peeled myself from bed, my growling stomach responding to the smell in an inarguable way. This was a rare occasion. Even on Saturdays and Sundays, we didn't bother with breakfast much. I pulled on a pair of sweatpants and hurried downstairs.

We didn't speak much over breakfast other than to discuss the passing of the butter and syrup as needed. In her customary way, Karen sliced her pancakes into tiny, sub-bite-sized squares and drowned them with so much syrup that they began to dissolve on her plate. She ground them into a soft sludge with the flat of her fork and scooped the mess into her mouth. This was her pancake *modus operandi*, and the sight of it both amused and saddened me. It occurred to me that, if things were not completely different today, as promised, and our silence developed into a real separation, that would be just the sort of thing I would miss the most. I took my time eating, savoring the moment, and still had two largish pancakes remaining when she finished and dropped her plate into the sink.

"They'll be cold if you don't eat faster," she warned, picking up a fashion magazine from the counter and relocating to the living-room.

"I don't mind," I called after her. "I'm just happy to have something round to eat."

The sun at the breakfast table warmed me like the blankets I'd kicked off upstairs had. The tension between Karen and I felt softer, dowsed in syrup perhaps. I watched her through the open doorway to the living-room as she claimed the sofa for her own—legs tucked beneath her bathrobe, her mouth and nose fortified behind the pages of her months-old magazine. For the first time in a long while, she looked *casual*. Leaving my remaining pancakes undisturbed on my plate, I followed her into the living-room and searched out the book on the origins of the New England whaling industry I'd been reading and sat down, cross-legged, beside her. Our toes touched, and she whistled Henry Mancini's "Baby Elephant Walk," her favorite song. We read together for a long time and then she closed her magazine.

"Come take a shower with me," she then said, shooting up.

I didn't argue and followed her upstairs to the bathroom. Beside the toilet, I caught her robe as she dropped it off her back and then stood still, arms raised like a child, as she turned and stripped me out of my sweats and t-shirt. We stepped into the shower together, and I was hard by the time she spun the water on. I stroked her shoulders as the water warmed up, and she leaned back, pressing herself against me.

"This is a nice surprise," I said.

She nodded, turning to look at me over her shoulder, blinking in the spray.

"Whatever I did to piss you off, I'm sorry," I said.

She wrapped her arms around me, flattening her petite breasts against me.

"Whatever it was, you're forgiven."

We kissed for a while, and then she reached down to wrap her hand around me, and I jumped at the alien sensation. I bent and took her nipple in my mouth. The water turned briefly cold, and she shuddered.

"That fucking water heater!" she said.

"*Ssh!*"

"Sorry!"

I kissed her belly-button, and she let go of me to tug on my wet hair.

"Stop!" she said.

I ignored her and kissed lower.

"Stop!" she commanded, tugging harder. "Did you hear something?"

"No."

I tried to kiss her again, but she backed away. The shower-stream hit me full in the face, and I bolted upright, spitting.

"Listen!"

This time, I did hear the doorbell ring.

The two FBI agents sat on the sofa and cradled the cups of coffee Karen had offered them without drinking it. Neither had spoken a word since sitting down, and Karen eyed them from the chair in the corner, her bathrobe folded under her thighs and her hands clasped together in her lap. She sat as still as the FBI men did, matching the obliqueness of their facial expressions. I was less cool, leaning way too casually against the fireplace mantle. My feet were bare, and I worried that one of the agents might suddenly lean forward and bash my toes with a hammer. The younger of the two agents was Indian or Pakistani in his nationality, I guessed, maybe wrongly, and was finely dressed in one of the nouveau Sixties Mod-style gray suits with thin tie that I'd been seeing lately on late night television talk show hosts. Scraping at the brim of his cup with his thumbnail, he appeared to be waiting for his partner to speak first as he glanced sideways at the man every couple of seconds or so.

This was the guy to get you talking, I figured.

His partner, on the other hand, was the guy who stepped in if you wouldn't. He was older, closing in on sixty, with a slight paunch that didn't so much give an impression of a lack of physical fitness as it seemed to provide a counterbalance to his tree stump of a torso. His arms and shoulders were huge, and it was clear that, under his much less pricey suit, he sported biceps like small pumpkins. His weathered face was framed by a graying brush-cut, and he looked like a meaner, bulkier Johnny Unitas. He crouched rather than sat on the edge of our couch. I tried to catch a glimpse of a gun hidden somewhere on his person, but he was already so lumpy that it was impossible to tell for certain where he might be storing it. I assumed from television programs that it involved some sort of shoulder holster.

"Shall we try this again?" Karen said, breaking the silence. "Won't you please come in and tell us what this is all about?"

Her hair was still wet from the shower. Slicked back against her scalp, it dripped on her shoulders, which she seemed not to notice.

"Sure," the younger agent said. He had a voice like a late-night soul dee-jay. "You see—"

The older agent cut him off with a look, and he resumed his smiling. We sat a bit longer, and I watched Karen's impatience grow. Her toes knotted the carpet, as if she were bracing herself to monkey-spring from her chair.

"Perhaps you gentlemen would prefer to finish your coffee in your car?" she said. "I have some Styrofoam cups, if you like."

"Thank you, no, ma'am," the older agent said, his voice rattling like a can of thumbtacks. "We're just collecting our thoughts."

"Uh-huh," she said.

He finished off his coffee and set the cup down onto the table in front of him.

"Hugo Farrell," he said.

"Christ, I should have known," Karen sighed, slapping her knee.

"What about him?" I asked, the blood already

rushing to my face.

"We're looking for him."

"Well, he hasn't been here," Karen said, without even looking at me.

I opened my mouth and then shut it again. Both men seemed to notice this, placing their eyes on me for an uncomfortable few seconds while Karen continued to speak.

"We haven't seen him in—how long now, Ivan?"

All eyes turned in my direction. *If anyone asks, I wasn't here*, Hugo's note had instructed. Lying to the FBI: this would be a turning-point for me. What if they already knew he'd been here? I blurted my answer before fully considering it.

"Um, two years?" I said.

The older agent furrowed his brow and squinted at me, as if trying to spot a lighthouse through a fogbank. If I could have picked one thing about myself to change physically, it would have been the sunset-colored blush that exploded across my face whenever anyone looked at me. I wasn't fooling this old salt of a cop, for sure. I held still, though, and met his stare head-on. At intervals, I tried to blink casually without thinking too hard about what blinking casually actually meant.

"That long?" he asked.

"Something like that," Karen said. "2009, I think? Chicago. I was presenting at a weekend ABA conference, so Hugo met up with us to keep Ivan entertained while I was busy."

"Uh-huh," I said. "Since then, he's been bouncing around a lot, I guess."

"You hear from him, then?" the younger one asked.

"Every now and again, he'll drop a postcard."

"Any lately?"

"No," I lied, unsure why I was bothering.

"Not for a few months at least. I think the last one came from Seattle."

"Seattle," the older one said.

I nodded.

"Why are you looking for him, anyway?" I asked.

"We just want to ask him some questions," the agent said. "Nothing to worry about."

He reached into the breast pocket of his suit-coat and retrieved his wallet. As his arm exited the folds of his coat, I spotted dull leather: the shoulder-holster. Without meaning to, I shuffled backward, away from him, and bumped one of the knick-knacks on the mantle with my elbow. I hurried to catch it before it fell, and the older agent took every step of the spectacle in as I bumbled around. When I calmed down, he removed a business card from his wallet and handed it to me. *Carl James Olsen, Special Agent*, it read. He handed another one to Karen.

"If Farrell contacts you in any way, I'd appreciate hearing about it," the agent said. "You can reach me or leave a message at that number. Just ask for Carl."

"Okay," Karen said, nodding, and I presumed that she would not hesitate to call the guy.

The younger agent produced a card from his pocket and handed one to each of us as well, revealing himself to be one Special Agent Khurram Shah.

"Indian?" I asked.

"Pakistani," he corrected sharply, snapping his fingers as if the word were the cue for a song. "And it doesn't matter."

Karen glared at me, and Carl glared at Khurram.

Agent Carl thanked us for our time before his partner could speak again and tugged him out of the front door. Karen shut and locked it as soon as they'd passed through, and we watched as they walked across the lawn to an Oldsmobile parked on the street.

"Fucking Hugo," she sighed, as they pulled away from the curb. "I'm telling you, I'm not surprised one fucking bit."

"Who knows?" I mumbled, receding back into the house and up the stairs before she could turn and look me hard in the face.

7.

For the next few days, ramping up to her continued trial date, Karen worked very late. I continued to wait up for her, always with various black apprehensions, but she paid little attention to me upon re-entering the house every night, throwing me only a cursory nod or, "Hey," before undressing, washing, and, very quickly thereafter, diving into deep sleep. She seemed to sense, as Agent Carl had, that I was full of shit with regard to Hugo. She had known the last time *she'd* seen Hugo, and, until I'd opened my mouth there, leaning on our mantel, she'd assumed that the last time I'd seen Hugo was more or less the last time she had. *Not true*, she now knew, though I'd avoided the subject all afternoon that day, after the FBI had spoiled what was apparently our one shot at a romantic interlude for the entire summer. I stuck to my story for lack of any better idea, but she only let me get away with it on the surface of things. She didn't try to depose me, but I got her cold shoulder in spades. We became mere roommates again.

I fought off the now very tired urge to compare Karen to Lyudmila and myself to Anosov, though that urge was reflex for me at this point.

It was a childish comparison.

Those final days awaiting the firing squad had been lonely ones for Anosov. Trotsky in exile, Lenin dead, Stalin dispatching anything that looked like a threat, Anosov could have used a voice on the other side of the door, surely. Lyudmila had visited him only once, however, for an apparently almost wordless exchange that Anosov reportedly described as "pleasant but ultimately unfruitful." One would like to describe it as a defining moment in Anosov's life, but you could only read so much into a description like that. I'd always wondered how the air between such close people could reach such an intractable state of upper altitude thinness—and, now, I was finding out exactly how.

According to Piroshev and Millar, the authorities who weighed in most heavily on my hero, Anosov, Lyudmila was really a cold-hearted bitch. Naturally, Piroshev and Millar were a little more adroit about it, but the consensus was generally that, once Anosov could no longer propel Lyudmila upward in society, could no longer provide her with access to the corridors of luxury and power that had beckoned her up from the trenches of peasantry and poverty, she simply moved on.

Piroshev and Millar, read now by only we dedicated few, really provided little information about the state of the atmosphere in his jail-cell, during or after Lyudmila's final visit. By that time, it was all over for Anosov, and both of them knew it.

Truly, in those days, they were fortunate to even be allowed that final visit, a privilege that I assumed, without evidence of any sort, was due to the esteem with which Anosov's captors held him. Perhaps they admired

Anosov, maybe relieved to have captured such a fierce opponent, or simply patiently waiting out the moment when they could put him to the firing squad, they nonetheless apparently afforded him certain accommodations in his cell. He was a good prisoner, no doubt—conversational, friendly, and gallantly accepting of his fate. He gave them no trouble. He advised them on their personal problems, confided his own female troubles through the heavy iron door after his block of stale bread was passed through each day. I imagined the camaraderie that bonds all military men despite battlefield opposition was thick between Anosov and his captors, the recognition that, but for the will of fate and god, their positions might be reversed, the uniforms exchanged, the Hague Convention of 1907 applying to one and not the other, the door between them locked and unlocked and locked again.

Of course, most of this was the product of my own imagination. I spent a lot of time on yard work these days, after all.

And I could imagine that, when a woman arrived, begging to speak with the prisoner, an exchange was allowed through the heavy door, perhaps under supervision, because he was Anosov and she was beautiful, even through her heavy veil. No one now knows what was said, but, clearly, it was indeed "ultimately unfruitful" as Anosov was shot shortly thereafter, his remains lost to the fields of mass graves dotting that Russian countryside. Lyudmila was gone by then, having arrived from and then returned to the safe folds of some former opponent's coattails, no doubt.

I had ingested Piroshev and Millar's accounts so early on in my life that this story had come to signify something like a personal eventuality to me. Possibly I was twelve or thirteen years old the first time I read that material, and, at that time, I took Lyudmila's lack of steadfastness to heart. It shocked me that she would not demand to be shot alongside her lover. The hollow loneliness that Anosov must have experienced in his final moments echoed within me for days afterward. I drew a picture of him in front of the firing squad for a school art project, which resulted in a frantic phone call to my mother from my teacher. Apparently, I went a little overboard with the red crayon. However, what may have upset my teacher more than anything was the word-balloon I'd drawn springing from Anosov's screaming lips: "WHY LYUDMILA WHY?!?"

I clearly had an overdeveloped sense of romance that was not normal for a boy of almost any age.

In any case, my mother didn't put an end to my Sunday afternoon habit of watching Humphrey Bogart and Lauren Bacall whispering to each other on our small black-and-white television. Alone herself for years, my mother didn't fear romance. My instinct that Lyudmila had wronged Anosov was not quelled, and I continued to believe this to be so to the present day.

No, the fact that love ended badly for Anosov rippled on throughout my life. In junior high school, I viewed every girl sidling up to me in the school hallway with a folded note as leading me off to the firing squad in some way. I liked girls; I wanted girls to hand me notes. But there it was. Romance was passion striated with fear and aversion. At some later point, I heard that it was better to have loved and lost than to never have loved, and that sounded pretty good, too. I didn't know which way to turn. Every new canard injected into my system simply resulted in greater confusion, all because of my early education in the inevitable relationship between love and a firing squad.

Even now, when Anosov's gloomy biography occasionally rattled me into outright pessimism, I forced myself to recall some of the earlier events in his life, the happier moments, such as the time he trained a grey dog to fetch his boots for him, or, better yet, his first meeting with Lyudmila, in her village, in the middle of nowhere. That was the account that brought home the whole point of love and marriage for me, at least when the twelve year-old boy within me wanted to believe the best of it all.

Regardless of what that boy, who sometimes seemed as dead and buried as Anosov to me and sometimes did not, now thought of anything, it was still a good story.

Anosov and Lyudmila first met on a cold November morning in 1915, as Anosov and Piorotkin, his comrade-in-arms since childhood, fled a detachment of Bolsheviks into a woods a few hundred kilometers west of Moscow. The two had just led a raid against the small army detachment guarding a caravan of wheat grain confiscated from nearby villages for hungry Muscovites. All but a few of the soldiers guarding the wheat were dead, and Anosov had directed his men to escort the seven wagons of grain back to the nearest village—after confiscating whatever portion of the wheat Anosov's group required to continue their resistance. This left Anosov and Piorotkin alone, along with their own few wounded, to forge ahead to determine whether the next village was free of danger and suitable for the group's recuperation. The two watched their men disappear back along the road with the wagons before moving forward with their group, making slow progress because of the injuries among them. They hadn't gotten far when the Bolsheviks, traveling in the opposite direction along the road, found them.

Anosov and Piorotkin were the only uninjured

members of the group, but the raid had left them fatigued and in less than ideal fighting condition, let alone able to protect their wounded from two dozen well-armed professional soldiers. Anosov quickly ordered his wounded men to make for a nearby tree-line of the woods while he and Piorotkin dove into the brush beside the road to hold the Bolsheviks off with pot-shots. They laid low while their men escaped, vanishing with practiced ease into the trees, and sniped away at the Bolsheviks, constantly shifting their positions, crawling along the ground, rolling from one firing point to the next, hoping to give the impression that many more than two men were engaged in the attack. It seemed to work for a moment, and the Bolsheviks, surprised, retreated and fell back behind a rise in the road. Bolsheviks were not famous for retreating, however, and Anosov knew that they would regain the advantage quickly. He aimed his rifle carefully at the center of the road and shot the tall hat off of the first Bolshevik head to peer over. When Piorotkin hissed at him that their men had made their escape, Anosov waved him along as he leaped up and bolted for the woods himself. Bullets chipping the wood from tree trunks beside them, the two plunged into the tree-line and did not stop running until they were deep within the wood, under a canopy so thick that the forest floor, where visible at all, glowed a faint, dead silver, as if lit only by a half-clouded moon.

It didn't take Anosov and Piorotkin long to realize that they'd run into the wood on one side of the road while their men had run into the wood on the other side. The road was long and effectively bifurcated the wood. The Bolsheviks were relentless and would be watching for darting figures on the open road. Once they realized they were not being immediately pursued, however, Anosov and Piorotkin stopped to discuss their options.

After a quick debate, they decided that continuing onward into the wood a bit and then circling back in a wide arc which would, hopefully, take them back behind the Bolsheviks seemed the best option. They were less worried about reuniting with their wounded men, none of whom were in mortal danger, than with warning their unwounded comrades who had traveled back down the road with the grain wagons. They would try to catch up with them only to run into the Bolsheviks themselves, and, while they were in better fighting condition than the wounded men were, they were still no match for the Bolsheviks and would be surprised and scattered without Anosov's leadership. Without Anosov, Piorotkin reminded him, they were frankly only a band of peasants who were slightly better armed than most other peasants.

With this, the two continued into the wood. Neither, however, was an experienced woodsman, and the thickness and darkness of the forest soon got the best of them. After several hours, they assumed that they were wandering in circles, but even determining that much was beyond them. They walked on, at first joking about their predicament, then, soon, in complete silence, the humor of the situation vanishing in favor of aching backs and knees, branch-scratched faces, and cold, reddening knuckles and fingertips. When the last of the light fighting its way down to the forest floor disappeared and the branches above their heads truly became a tangled nest of darkness, they gave up walking and simply huddled together at the base of a tree, shoving the toes of their worn boots beneath the dead leaves and loam. Piorotkin's head on his shoulder, Anosov slept, wondering whether his men had made it to the village with the grain and whether they had survived much more than that.

Both men survived the night and awoke to see that the oak that had sheltered them stood at the crook of a narrow but well-worn footpath. They clapped hands and hugged at the sight of it but soon fell to bickering over whether they should walk right or left along it. Both directions looked equally well-forested, each end of the path curving off behind row after row of the same thick trees they had been pushing through for a day. Piorotkin suggested that he play left to Anosov's right and that they arm wrestle for the direction, but Anosov seemed not to hear him as he considered the options, which seemed to Piorotkin to number only two.

"My friend," Anosov said finally, staring down at the path, "we should each take a direction."

This suggestion seemed, at first, mad to Piorotkin, who could think of nothing worse than dying alone in the woods. Anosov explained that the important thing was the safety of the men and that, if they split up, at least one of them should make it back to the main road, to which the path presumably led, and could then see to the safety of their group. The other would eventually realize his mistake and turn around, but the sooner it was verified that the Bolsheviks had or had not destroyed their outfit the better, let alone the wounded they had also accidentally abandoned. Piorotkin admitted the sense in this suggestion.

"Besides," Anosov assured him, "that is the beautiful thing about a path. Both ends lead somewhere, else it would not exist. Neither of us will die now in this wood."

With that, Anosov and Piorotkin embraced and set off down opposite ends of the path, Anosov to the left, Piorotkin to the right. Anosov stopped to watch his friend disappear around the first curve, not realizing that it would be the last time he would ever see Piorotkin alive. He waved goodbye to his friend, who did not turn to see the gesture, and then continued on leftward down the path, which, unbeknownst to him, plunged him deeper yet into the wood.

    Anosov walked on for hours. Hungry and sore, he suspected that Piorotkin had taken the proper turn on the path, but they had walked so far the previous day that it was impossible to say with certainty. He held to his own words and hoped, eventually, to at least find the end of the path in this direction, wherever it might lie, whether it be at the forest's opposite side, a road and his comrades, or some simple woodcutter's cottage. The thought that one of things—or *anything*—might be just around the next corner kept him moving forward, even when he knew that, with every step, the hoped-for result of finding the main road and his comrades grew less and less likely. Eventually, exhausted, he sat down, and, within seconds, was sound asleep.

    A woman's voice awoke Anosov as darkness began to fall once again. Startled, he opened his eyes to find standing before him a peasant girl, perhaps sixteen or seventeen years old, with wheat-colored hair curling out from beneath a bright red babushka. She had the chapped cheeks and hands of a country girl, but her smile was wide and her eyes were blue. Her feet were bare but slender, with narrow, clean toes. She did not have the feet of a peasant. She was beautiful and, Anosov, immediately felt, as much a stranger in this wood as he. Her smile broadened, and Anosov realized that she was laughing at him.

    "Who might you be?" she asked in an odd accent, typical of the peasants of this region but also slightly formal and antiquated.

    Anosov jumped to his feet, brushing his hands clean over his leggings, shaking the sleep from his head.

    "Anosov," he replied, holding out his hand.

    She didn't take his hand and seemed more interested in his own feet, which, although removed from their boots, were thickly bandaged with strips of cotton.

"Are you injured?" she asked.

"No," he said. "For marching."

He walked in place as though he were explaining what he meant to a foreigner, and she wrinkled her brow at him.

"Well, you'll freeze out here," she said. "Whatever are you doing here?"

"Lost," he admitted.

"Come on, then," she said, walking back down the path in the direction in which Anosov had originally been headed. "You'll need soup."

Anosov laughed, forgetting his exhaustion.

"Yes, you're quite right," he said. "I do need soup."

"I thought so," the girl said. She beckoned him onward with a cock of her head, and he set off after her.

"What is your name?" he asked her, as they rounded the next curve and entered her village, which Anosov would have stumbled into himself if only he had managed to walk a little further on his own.

"Lyudmila Ekaterina Miroshin," she answered, glancing back at him with her wide, blue eyes.

Piroshev and Millar simply sum up the rest of the meeting. Smitten, Anosov forgot his men, his friends, and stayed with Lyudmila in her backwoods village for a month. She fed him, wove and embroidered a vest for him, and, when he remembered his responsibilities at last, she left with him, never again to return home.

It was the end of Anosov the solitary, Robin Hood-like figure who led his men into combat with daring and with an Errol Flynn-like wink and smile. It was the beginning of Anosov the lover, Anosov the would-be husband, Anosov the cuckold, and, eventually, Anosov the prisoner and martyr. Piorotkin was the first casualty of their love; Anosov himself would be the next.

It was a story without a happy ending, but, if you ended it at this point, with Anosov in his excellent vest striding out of that village with a beautiful woman on his arm, it comes off like a fairy tale. Hero goes into dark woods, comes out with princess. At certain points while reflecting on my own marriage, I considered myself to be like Anosov at this stage of his biography: victorious despite having briefly lost his way. At other points, however, I assumed that some sort of firing squad loomed ahead for me just as it had for Anosov.

This was the context for my outlook on love and marriage, the plotline I probably had always expected my relationship with Karen to follow—subconsciously. My pessimistic predilections arose from my early identification with Anosov, probably, but, as I'd often noticed while avoiding direct argument or physical confrontation with others, I was myself no Anosov. While Anosov might have trounced my schoolyard bullies, he was Lyudmila's hapless victim all the way.

I didn't think Karen and Lyudmila were particularly alike in the manner in which they related to men—Karen couldn't possibly use *me* for any gain in social position—but I liked to think that I was as unlike Anosov with regard to his romantic behavior as I was with regard to his revolutionary behavior. I didn't have to leave the ball in Karen's court every time; I was capable of leaping into action Anosov-style every now and again myself, though I could not remember the last time I had done so. I didn't want to be Karen's roommate; I wanted to be the object of her passion, though I wasn't sure it was still entirely possible as Karen, likely, did not associate objects of passion with either of the words "unemployed" or "librarian."

Still, the night before her next trial date, I again waited late into the night for her, and, when she finally staggered through the door, exhausted, I startled her by leaping up to help her with her bags and offered to make her something to eat. She shook her head and sat down on the couch to remove her shoes.

"What's gotten into you?" she asked me without looking up.

"Nothing," I said. "I guess even I get tired of, well, whatever it is that I do sometimes."

"You've been watching daytime talk-shows again," Karen laughed, leaning back and loosening up at last.

"Only on Thursdays," I said.

"I hear they give away free cars now."

"Only on Fridays."

Karen laughed again but closed her eyes.

"Man, what a day," she sighed.

"Tough one?"

"Uh-huh."

"All set for tomorrow?" I asked her.

"Uh-huh."

I turned off the lights in the living-room, one by one, as her breathing softened and deepened. She balled her hands into fists and then relaxed them, rubbing her palms over the couch's textured upholstery.

"Want to go away for the weekend?" I asked her when all of the lights were off except the one over the stairwell leading upstairs.

"Be serious," she sighed.

"I am serious," I said, pulling her gently to her feet to help her upstairs. "Next weekend. Let's go. No big deal. You can bring some work if you have to."

"Daytime talk shows rock," she giggled.

"Just wait till I get the free car," I said as we

mounted the stairs.

Upstairs, I helped her out of her jacket, blouse, and skirt, peeled her stockings off, and then re-hangered her suit like a Victorian valet while she cleaned up in the bathroom. When she emerged, I folded back the covers on the bed for her and tucked them in tightly around her after she'd climbed in. I clicked the lamp on the nightstand beside our bed off and pecked her on the cheek before lying back myself. To my surprise, she rolled over and wrapped her arms around my waist, tucking the tip of her chin into the curve of my neck.

"Let's do it," she whispered. "Let's get the hell out of here for a few days."

"Okay, great," I said. "We'll head west, see some water."

"Sounds nice," she mumbled, falling asleep. "Do we get a chauffeur with the free car?"

"Who needs one? We have you," I said.

She replied with a soft snore, like a cat's, her breath warm against my neck.

8.

Karen's backed-up desk work caused off to put the trip off for an extra week, to just before Labor Day, in the end. However, for the next week, she returned home every day with some new purchase that would make our trip more fulfilling: walking shoes, birding guides, mystery novels, even massage oil, as if we would be gone a month rather than two days, as if we would pay any attention to any bird that came anywhere near us in Saugatuck, the touristic beach town on Lake Michigan which was our destination. We chatted about whether the beach would be too crowded or, worse, as had happened to us on previous getaways, whether the beach would be simply unusable due to the apparently semi-seasonal mass suicide of a very odorous species of fish. We reminisced about the restaurants in town and a bar once visited by Hemingway, about the arts and crafts fair that occupied the whole of the downtown area each summer. She browsed the internet for other area attractions just in case the dead fish washed up onto the beach again and called to check whether our favorite hot dog joint in nearby Grand Rapids was still in business.

It was the most we'd talked in ages, though, for that week, we still rarely ate a meal together and the twin conversational poles of work and trip constituted the entirety of our interaction. I ran out of things to say about west Michigan after we'd covered the basics, though, and small-talk about her office goings-ons, such as who exactly was covering for her, who he or she was, what they were like—just earned me eye-rolls and deep sighs. Once, I mentioned a story I'd seen on a television news program about a local man who'd been arrested for keeping two Siberian tigers in his basement, but she just changed the subject back to the trip.

The plastic bags of vacation accoutrements she'd bought were left lying on the kitchen counter for days. As much as I was looking forward to the trip, it still occurred to me that this détente was the sort that had brought about World War II. I was as pent up and ready to break free as the German people had been two decades after the imposition of the Treaty of Versailles, and I assumed the same of her. All either of us needed was our own, personal Hitler to lead the way. Was Karen Hitler? Or was I? Was she the German people? Who were the liberating Allies?

I had no idea.

Analogies to military history had only ever failed me.

Finally, though, the big day came. The interior of the car was over eighty degrees according to the digital thermometer in the dashboard when we climbed in to leave at 8:00 AM. The heat had been climbing for days prior to our departure, which had Karen miserable in her business clothing by evening every night but which she said meant we'd have great beach weather. That morning, though, we were one glorious block away from home when we discovered that the air conditioner was no longer pumping out anything but the dusty sort of atmosphere that follows city busses around, and our thighs and forearms were already sealed to our black upholstery. We rolled the windows down and sped to the highway regardless, but an impossible traffic jam piled up behind a point of Michigan's usual summer highway repair scrambling stopped us upon sliding down the highway entrance ramp.

"Jesus Christ," Karen said, tightening her grip around the steering wheel.

I pushed a CD into the dashboard stereo and tried to coax her into singing along with me, but she wanted nothing to do with Irish folk music, which was never a sign of anything good in anybody in my opinion. Instead, she stared down the unmoving traffic as though she could telekinetically fling the cars locking us in from the highway. After a few minutes of stop-and-go, she began to hum along, but only in a spitty, sarcastic way. I'd never heard anyone hum angry before, but Karen managed it. I stared out of the passenger-side window and tried to enjoy myself, but the traffic jam lasted all the way out of the Detroit Metro area. Past Wixom, we picked up speed, but Karen's mood stayed where it was for the balance of the trip.

It hadn't taken long for Karen to revert to her after-work demeanor. The planning of the trip would turn out to be the point of the venture, I feared. Presuming that anything I did or said would only further irritate her, I did not try to cheer her up. If the Irish music couldn't do it, what could?

Instead, I enjoyed my sideways passenger-window view, settling into the flat groove of mid-Michigan's farmland-and-strip-mall vistas. We passed oddly placed subdivisions of enormous but identical houses in places where there had been only a small pond or a service road before, clustered together for safety in the shadows of gigantic signs reading "From the Lower $350s & Up!" and punctuated with billboards advertising the rightwing AM talk-radio shows. Miles of furrowed cornfields between these things were occasionally graced by the shadow of a spiraling hawk or the sudden explosion of sparrows from a lone tree's branches, but, otherwise, mid-Michigan was a portrait of a nature beaten into dreariness by underfunded real estate developers.

 Still, the twelve year-old me hadn't been laid totally to rest, and I still felt the giddy excitement I had when I was a kid piling into the backseat of my mother's Pinto, along with the three hours' worth of books and toys and blankets she'd wrapped in around me, as we prepared to drive to Gatlinburg, Tennessee or some other pre-packaged destination. Those were my fondest childhood memories. I couldn't take a car trip now without packing my mother into the suitcase, and Karen couldn't manufacture a bad mood powerful enough to dispel my Pinto nostalgia entirely. I sat back and let Karen be, and, eventually, when, nearing Okemos, I laid my hand on her bare knee, she didn't push it away.

 The bed and breakfast we'd booked in Saugatuck was an old Victorian Painted Lady done up in forest green with gold and burgundy trim. I counted only three windows on the upstairs floor as we entered and none on the ground floor that I could see that weren't attached to simply functional rooms—kitchen, living-room, or dining-room, and a frosted window over what I presumed to be a bathroom. The brochure for the place had featured only a pencil drawing on the front that made the house look much larger than it was. Stepping up onto the porch, a rail-thin fifty-something man in sandals and a weather-worn polo shirt opened the door before we could knock.

"Hi, there," he said. "The Tracys, I presume?"

"That's us," I said.

"Welcome," he said, holding the door for us. "I'm Tim. I run the place."

"Right," I said. "We spoke on the phone."

"Yep."

He asked us if we'd had trouble finding the place, and Karen shook her head and described the traffic-jam back in Detroit.

"Traffic, yeah," Tim said, nodding. "Bummer. Don't get a lot of that here, which I love. Let me show you around and get you booked in."

He turned, and we followed him inside.

The dining-room and living-area of the house, visible upon first entry, looked to have been meticulously restored in Victorian style—although with electricity and other mod cons—and was replete with beautiful woodworking, floral arrangements, and a couple of carefully placed Tiffany-esque lamps. The floors were hardwood, and both main rooms featured stained glass windows, antique furniture, and enormous bay-windows framing the tree-lined road outside. Tim guided us to a corner of a china cabinet in the large dining-room where he penciled our arrival-time by hand into a spiral-bound ledger and swiped Karen's credit card through a tiny card reader attached to a smart phone.

He handed us an old-fashioned skeleton-type room key on a long leather strap with a room-number Sharpied onto it and then led us up a creaking staircase to a bright attic room with a white painted ceiling and floral wallpaper of the sort I'd last seen visiting my grandmother's house as a child. A single, large window overlooked a backyard swimming pool and, beyond a line of trees, the silver horizon streak of Lake Michigan. Tim told us where we could find anything we needed that wasn't already in the room, wished us welcome again, and then shut the door behind him. A good host, he knew when to vamoose.

We froze in place, listening to him tromping back down the stairs. Every step sounded like a tree tipping over. Karen walked across the room to peer into the bathroom, and the old floorboards creaked just as loudly.

"Guess we won't be making much noise in here," she laughed.

"Guess not. It's nice, though, isn't it?"

"Yeah," she said, leaning on the window-sill and looking outside. "It is. Nice pool, too."

"Looks like it. Got your swim suit?"

"Four or five," she sighed, "but I'm a beach girl."

I joined her at the window and looked down. The walls of the swimming pool outside were painted to look like a coral reef, complete with psychedelic fish, hammerhead sharks, and dolphins. It was impossible to tell how deep it was because of the decoration, and I wondered if I could survive leaping out of the window into it. Karen turned away from the window and cranked the air conditioning on full-blast, and we both spent a few minutes just standing in front of the central air vent. We stripped out of our clothes and lay down on the surprisingly hard bed together and then, at some point, fell asleep under the gingham canopy.

We didn't wake again until after the sun had set. When we did, we were hungry, so we showered and dressed and made our way into town for dinner. Winding our way around the Lake Michigan inlet on the way into town, we slowed down to get a better look at the small but brightly painted homes that all looked like wedding cake toppers lining the main drag. The traffic flow thickened and slowed to a crawl the closer we came toward the downtown grid, and Karen busied herself pointing out every feature of each of the little houses we passed that she thought we might adapt.

"Check that dormer out, Ivan!" she said, pointing at a peaked roof that might have been stolen from an oversized cuckoo clock. "We could do something like that, don't you think? You think you could figure out how to build something like that?"

"Not in a million years," I said.

"You could do it if you wanted to. How hard could it be? People that do that sort of thing don't even have high-school diplomas half the time."

I just drove and didn't respond, wary of the slow-moving bumpers in front of me and enjoying being behind the wheel for once. Pulling into the downtown area, the town looked the same as it always had, a tight beehive of a gift shops and little art galleries and boutiques, nestled tightly against a waterfront strip with a well-populated marina. Strolling tourists sidled past display windows, drifting in and out of fudge and ice cream shops. Out over the water, at the end of the marina, a single, stunted firework exploded in a brief shower of red sparks as we drove past, briefly exciting Karen until we figured out that it was probably just some hand-held, illegal munition carted up from Ohio. Karen pointed spotted a restaurant around the corner from the marina that looked good to her, so we drove a few blocks out of downtown to park and hiked back. My legs ached with the strain of just a few blocks' worth of exercise, and it occurred to me that I could not remember the last time that I'd walked a greater distance than the front porch to the driveway and back. Not good: I was pretty sure that, after a certain age, muscles allowed to gelatinize just sort of stayed that way.

We walked in and found a table in a nice corner beside a window overlooking the water and ordered beers and hamburgers and watched a boat covered in green and red Christmas lights mooring in its slip. A sixty-something woman in a striped polo shirt and khaki mini-skirt stood on the prow with one leg propped up on the stainless steel railing, exposing her pantied crotch.

"That boat is decorated for Christmas already," Karen said.

"She's on a boat?" I asked.

"Look lower."

"Oh, that," I laughed. "Tis the season. In about four months, anyway. What are you buying me?"

Karen absorbed the question with narrowed eyes and tapped her beer bottle on the tabletop rather than answering even in jest, giving the distinct impression that the question might be mooted entirely by the time December rolled around. I suddenly felt as though I'd walked into a bathroom at a dinner party to find the host in the process of using it. Thankfully, the waitress brought our hamburgers over on a tray shaped like a ship's steering wheel, giving us something else to do for the moment. We devoured the burgers like starving wolves, and I watched the woman on the boat put her leg down and retreat from sight, toward the back of her boat. When we finished eating, we sat still, looking out at the water, pretending like we weren't just trying a little too hard to come up with something to say next. Karen knocked her foot against mine under the table, and then snapped it back a little too eagerly.

"Sorry," she said.

"That's okay," I said. "What do you want to do

next?"

She leaned back in her chair and stared outside again.

"I don't know," she said. "Is it too late to swim?"

"This late? After dark? Who knows what lurks out there beneath the waves?"

"Too many movies for you."

"They're my survival guide. I wouldn't have survived Horror High and Zombie Hell Camp without them."

"Whore High? Was that woman on the boat a counselor?"

"Never mind."

I reached across the table to hold her hand. I expected her to pull it away, but she didn't.

"That's nice," she said.

"You have the second nicest hands I've ever held," I said.

"Yeah?" she smiled. "Who had the nicest?"

"Ladybird Johnson. But I'm not supposed to talk about that."

"Oh, okay, then."

She slipped her hand free and pushed her hair back from her ear. Her eyes glittered, and I noticed for the first time that she'd freckled more than usual over the course of the summer. She smiled in the nicest way possible and leaned across the table to kiss me. Her lips tasted like salt from the french fries, and I couldn't resist licking them clean as she withdrew.

"Gross," she moaned, wincing and wiping her mouth with the back of her hand.

"Mmm," I said. "Like the sea!"

I kissed her again, and, when we parted, we stayed close, leaning over the table like high-school kids.

"How about dancing?" I asked her.

"You're kidding."

"Why not?"

"Are you sure the monsters at Horror High haven't possessed you? Is this my Ivan, or his evil twin?"

"What do you care? As long as I can shake a leg, right?"

I hated dancing. She adored it. That's all there was to it. I got a recommendation from the waitress as we paid our bill, and we headed off to find the place.

It didn't take us long to figure out that Saugatuck's premier dance club back out on the Blue Star Highway was a gay bar. It was karaoke night, and the sound of a deep voice belting out "Dancing Queen" hit us the minute we opened the door. Three bartenders in body-formed, sleeveless t-shirts cruised back and forth behind the bar, trading drinks for cash with choreographed precision. They were uniformly well-sculpted, good-looking guys, in contrast to the rest of the men in the crowd, who were an older, graying group, largely. Hair color aside, they were the more jubilant cousins of the people mooring boats in at the marina downtown without question. It had been a long time since I'd walked into such a crowded room, but Karen stepped grabbed me by the wrist and yanked me in. She guided us toward the bar as if she owned the place, dragging me across the dance-floor to the bar, past the deep singing Abba fan onstage, and then released me beside a mirrored support column while she shouted an order for two rum and Cokes at the nearest bartender. Once we had them, we stepped away from the bar and half-danced on the edge of the dance-floor while sipping the drinks. It was hot. Someone bumped into me, spilling my drink out over the back of my hand.

"Shake it off," Karen shouted, bobbing her head to what I thought was a latter-day Madonna tune. I wiped my hand and wondered if I would like dancing more than I used to.

I never had, other than jumping up and down at a Descendants show when I was sixteen, maybe. Everyone else was having a good time, though, and Karen was smiling out over the edge of her plastic cup, thrilled to be in the middle of a happy bustle. I couldn't help but smile when Nick Gilder's "Hot Child in the City" took over from Madonna. A favorite tune of my childhood.

"This place is great!" Karen shouted, knocking back the rest of her drink and freeing herself to lean into some sort of a dance involving an arched back and chicken-winged elbows striking me in the ribs.

I didn't know any actual dances, so I imitated her as best I could as she picked up speed and lured me deeper onto the dance-floor. I did what I could to keep up, and I couldn't remember if she'd always been such a frenetic dancer or if we'd simply never done this sort of thing before. When the DJ played "Fox on the Run," another staple of my past—and which always reminded me of my childhood babysitter Marisa for obvious reasons—I managed to stop thinking for the first time in a while and just *move*.

We danced through three straight songs and then stumbled toward the bar for another drink. I could hardly breathe, but I didn't mind at all and realized as Karen handed me another plastic cup that I was smiling.

Then someone yelled, "Hey, *chica*!" in my ear, and a man grabbed Karen by the hand and spun her away.

"Roger!" she shrieked, allowing herself to be wheeled around. When she stopped spinning, she spun her new partner back to me.

"Ivan, look! It's Roger! You remember him from the holiday party at the firm?" she said.

I did not, but I smiled and shook hands with the

man anyway. Roger was a well-built man a few inches taller than I was, although with thinning hair and a white Tom Selleck moustache yellowed around the edges from cigarette smoke. He wore gold wire-rimmed glasses, and his whitened teeth were offset and made luminous in the colored light by viciously tanned skin. A shock of thick hair curled out of his open shirt collar.

"I can't believe you're here!" she shrieked.

"I can't believe *you're* here," he said. "I'm *always* here. Glenn and I have a summer place in Douglas."

"And the famous Ivan!" he yelled over Karen's shoulder at me. "Karen is always telling me about your never-ending quest for knowledge ... I envy you! I'd absolutely love to stay home and just *read*—I just don't have the time."

Roger waited for me to reply, but I couldn't think of anything to say.

"Ivan's thinking of law school," she offered, much to my surprise, "but he hasn't made up his mind yet."

"God, don't do it!" Roger exclaimed, shaking his head firmly. "Then again, we had a law clerk in our office last summer who was, what? Thirty-eight years old? Is that right?"

"Thirty-three," Karen said.

"Sure," I said, failing to stop myself glaring at my wife. "Well, I've got him beat by almost a decade."

He laughed and insisted that we join him for drinks. Karen accepted on my behalf before I could offer an excuse, and we shortly found ourselves packed into a tight booth with Roger and his partner, Glenn, also a lawyer.

"You should be proud of young Karen here," he told me after ordering a round of Tom Collinses. "She's turned out to be the best hoofer in the firm."

"And a few other firms, too," Glen added.

Glen was short, bald, and bespectacled. No other qualities sprang to my mind as I watched him suck his drink through a red, plastic stirring straw.

"Is that right? I didn't know you got around so much, Karen," I said.

She shrugged.

"Are you kidding?" Roger said. "We hit the clubs every Thursday night after the staff meeting! She was a work in progress, but she's come quite a long way."

"Thanks to you," Glenn said.

"Thanks to me, that's right," Roger laughed. "I don't mind saying that I've always had a knack for slacks, if you get my drift."

I didn't get his drift, and I hadn't disliked anyone so intensely in quite a long while. I wasn't sure what to do with it. Most of my little hatreds were abstract, focused on humanity in general, not an individual people who mostly seemed to mean well and just as often surprised me by being more interesting on some level than first appearances would lead one to believe. Here, now, though, I wanted to get away from Roger, and I wanted scream at Karen. Law school?

"Every Thursday, huh?" I said.

"Uh-oh!" said Glenn, covering his glasses with his tiny hand.

"Did I put my foot in it, Speckles?" Roger said to Karen.

She blushed again and shook her head.

"Don't worry about it," she said.

"Speckles?" I asked.

"On account of my freckles," she said. "Roger said it once at the club, and it caught on. Drives me crazy."

"Hilarious."

She patted me on the knee, indicating that, whatever might occur to me to say next, I should keep quiet.

"Did you see Paul Berkley in the office last week?" she asked him, but he waved her off.

"Please! We're on vacation, kid! I don't even know that name."

"I really don't know it," Glenn said.

He rapped his oversized ring against the table's edge, and I realized he was about as pleased by this chance meeting as I was. Our eyes met and exchanged our mutual disappointment. We'd both wanted to be alone with our significant others; we'd both wanted the firm left far behind in Detroit.

"I don't know it, either," I echoed.

Despite our obvious displeasure, Roger and Karen persisted in discussing the despicable Paul Berkley with great enthusiasm.

Our drinks arrived, and Glenn and I sipped ours as if expecting cockroaches to swarm out of the cups. Karen's and Roger's remained untouched for quite some time, and I soon remembered why I hated disco as the DJ spun some really, really extended dance mix of "Roller Coaster." My temples throbbed; the strobe light we'd settled beneath threw Karen into a stop motion pantomime of bowing, nodding, half-dancing, laughing. I endured it as long as I could and then, apologizing, tugged at Karen's arm and simply walking from the club, compelling her to trip after me lest she stumble and fall. Near the door, she simply dug in her heels and refused to move, but, I moved her anyway, suddenly remembering like a recovering amnesia victim that I was, in fact, much stronger than she was. I hauled her past the bartenders in their tight shirts, past the DJ, and past a woman at the pool table in skinhead bracers and Doc Martens, at least a decade too young for this bar, who looked as if she'd like to drive her pool cue straight through my rectum.

She would have been right to do it.

9.

The ride home from Saugatuck was exhausting. Karen drove in silence while I stared through the glass at the passing landscape. I stared on even after the darkness outside left me simply staring at my own reflection in the window. All the way home, there I was: the baggy-eyed version of the kid I used to be. Even translucent, I could spot the gray in my short hair and the crow's feet around my eyes, and the fat cheeks that had once been sort of gaunt and hollow. I had thought that I looked tough when I was seventeen. Now, I was no different than any other middle-aged guy pushing a shopping cart in the parking lot of the supermarket up on Woodward. No, I had never actually been tough or mean, but I had once tried to look the part. Who didn't in a Minor Threat t-shirt? What skinny frame didn't a leather motorcycle jacket add some bulk to? I looked like an old man, now, propped up on life's lawn chair, waiting to talk college football with guys from the bowling league. I was grateful when passing car lights punched through my reflection and I vanished entirely.

Once home, we slept—briefly—and then Karen woke up to her alarm clock's regularly scheduled 6:15 a.m. blast and left for work without a word. She didn't call me during the day to say hello, to ask what I was up to, to tell me about a particularly vexing conversation, to ask me to leave some dinner for her, or for any other reason. She worked late, making up for the time she'd taken off over the weekend, I presumed, and she went to bed immediately upon returning, dismissing my greeting and offer of a microwaved TV dinner with an exhausted nod. A few more days slid by in similar fashion, and, when Thursday rolled around and she came home very late once again, and I waited in bed, gritting my teeth in the dark as I stared up at our mysterious ceiling, imagining her dancing with Roger or, worse, with some other lawyer asshole. When she rolled in around one a.m. and tried to slip discreetly into bed beside me, I sat up and squinted at her through the dark.

"Out dancing?" I asked.

"You know where I was," she sighed, pushing her way into bed.

"I don't really, do I?"

"I'm tired, Ivan. Just go to sleep," she snapped, lying back and rolling away from me.

"How am I supposed to sleep with you coming home like this?"

"What's new about it?" she said, sitting up again. "I've always come home late. It's my job."

"Going out dancing is part of your job?"

"I told you I wasn't dancing!" she nearly screamed, thudding her small fist into her pillow.

"You did not," I countered. "You dodged the question."

"Don't be an asshole," she groaned. "I'm just so, so

fucking tired."

"Of what?"

"Of who?" she corrected me.

"Well, I'm tired of you using your job to avoid talking to me for even five seconds. You know you were wrong to lie to me about working late on Thursday nights. Why didn't you just tell me you were out with co-workers? Did you think I would be one of those jealous asshole husbands?"

"I so can't do this right now, Ivan …"

"When else? You're never home. When you are, you don't say shit to me."

"I need sleep. I don't need this," she groaned, slugging her pillow again, weakly, and stepping back out of bed.

"Don't be a bitch," I said.

"Excuse me?" she said. "What did you call me?"

I sat still and stared at her, at a loss. I wasn't breathing. I was tense, my face heating and reddening though she could not see it. The next word I might say could only be worse. I laid back down and kept my mouth shut. She repeated her question, and, again, I did not answer.

"Fuck you, then," she said.

She walked into the hallway, and I listened as she pulled some spare blankets and pillows out of the linen closet and stomped downstairs with them.

I slept alone that night, and for the next several nights. Eventually, Karen returned to the bed but only out of a need for the physical comfort of our carefully selected mattress and the preservation of her back. We retired separately each night and did not cross the invisible line running vertically between us along the length of the mattress. We did not speak, morning or night, and, in the days that followed, the silence solidified into an intractable mutual disdain that for the first time seemed me to be something could coalesce into a divorce instantly, the moment either of us happened to bring it up. I saw it, smelled it, pressed my palms against it as I forded my way through the fog in the house, and, on some level, savored it as some signal of impending finality, which was sounding good to me regardless of the form it might take. Regardless of my financial inability to house and feed myself without her.

It worked both ways, this silence, and, insidiously, it devoured time, digesting the days and weeks that should have been the substance of our marriage itself, given that a marriage is a form of time travel, a journey with easily commemorated guideposts. You are young at its inception, and, afterward, you are young no longer and are left wondering where exactly the time was spent and why, at the end of it all, the only happy day you can remember is that first one, the day on which the journey started with a walk down an aisle. Karen and I appeared now to be zooming toward a pathetic end-point with amazing alacrity. During those quiet those weeks, I did not fight but instead savored our trajectory out of sheer exhaustion.

More than a month passed. We spoke as necessary to get the bills paid and the lawn mowed and then raked and whatever else was necessary to maintain at least a nominally peaceful cohabitation. We went to the movies once, driving the few miles to our local chain theatre without saying much of anything and sitting beside one another in the dark theatre in the same fashion in which we slept together, like two strangers seated together only through happenstance.

Afterward, I realized that I had, for some length of time in the middle of the movie, actually forgotten that Karen was there at all, and I wondered whether she had at any point noticed that I was there myself. She was away from the house so often that I developed a routine which did not depend on her presence in virtually any way, other than the provision of funds necessary to keep the house from being foreclosed upon. I woke, made breakfast, washed the dishes in the sink, stood out on the porch in my bath-robe for a few minutes, at first warming in the morning sun and then shivering in the crisp autumn air as the last shred of Indian summer dried up and crumbled away, only to spend the rest of the day in my study reading. Eventually, night would fall, and I would watch television until I was sleepy, and, then, whether Karen was home or not, I retired. I did not sit awake, waiting for her any longer.

I allowed the simple avoidance of conflict that my marriage had become to tear off and swallow everything else.

Then, on Halloween, I waited on my porch for trick-or-treaters in the same store-bought Zorro costume I'd worn for the past three years. Karen and I had previously passed out candy to the neighborhood kids together, which we'd always enjoyed despite the decreasing numbers of children each year in our rapidly aging neighborhood. In prior years, we'd sat on chairs at the top of the porch stairs, between our jack o' lanterns, one carved male and one female, holding our own private costume contest, rating each kid's outfit with a secret code designed not to reveal what we were up to and embarrass the kids with the poorer costumes.

"Hey, *Citizen Kane!*" I would say, reaching for the candy bowl, when a particularly good costume approached.

"No, *Ishtar*, I think," Karen would counter, reaching for significantly less candy.

It was a shaky code, considering that we rarely agreed on the quality of movies. I didn't think that *Ishtar* was as bad as everyone else in the world did, for instance, but it was a fun system. The winning kid, who had to really blow us away would earn a mutual "*Casablanca!*" from both of us and would receive an entire twelve-pack of full-size candy bars in his or her sack.

The kids thought we were totally insane, shouting nonsense words at them, but they liked the large handfuls of Hershey miniatures that even the least well-costumed among them received from us. Sometimes, between visits, Karen and I would cautiously approach the idea of having a kid of our own, always on the pretext that it would be fun to come up with costumes for it that might be better than the ones our neighbor kids managed to come up with, though that conversation never really stepped past the hypothetical for us.

This year, the tradition died. Karen had opted to attend her office Halloween party rather than to join me on the porch. I sat alone, rating the few kids' costumes silently, either whispering or simply thinking of my movie title ratings, cradling a salad bowl full of candy against my sword-belt, waiting for hordes of children to ascend the porch-steps. They were slow in coming, though, possibly due to an asinine new local regulation fueled by religious conservatives that trick-or-treating be allowed only for a ninety-minute period on a non-Sunday.

In any case, I was the only one anywhere in sight wearing a costume. My *Sounds of Holy Terror* sound-effect album barely registered over the wind rushing through the enormous tree's branches. Beneath the tree's creaking, chains rattled and Satanic laughter drifted faintly only out through my screened door without a shred of the chilling effect the record had had on me as a kid, when I listened to it almost nightly after dark on the floor beside my mother's record-player.

I began to eat my candy out of boredom, and, before long, I had eaten enough that any trick-or-treaters were as likely to receive a handful of empty wrappers as they were of candy from my bowl. It was after eight before the first kids arrived, well outside the Halloween timeframe erected by the municipal assholes, and I was grateful for this minor rebellion. The kids might be alright, after all.

I stepped forward to the top of the stoop and dropped big handfuls of candy into their outstretched pillow-cases and plastic pumpkin pails.

"Here you go, here you go," I said, wanting, as always, to say something a little cooler, a little more Halloween, a little less *adult*, to them but, as always, coming up short.

"Ooh, are you Batman?" I asked a very young boy dressed in an utterly unmistakable Batman box-costume, which not only had the Batman insignia emblazoned across its flapping, plastic breast but also the word "Batman" itself, a flagrant bit of self-advertising that I didn't think the real Batman would have gone in for.

The boy, who was maybe five, nodded his head behind his plastic mask, its rubber-band tight around his reddening ears.

"Say hello to Robin for me," I told him, and he nodded again.

Did kids today know about Robin?

The other trick-or-treaters beamed and grinned through green makeup and rubber masks, slobbering around glow-in-the-dark plastic fangs, pushing and pulling at each other's capes and glitter-coated wands. I'd loved trick-or-treating as a kid, and, although missing Karen, I loved it now. A miniature Alice Cooper in full leather and face-paint mumbled a muffled thank you to me through immobile black lips, and the tiny faerie queen gripping his hand, no more than five or six years old, sneezed instead of saying anything and covered her mouth with the glittery tip of her star-wand. I barely resisted dumping my entire bowl into her bag. Two wounded soldiers shouldered plastic machine guns and gritted their teeth through torn pillow-case bandages. A vampire in an actual tuxedo swept his cape around him, leering at the bared neck of a slightly older ballerina whose tutu sprouted from beneath the hem of an unnecessarily thick winter coat. They rotated up and down my stairs and then hurried next door. From the edge of my porch, I watched them repeat their routine, screaming and holding their bags out for Ellen, who leaned precariously out of her door to get the job done as if her feet were glued to the carpet inside. She hadn't dressed up and wore only jeans and a long, bulky, wool sweater that made her look like a human head sewn onto the end of a sock.

"*Hola*, Señor Zorro!" she called, waving, catching me looking, as the kids moved on to the next house.

"Happy Halloween!" I yelled back.

"Come over and say hello! Leonard's abandoned me tonight."

She held up her bag of candy as bait, and I walked on over.

"Nice costume," I said, stepping up onto her porch.

"I was about to say the same thing. Care for a beer?"

"Sure. Even the Hero of the People thirsts."

She winked and set her candy down on a wicker chair.

"Be right back," she said.

I stood on the steps and looked back across the yard. My own porch looked distant, not so far away, as if

I were remembering it from years ago rather than seeing it now across adjoining lawns. The chimes hanging over Ellen's front door shivered, a lonelier and more Halloween sort of sound than my old record managed to be. Its tinkling reminded me that, wherever Karen was, she certainly had a drink in her hand and was giving me maybe a second thought but probably not a third. I felt outside myself looking over at my porch, staring into a place I'd loved but which I was beginning to feel was no longer mine. Ellen returned with two cans of Black Label, popped one open for me, and then sat down beside me on her porch steps. The beer was cold, and I shivered in the wind in a very un-Zorro-like fashion.

"So where are all the kids this year?" Ellen asked.

"I was wondering the same thing myself."

"They used to parade up the sidewalk by the dozen," she said. "When Leonard was little, I'd lead him along by the hand, and we'd have to wait five or ten minutes for our turn at some of the houses."

"You can hardly give the candy away now."

"Parents are afraid. That's the problem."

"Afraid of what?"

"The same old stuff. Razor-blades in apples, strange men in cars."

"We told the same stories when I was a kid," I said.

"I know. Me, too. Maybe that's the problem. Our generation told too many stories, and we scared ourselves to death."

"So now we make stupid laws like this hour-and-a-half Halloween bullshit," I said. "How much trick-or-treating can you even do in ninety minutes?"

"Not much in this neighborhood," Ellen agreed. "It takes a half hour just to cover one block. Or at least it used to."

I shrugged and drank some beer. Across the lawn, a cluster of kids dressed like television cartoon characters clambered up onto my porch. They rang my doorbell, and I shouted at them to come on over. It took them a second to figure out why I was shouting at them, but, when they did, Ellen and I were again besieged by grabbing hands with the smell of chocolate and latex upon them. She laughed in a bright, becoming way while filling their bags from both of our bowls. Her eyes lit up as she bantered with the kids in the practiced voice of an experienced parent, and I saw why she didn't need a costume to ingratiate herself. She addressed them by the proper names of the cartoon characters they were dressed as, thrilling them, even challenging one little girl to demonstrate the martial arts prowess for which her character was apparently famous on the front lawn. We laughed and applauded as the girl spun and kicked at invisible enemies on the lawn, stirring up dead leaves around her ankles.

"Hyah!" she yelled in a little helium squeak.

Ellen clapped and gave her an extra piece of candy, and, when the kids moved on to the next house, she stood at the edge of the porch waving even after they'd stopped paying attention.

"Oh, I miss that," she sighed.

"What's that?"

"That age. Now that Leonard's in high school, I sometimes forget how much fun we had when he was eight or nine. He wanted to know everything, then. He was full of questions. We had all these activities we did together. Halloween. Birthdays. Trips to the beach in the summer. Now, I don't even know where he is tonight."

"That must be hard."

"Oh, not really. Not usually. It's normal. Healthy, really. I just get nostalgic every now and then. I appreciate him in the moment. Watching them change is half the fun."

"I can imagine."

"No plans for kids yet?"

"Not really. I don't know. It occurs to us every now and again, but then it never seems to go much further."

"Karen works so hard, I can understand. Me, I never really did. At least not until Leonard's father died. Motherhood seemed inevitable when I was younger. I didn't question it."

"Well, he's a good kid. A smart kid," I said, even though he didn't seem any more brilliant than any of the junior thugs I noticed flexing their biceps around town.

"I know," Ellen said, nodding. "Too smart for me. That's where he goes wrong, I think. I never had all of the answers to his questions. Even when he was little, he had some real hum-dingers. Stuff I never learned in school."

"Kids seem more sophisticated now than I ever felt like I was, then."

"I know what you mean, but, when I stop and think about it, I thought I knew everything back then, too."

"Yeah," I said. "Same here."

"No, I mean, I *really* thought I knew *everything*. Nobody could tell me anything at all. My poor parents … But that sort of confidence goes a long way. When I pay close attention to Leonard, he's not really sophisticated. Nor any of his friends. They're just big galoots hooting and jumping up and down and getting all excited, just like six year-olds. It's sort of funny to think about when I find myself intimidated by teenagers at the mall or something. They're just sure of themselves, that's all. They'll figure out that they don't know anything about the same time we did."

"We must be officially Old now to fall for that,"

I laughed.

"It's the cycle of life," Ellen said. "What goes around, comes around."

"Right."

She emptied her beer can and set it back behind her on the porch floor where the wind wouldn't knock it around. The streetlight back-lit her, igniting her blonde hair into a blue-white aura. She shoved her hands into her jeans pockets and rolled her shoulders back, stretching, accentuating the size of her breasts a little too nicely. My palms sweated around my beer can, and I entered an old but always familiar frame of mind as I watched her. At age seventeen, I would have asked her to a movie at this point. (No, not true, I reminded myself: I would have thought about it for several long, painful minutes only and done nothing at all.) At twenty-one, I would have invited her back to my apartment. (Probably also not true, unless I'd had a lot to drink.) She smiled at me, and I realized that I could kiss her now and maybe she wouldn't mind, or, if she did, she might do it anyway just because she was bored or lonely.

"Hey, is that Karen?" she said, standing and leaning over the porch rail.

Someone moved in the shadow of the enormous tree beside my house and then hurried across the lawn toward the back door. A slim figure. A woman, alright. There, she stopped and lit a cigarette, ruining any further attempt at stealth, and an orange ember rose and fell in the darkness, briefly illuminating a woman's face before being falling to the ground. The woman paused and then moved around the corner of the house, out of sight.

"I didn't think Karen smoked," Ellen said.

"She doesn't," I said.

I tumbled down the stairs and covered the yard in a few short steps, my left knee clicking. Hurling myself inside through my open front door, I locked it behind me and rushed to the kitchen as quietly as I could, leaving all of the lights off, relieved to see that the back door was still locked. All was well, and there wasn't a sound inside or outside the room. I peeled my Zorro mask and cape off and peeked through the curtains in the window but saw nothing out of the ordinary. The back yard was empty as far as I could tell. I watched for a moment or two, but, then, as I was about to give it up and step away, the orange tip of the cigarette reappeared in the shadows beneath the enormous tree's overhanging canopy. The ember glowed hot, again, and then faded out, but, now that I knew where to look, I discerned the figure holding it. I stayed put and waited for the woman to make a move, wondering if I should stop looking long enough to call the cops, but the mystery woman made no further movement toward the house. She dropped the cigarette and crushed it out with her toe. As my eyes became accustomed to the dark, I saw that the woman wore a long black coat with a large hood. It cloaked her face pretty well, but what I could see was thin and pale. Her silhouetted head twitched as she glanced from side to side, from the fence bordering the alley behind the yard and then back to the house again. She didn't seem to see me and didn't move toward the house again, so I parted the curtains and made myself known.

"Hello? Can I help you?" I yelled, cracking the door open.

She stepped out from under the tree, and the light from the sky and street caught her as she stepped closer to the door. She had dark eyes and pretty, elfin features and didn't look to be more than twenty-five or so. Nervously, she fidgeted with the folds of her coat.

"Ivan?" she whispered, stepping up to the door.

"Yes?" I replied, holding the door so that I could

slam it shut if I needed to. "Who are you?"

"I'm *Francine*," she hissed, pointing to her chest as if anyone else were around who might make the same claim.

"Francine?"

She nodded. The name bubbled up from my memory as a word scrawled on a piece of paper that I hadn't thought about in weeks and weeks. Hugo's handwriting. This was his girlfriend, the one I hadn't really believed existed.

"Hugo's Francine?" I asked her, double-checking.

She smiled in a way that made me think she was about to cry. I thought about what would happen if Karen arrived home at exactly the wrong moment and found me standing in a dark kitchen with a strange woman, but I opened the door anyway.

"Come in," I told her, stepping aside.

I shut the door behind her and circled around the table to stand between her and the rest of the house. She took in the lay of the room before proceeding further, scanning the room from corner to corner: the windows, the furniture, the basement door, and the entry-way into the dining-room behind me.

She wasn't subtle, checking out every possible exit, but I tried not to expect the worst—whatever that was. Hugo's taste in girls was never that bad. His sporadic dates were always much nicer than he was. He had never been one to take up with the junkie high-school punk chicks who burned themselves with cigarettes or stole money from their parents' wallets or anything like that. The girls he'd gone out with in college, before he dropped out and disappeared almost entirely, were simply pretentious, more often than not. They shared his grandiose visions of a political utopia, or were vegans or diehard fans of pseudo-intellectual bands like The Residents, Einstüerzende Neubauten, and Nick Cave. They bored me silly, but that was the worst of it. This girl was nervous. The FBI agents' nearly forgotten visit aside, it now hit me that Hugo really was in some kind of trouble and that this girl probably had something to do with it. *Congratulations, Hugo*, I thought. Francine didn't look capable of anything more arduous than digging a hole to hide in, however. She was a pile of twigs, bound together with fraying terrycloth, something that might have fallen out of a tree like an abandoned bird's nest.

"Can I get you something to drink?" I asked her, pulling out a chair at the table for her.

She sat down and shook her hood off. Her hair was dyed black but badly, in a shoddy way, as if it had been done furtively in a gas station restroom with a can of shoe polish, like in a movie. A smudge of dye even remained like a birthmark on her forehead, just under her hairline. She rubbed her hands together and shivered. I wondered how far she'd walked outside in her thin coat, and I tried to remember whether we had a warmer one stored somewhere in the house that I could offer her. She asked for a glass of water, and I filled one for her.

"So where's Hugo?" I asked as I handed her the glass, but she only shrugged.

"I don't know," she said.

She drank the water in a single swallow, and I filled it again for her. This time, she relaxed with it, sipping carefully.

"You don't know where Hugo is at all?" I asked her again.

"No," she said, furrowing her brow, thinking it through.

"He left a letter for me here?" she asked, and I nodded.

"Yeah," I said. "I forgot all about it. I didn't think

you really existed, to be honest. That would be just like Hugo, to leave me a letter for someone who doesn't exist. I thought if I opened it there'd be nothing but a drawing of a penis or something inside."

She grinned, suddenly and surprisingly pretty, and almost laughed.

"I exist," she said. "Can I have it, please?"

"Sure," I said. "Wait here."

I ran upstairs and found Hugo's letter in the book, where it might have gathered dust for twenty years if Francine hadn't actually come for it. I brought it downstairs and handed it to her, and she ripped it open and read it while I waited. I followed the track of her eyes as she scanned the text, and there was a desperate sort of insistence to the way she hurried through it, as if she were thrashing through brush to find one key phrase or sentence. Through the paper, I could read Hugo's careless handwriting, but there was something else in the envelope, a card or piece of cardboard, as well. She pocketed it before I could get a better look, and, when she finished, appeared no more satisfied than she did before reading it. She hadn't found her key phrase; whatever she'd hoped Hugo had left her was not in the letter.

"What does he say?" I asked her.

"Nothing."

"Can I see it?" I ventured, feeling clumsy and rude for even asking.

She only frowned and folded the envelope and its contents in half and stowed it in her pocket.

"Thanks for the drink," she said.

"Can I fix you something to eat?" I asked.

She seemed to consider it but then stood and set her glass in the sink. A police siren wailed in the distance, and she tensed as it approached and faded. She pulled her hood back up over head and removed a pack of cigarettes from a pocket. Without lighting it, she pulled a cigarette from the pack and pressed it between her cracked lips, fingers shaking.

"Hey, are you okay?" I asked her.

She opened her mouth to answer but then deflated. Without lighting the cigarette, she eased the back door open and crept back out, crunching toward the darkest back corner of the yard through the fallen leaves. There, the chain-link fence shivered as she climbed it. After she was gone, down the alley to the east, the fence swayed and creaked a little but soon settled into the familiar quiet of the hour before.

10.

Karen returned from her party just as the police were reversing their patrol car out of our driveway.

"What happened?" she gasped, running inside.

"Nothing," I sighed, rubbing my eyes. "Ellen thought she saw someone trying to break into the house, and she called the cops. But no one was breaking in."

"Why would she think that?"

The armpits of her skintight, lycra cat costume were sweat-stained, and her whisker and nose makeup was smeared around her mouth. None of that detracted from the effectiveness of the imperious gaze she focused upon me as if I were the subject of one of her cross-examinations.

"What happened to your costume?" I asked, attempting to deflect.

She held what was left of her velvet tail in one hand and frowned.

"Why did Ellen think someone was breaking in?" she asked again.

Once, we had been able to argue without either one of us acting like a lawyer, but that had been a long time ago. Karen didn't know how to stop doing her job now.

It didn't help that she was correct in suspecting that I was, once again, full of shit.

"I don't know," I answered her. "Probably some trick-or-treater jumping the back fence."

"Hmmm," she said.

She circumnavigated the living-room, checking all of the windows, pushing the locks in harder, testing the integrity of the panes of the window with the flat of her hand. I sat still in the chair as I had while the police had questioned me about what I had and hadn't seen in the yard and waited as she double-checked each window in the living-room and dining-room, suddenly less concerned with my story than with the integrity of the house. I stayed out of her way until she worked her way back to the front door, locking the deadbolt and drawing the chain, and then headed for the kitchen to do the same with the back door. Realizing that I had not locked the customarily sealed back door after Francine had used it, I tailed her.

"Why was the back door unlocked?" she called from the kitchen, ahead of me.

"The police wanted to see if the back door had been messed with. I opened it to show them it hadn't."

"Oh," she said, apparently convinced.

She locked, unlocked, and locked the door again, until she was satisfied.

"Did they check the cellar doors, too?" she asked.

I'd forgotten about the wooden hurricane doors leading directly down into the basement from the back yard. We hadn't used the doors in years, and they were padlocked shut.

"They didn't ask, and I didn't think to mention them."

"Well, I guess I'll have to do it, then," she sighed. "Whatever."

I sat down at the kitchen table as she opened the interior basement door and flipped the light switch just inside. Craning her neck, she peered down the stairs and cocked her ear, listening. She stepped on the first downward stair and started quickly back when it creaked beneath her weight, almost tripping on her ruined cat tail. She gave it another try and reached the second step down before stepping back.

"Oh, cut it out," I finally said. "I'll check. Why don't you go and wipe your face off?"

She started to speak but then stopped, for once, and stepped aside. I brushed past her, stomping down on that first squeaking step as if there were no sillier thing in the world than to be apprehensive about a basement potentially containing any number of burglars, murderers, and thieves. In fact, although knowing that there was no one in the basement, I still wanted to turn around and let Karen lead on.

Anosov would not have approved.

The basement was not dark, dank, moldy, scary, or exuding any other quality worthy of panic or horror. It was just a large, square room, covering most of the space between the house's foundation, unfinished, all concrete and cement. We used it for storage and for laundry and not very much else. The furnace and water heater occupied the room's central space, nestled up against the west wall, and the washer and dryer lined the wall closest to the staircase. A carpenter's work-bench that Karen had purchased for me the year after we'd moved in with the apparent idea that I transmogrify into her father under the magical spell of homeownership sat untouched on the furthest end of the room. Beside the washer and dryer, the hurricane doors capped off a short staircase leading up to ground-level and the back yard. As the washer and dryer had come with the house when we bought it and the work-bench had been assembled from a series of long cardboard boxes that fit neatly through the front door of the house and the basement's kitchen entrance, we had never before opened the hurricane doors other than to replace the padlocks that were on them when we'd bought the place with new ones. Unless the furnace or water-heater needed replacing, I couldn't imagine any reason why we ever would. They were vestigial, the sort of doors you'd find on a farm house's root cellar, an unnecessary entryway that served no practical purpose except to provide Karen with another point of insecurity.

In any case, the basement, utilitarian as it was, was clean and well-lighted and was not one of those crumbling foundational holes that people in Michigan liked to call "Michigan basements" and which people in Ohio no doubt called "Ohio basements." Other than a roughly three foot-by-three foot square directly behind the furnace, there was no possible hiding space as seen from the bottom of the staircase. Even if anyone had tried curling up behind the furnace to lie in wait, the naked bulbs illuminating the room from several spots in the ceiling, would have thrown a give-away shadow across the floor.

At first glance from the top step, it was plain that basement was empty. However, Karen's jitters stayed with me as I crept down and padded my way across the concrete floor to the hurricane doors. I stepped up to the topmost of the three steps approaching the doors and pushed against them, expecting the slight pressure to meet resistance. To my surprise, though, they banged right open. Shocked, I twisted around to look around the basement again, but, as always, nothing was out of place. The padlock that had secured the doors from the outside was gone, however. I climbed my way up and outward into the backyard.

The temperature had dropped in the last hour, and I shivered in my thin buccaneer's shirt. Ellen's lights remained on next door, but she'd called it a night after I had assured her that all was well, just before the police she had already called had streamed onto the street. I looked up at the second-story window that I suspected to be her bedroom, and a light was still on inside. I strained to pick out any detail behind the filmy curtains. As a kid, my friend Toby and I had roamed the narrow streets of our neighborhood on the west side of Grand Rapids, freezing expectantly in front of every such illuminated window, hoping beyond hope for even a quick glimpse of a naked woman. Just as we had never seen anything then, I saw nothing now and felt like a creep for looking. I walked to the back of the yard and leaned over the fence that Francine had vaulted in her escape and studied the length of the alley, first one way and then the other, just for the sake of playing the role of concerned homeowner. But for a skinny cat gliding from one side to the other, the alley was empty. I paced the length of the fence, kicked some leaves on the ground near the open hurricane doors, and then climbed back inside.

When I shut the doors behind me, I something metal glinted on the basement floor at the bottom of the stairs. I picked it up, smudging my fingers with the rust coating it, saw that it was part of the hurricane doors' padlock, the curved end that looped through the fastening eye on the back of the door. It had been snipped cleanly in two, the sheared ends of the shackle smooth and bright compared to the dull, worn metal on the exterior of the piece.

Someone had been inside the house, just as Karen feared. I caught my breath and thought hard about whether I had checked every inch of the basement, but there really wasn't anything else to check. No one was there now. It was possible that this all could have happened some time ago, but, given Francine and the shininess of the sheared lock, it seemed unlikely. I hadn't seen Francine go anywhere near the hurricane doors, but I couldn't imagine a better candidate for a mysterious break-in, regardless. Had she been inside and out again before Ellen and I had even spotted her lurking under the tree? Had she gone in while I was handing out candy on my porch to look for Hugo's letter and, then, failing to find it or thinking better of it, simply gone back out in order to ask me directly? If so, why did she loiter around my backyard at all when she could just have knocked and asked me? Where had she been hiding whatever massive tool she had used to snap the padlock?

I was no detective, and answering the seven dozen other questions springing to my mind as I stood holding the severed padlock was beyond me. I'd wanted to just trot down the stairs from the kitchen, confirm that the door was secure and that my wife was paranoid, and then head back upstairs to tell Karen that there was nothing to worry about, that all was well, and that she ought to give me a little more credit than she usually did. It seemed clear enough that Francine must have broken the lock, so I resolved to dismiss all related questions of how and why she had done so and just forget about it. The reason she had come to the house was for Hugo's letter, and it again seemed safe to assume that, if she had broken into the house, it was to get the letter. She had not gotten it that way, but she had gotten it and was gone now. End of mystery.

I slammed the hurricane doors shut from the inside and jammed a piece of pine wood from the unused workbench through the handles. A good, strong pull from the outside would snap or dislodge the wood but probably not without making a lot of noise. I'd buy a new padlock in the morning. In the meantime, I gathered whatever junk I could find around the sparse room and piled it in front of the stairs. If someone did manage to break the wood and open the door without alerting me, the noise they made would be impossible to miss. Satisfied, I whistled my way upstairs.

Karen was waiting for me in the kitchen, sitting in the same chair that Francine had occupied.

"Everything okay?" she asked.

"Of course," I said. "All normal."

"Sure. Coming home to find police in my driveway is really normal."

I opened my mouth, but nothing came out. Karen scowled and informed me that she was going to bed. I followed her up to the bathroom and brushed my teeth while she molted her costume. She turned her back to me so that I could help her out of it, and I noticed that the zipper along her spine was undone somewhat, exposing two or three inches of bare skin between her shoulders.

"That costume looks like it tried to make a getaway," I mumbled.

"It's just a cheap piece of shit," Karen said. "I should've had my mother sew me one when she offered."

"She offered? I thought her arthritis was too bad for sewing anymore."

"It is, but she offers anyway. You know how she is."

"Right. You dance?"

"Tonight?"

"When else?"

She shrugged instead of answering, and I half-expected to see bruises, scratches, or hickeys on her bare skin when she finally tore the cat-suit off. Her body sported no such markings.

"I missed you tonight," I told her. "There were some great costumes."

"I'm sure," she said.

She turned and reached for a wash-rag hanging from the ring over the sink's basin, twisted the faucet on, and wiped her face.

11.

    I lay beside Karen in the dark a few nights later, imagining myself in Ellen's bright, unfinished bedroom instead. I wrapped my arms around Karen and wondered how Ellen would fit within them. Would I even find a waist to wrap my arms around, or would I simply lock them around her and sink into something deep, settling into the warm expanse of her naked back, pressing my chin into the nape of her neck as I gathered her large breasts in my hands? Karen's breasts were smaller; one of my hands could almost enclose both of them. I could stretch my hand from nipple to nipple, index finger to palm, holding her to me with my other arm. Her feet not quite reaching my own, my mouth pressed against the back of her head, I could pull her onto me with the slightest movement and thrust her off of the bed and onto the floor almost without meaning to. Ellen would encompass me, and I suspected that she wouldn't even budge on the mattress, no matter how fervent my nuzzling. Ellen was a bottomless bowl of porridge, Karen a plateful of raw kale.

I was still holding myself when my rarely used cell phone blared out its "Battle Hymn of the Republic" ringtone on the desk in my library, jerking Karen awake.

"Damn it," she sighed, rubbing her eyes with the back of her hand.

"I'll get it," I said.

"We need to just cancel that thing," she groaned.

"Go back to sleep."

I staggered into the study and picked up the phone.

"Hello?" I said.

"Hey, man!" the voice on the other end hissed. "Hey!"

"What?"

I couldn't focus. The signal was fuzzy.

"Dude, it's me," the voice said. "Can I come over, man?"

"Who is it?" Karen called from the other room.

"Okay?" the voice said.

"Hugo?" I croaked.

"Wakey, wakey, this just in!" he shouted. "I'll be there in ten minutes. Back door. Leave the lights off."

"Hugo?"

The phone clicked and went dead. I went back into the bedroom and fumbled in the closet for a pair of sweatpants.

"Hugo's coming over," I told Karen.

"Oh, no, he isn't!" she spat, wide awake and jumping out of bed. "He is not coming here!"

But he did.

Karen and I sat in the kitchen, in the dark, watching the back door. I rubbed my eyes, but Karen was alert, her feet planted flat on the floor, her hands knitted together in her lap. She stared straight ahead at the door with the same deliberate expression she'd worn in the presence of the FBI agents. She was screwing herself up to eject Hugo, I could tell, and she was ready to battle the both of us to the death, if necessary, to get it done. I started to speak, to try to ease her down, but my half-stutter dissipated into the corner of room, ineffectually. I had nothing much to say, it seemed. I wasn't any happier about the possibility of Hugo popping over for a dead-of-night visit than Karen was, and I was at a loss over how to stop him other than phone the FBI.

    Hugo had always teetered on the edge of trouble but had always managed to lean back from the precipice. In school, Hugo's back-talk constantly landed him in Mr. Cane's after hours detention class, where, even then, he never shut up, even to the point of provoking Mr. Cane, who was a nice, soft-voiced man simply biding his time until retirement, into red-faced rage. Yet, somehow, it never went any further than that. The kids who repeated wood shop class over and over again were there just as frequently. Hugo had had occasional shouting matches with the cops who regularly swept us out of the mall near our school, but nothing more serious than that. They yelled, he yelled, they yelled again, he flipped them off, and we ran for our lives. Every time. At the end of the day, he had always done his homework, eaten dinner with his parents, and he eventually graduated with a decent enough GPA to get him into the same college I enrolled in. It was incongruent to me. FBI agents were mythical creatures that one wasn't any more likely to encounter in the course of a normal day than Bigfoot.

    I couldn't believe that whatever he'd done to get himself in trouble with the FBI wasn't something easily worked through, if he would only accept a little helpful advice and apply a little common sense. Karen was a lawyer, after all. She didn't like him, but she would help him if I asked her to, even if only to refer him to a good criminal defense attorney. And I would ask her, even though I would surely never hear the end of it. I would do whatever I could to help him out. That's what friends did, I'd been told, even in times of dark duress, and, other than Hugo, I no longer had many friends to speak of. None, in fact. He was a bit of an asshole, but he was a rare commodity: a human being other than Karen who cared whether I lived or didn't. In the forty minutes we waited in the kitchen for him, I resolved to help him. There was always a chance that Karen would simply kick him back out into the night no matter how I plead for his life, but, to my relief, when he finally tapped quietly on the door, hissing my name around its seams, she stood up and without hesitation let him in.

He held his breath as he slipped inside, setting the door back in place with quiet care. He sighed and dropped something with sharp corners on the floor. Even with the lights off, I could see that his physical condition had not improved since his last visit. He was even more haggard, and his clothes were dirtier. His body odor was strong enough that I would have been able to find him in the room no matter how dark it was.

"Thank god," he sighed, reaching for a chair. "It's been a hell of a night."

"Not so fast," Karen said, iron-gripping the chair to the floor. "I can't have you here."

"Come on," he groaned, and I eased the chair from Karen's grip and held it for him while he sat down.

"Thanks, man," he said.

Karen pulled the window-shades down and flipped on the lights. The light was shocking, and Hugo squinted, blinking.

"Can I have something to drink?" he asked.

I filled a glass of water and set it in front of him. He drained it in a single swallow, so I refilled it. He did look worse than he had the night he'd slept on the sofa—thinner and less imposing, a wet fern. His hands shook, and he looked tiny inside his clothes. His cheeks were hollow beneath a few days' worth of patchy stubble. I sat down beside him, feeling larger than him for the first time.

"You have five minutes before I call the cops," Karen said.

He drummed his fingers on the tabletop and scowled.

"I'd really appreciate it if you would just hold off on doing that," he said.

"What do they want you for?" I asked.

"That's a story best told over breakfast, I think."

"I don't think so," Karen said, standing up. "I let you this far into the house, but, if you want to go further, you'll have to convince me that Ivan and I aren't going to end up in prison for doing it."

"You'd only help a friend if there were absolutely no possibility of negative repercussions?"

"You aren't *my* friend," Karen said.

"You don't have any friends," he snapped back.

"Hugo ...," I said.

Karen's face reddened, and her expression hardened.

"I only need to make one phone-call," she said, composing herself.

"I know, I know," Hugo said, easing up. "I'm sorry. Really. Honest to god. I'm sorry, Karen."

"Good," she said. "Stay that way. I like you better."

He looked at me, hoping for assistance, but I only studied the tabletop.

"Did Francine come?" he asked me.

"Who?" Karen asked.

I tried to signal him away from the topic with a subtle head shake, but it was already out.

"What are you talking about?" Karen asked again.

"Francine," Hugo said. "My girlfriend. I asked her to stop by here and pick up a letter I left for her."

"When did you leave a letter?" she asked.

I hung my head and waited for it.

"A month or so ago. That's about right, isn't it, Ivan?"

I could have killed him. He'd been canny once, a master of innuendo and inter-personal black ops. The guy who had, at age nineteen, organized a human chain to stop the CIA from recruiting at our campus job-fair was now about as canny as Little Red Riding Hood walking up to her grandmother's front door, basket in hand. He smiled at me as if I would approve, while Karen seethed. They both stared at me, waiting. I just snapped my hanging jaw shut and shrugged. My lack of full disclosure to Karen was not Hugo's fault, and he could not have known. Lies beget lies. Staring back at the tabletop again, I sucked enough oxygen to manage the job in a single, quick sentence and told Karen about the Halloween incident, that Ellen hadn't mistaken a trick-or-treating kid for a burglar but Hugo's girlfriend. She added it up in her mind and then walked to the window and peeled back the blind, peeking out.

"So you lied to the FBI?" she demanded. "You'd seen Hugo and didn't mention it? Some woman was in our house, and you lied to me completely about that?"

I stood mute.

"Yes or no?" she said, over her shoulder again.

"Yes," I said.

"FBI?" Hugo asked. "They were here?"

"Yeah," I nodded at him. "And I'm sorry, Karen.

I just thought there'd be less harm done if I kept some of the details quiet. I didn't think it would help things between us."

"Things between us?" she said, turning around.

"You know," I said, not wanting to spell it out in front of Hugo. "Things."

"Right," she nodded. "Things."

"Trouble in the bedroom?" Hugo asked.

"Shut up," she told him.

"When were the FBI here?" Hugo asked.

Karen told him, and he chewed it over, thinking hard. He was counting, tapping his fingers on the table in the finger-math style he'd learned from the alternative school his parents had sent him to when he was a child. His mouth worked as he added, and, when he finally came to a conclusion, he appeared even less comfortable than he already had.

"That's not good," he said. "Not good at all."

"Do you want to tell us what's going on, or not?" Karen demanded.

He thought about it, exhaling, deflating.

"Maybe I shouldn't," he said. "Maybe I should just leave."

Karen looked at me, and I shook my head. She rubbed her eyes and sighed.

"We can't help you if you don't tell us what's going on," Karen told him.

"You're going to help me?" he asked.

"Are you asking for our help?" she asked him.

"Well, I wasn't ..."

"Just say yes, Hugo," I told him. "Why the fuck else are you here?"

"Fine, then. I am asking."

"Well," she said, "all I can really do professionally is recommend a good criminal defense attorney. We have no attorney-client privilege with Ivan listening in, just so you know. You waive privilege for Ivan, you waive it for anybody, ever. So what you want to talk about is up to you. I am not offering to represent you as your attorney. I may not say anything at all."

"Are you going to call the cops on me? That's what I want to know."

"Just turn yourself in and make it easy on everybody. You think you're better at running than the police are at finding?"

"Hm," Hugo said, rubbing his temples. "As to that."

He stood up and paced the length of the kitchen, stopping to lean against the frame of the room's interior doorway and peer deeper into the darkened dining-room and the living-room beyond. His shadow stretched across the wooden floorboards from the kitchen doorway into the dining-room like the stroke of a large scalpel.

"Francine took the letter?" he asked again.

"Yeah," I said.

"Good."

He bent his chapped lips into a pained smile and stepped back to his chair and sat down, clapping his hands together as if warming them before settling back into the confines of his shrunken body with a shudder. His clap was weak and unconvincing, and I suddenly wanted to hang onto him the way I'd hung onto Otto, my family's old dachshund, as we drove him to the veterinarian to be put down after he'd been diagnosed with cancer. I'd known Hugo from the point of his original coalescence from the cosmic dust of high-school and I didn't want to know his ending, too. It was bad enough to stand witness to both the beginnings and the ends of dogs. It was unbearable to do it with people. Not much remained of my early years now—just an album full of photos, some boxes of books and letters, my mother's incense burner, and Hugo.

I imagined this being the last time I ever saw him, and it felt a lot like it did when I thought too hard about how long it had been now since I'd last seen my mother or father. When you're young, the artifacts that surround you seem eternal, fixed in time, impossible to dislodge from the totality of the small universe that spits you out. Soon enough, though, they crumble away and leave you with smoke and memory and an unfortunate collection of deep holes. You never quite feel at home again after that, except when the right song plays on the radio, or a certain smell wafts through the room, or an old friend, who knew your parents and played with your dog and sat in the back of your family car, drops by, and you sit together the way you always did, talking, laughing, and reminiscing. Only then does the museum come to life. Only when Hugo was around did I really feel that way.

"So talk if you want to," Karen said when he did not immediately begin.

"Okay," he sighed.

"Have a beer if you like," I said, pointing at the refrigerator.

He got up and removed three bottles from the refrigerator, but Karen demurred when he tried to offer her one. I didn't often wake up in the middle of the night to drink and the entire prospect sounded terrible, but I didn't want him to drink alone either. I took a bottle from him and twisted the cap off. He sat down with the other two bottles in front of him.

"I appreciate it," he said.

"Hey," I laughed, trying to lighten the mood. "I still owe you for Ed Young."

"I guess you do," he chuckled, looking just a bit like himself as he did so.

In the tenth grade, a football player named Ed Young had decided that I was the closest thing to a four-eyed geek he could find to pick on. He punched me in the stomach in the hallway and wrote "Fag" across the front of my locker with a permanent marker. In response, Hugo initiated a campaign of psychological terror against the kid, inventing an arbitrary nickname for him and thrusting it at him every chance he got. Some of our friends joined in, and we all hounded Ed through the hallways, chanting the nickname, laughing. The name caught fire, and, eventually, even his friends tormented him with it. We found it scrawled in purple magic marker across the desk he occupied for speech class at some point, and neither of us had put it there.

"*Ting-tang!*" he'd hear down every hallway, in the cafeteria, between the stacks in the library.

"*Ting-tang!*"

It meant nothing, but, when Ed menaced me thereafter, all I had to do was chant the magic word to paralyze him. When he eventually snapped, he didn't pick me to beat up but Hugo, who, as it happened, was the only one of my friends who could actually fight. Ed took a swing at him at a school football game, and Hugo ducked and pushed him down a flight of stadium stairs.

That Hugo was nowhere to be seen now.

"We're waiting," Karen said, growing impatient.

"It's a long story," he said.

"The Cliff's Notes version, then."

He swallowed half of his first beer in a single, long gulp and shook his battered jacket from his bony shoulders.

12.

"I had a temp gig with this software development company in Arlington, Virginia, just outside of DC, doing some technical writing," he began.

"Since when do you do that sort of thing?" Karen chuckled.

"Since always," Hugo snapped at her, rubbing his eyes. "It's what I've always done, I'll have you know, not that you've ever cared to ask. Tech writing, desktop publishing, some low-grade graphic design ... That sort of thing."

"I beg your pardon," Karen allowed, not quite begging.

"A guy's got to make a living, right? And it works for me. I don't have to sweat too much, and it requires at least a bare minimum of cranial activity. And it's easy to do on a contract basis, so I don't have to put up with too much bullshit worrying about whether I'm going to get fired or get a raise or any of that other crap that lifers in cubicles have to deal with."

"God forbid," Karen said, and, before I could tell her to just shut up and listen, Hugo did it for me.

"You want to hear this or not?"

"I'm sorry," she said flatly, making it clear that she wasn't, really.

"Close enough," he said, not buying it.

"Anyway, yes. In case you were wondering, that is the sort of thing I do to make a living. I don't ask much out of the material plane, but I need this and that. I'm not a Luddite or a monk, after all. And you know what? I'm good at it, too, and I have a few agencies here and there that will get me gig almost anytime I need it. And, when I don't need it, that's fucking fine with me."

"Okay, cool," I said, hoping to get him back on track.

"So I had this job at this company. And they're all the same, right? One company to the next. I don't really care what it is they want me to lay out or write. Some engineering process, almost always. How to use this piece of equipment or operate this truck, that sort of thing. Harmless stuff. In this case, not so much."

"What was it?" I asked.

"I'm telling you," he said. "The company they sent me to was a software design company that designed databases and whatnot. Not really my bag, but it doesn't need to be. I don't know how to build a car, either, but I've put together how-to manuals for assembly lines and that sort of thing, too. This place was doing some gigantic project for the government and had designed some kind of new software program to handle a huge amount of data. My job was to plant my ass in front of a cubicle and make the how-to instructions for the program all nice and neat and easy-to-understand. Engineers suck at making anything easy-to-understand. I had to go around to all of the software engineers who had worked on the program and interview them and get them to tell me how operate it, then draft it all up, and run it by them again so that they could test it out the way I'd written and make sure someone else could actually follow the instructions. And I needed to lay it all out with nice screenshots and graphics and whatnot, too.

"So it sounds pretty straightforward, right? It should have been. Usually, I work on more hard engineering projects: trucks, cars, even the robots that spray paint on car bodies on auto plant assembly lines. It didn't scare me off that the company's client was the government. I've worked on contracts like that before, for a company working with the US Army to develop a new amphibious cargo truck. I don't have a problem with tools, only how they're sometimes used, see?"

"That's another conversation," I said.

"Totally," Hugo agreed. "Anyway, so this was a monster database, but what the actual data was wasn't anything I really needed to know in order to do the job. The software program would've worked with any kind of database. I guess the innovation in its design was just that the amount of data was more than other commercial products could handle, coming in at some huge, constant rate. And the government just likes to shell out taxpayer money for its own proprietary crap, anyway. But, even though I'd passed security clearance, I still wasn't seeing the actual data that was supposed to run through the database. Instead, they pumped it full of crap from a bunch of phone-books or something—"

"Wait a minute," Karen interrupted. "You passed security clearance?"

"Sure," Hugo shrugged. "I didn't have a criminal record or anything."

"How is that even possible?" she almost laughed.

"Name one criminal activity I've ever engaged in."

"Well ..."

"Exactly," he said. "Exercising free speech isn't criminal, at least not yet—and nothing else is criminal if you don't get caught."

"I don't know about that," she said.

"Anyway," I said, putting a stop to it, though I was also surprised that Hugo could pass any kind of security clearance test.

"Anyway," he continued, "I had to work with the software engineers, as I said. Mostly, they were a pretty buttoned-down crowd. Very DC, very business casual. Not a sense of humor between them—except for one. And she was hot, too ..."

"Francine," I guessed.

"Francine," he nodded. "Yep. She was a tamale. I was surprised to see that she didn't have the usual pictures of herself on vacation with a husband or boyfriend or photos of kids, all that sort of thing, on her desk. Just clipped photos of animals and pyramids and whatever, clipped out of *National Geographic* or some other magazine. And, on her monitor, a little clipped photo of Iggy Pop. You know the one. That still from that live Stooges gig where he's up walking on the crowd, covered in peanut butter?"

"Uh-oh," I said.

"Right?" he grinned. "So I asked her about it. Told her how many times I'd seen Iggy. Remember that first show we saw at Cobo in Detroit, Ivan? Junior year in high-school, when he opened up for The Pretenders? Still can't believe he was anyone's opening act, but, man. Anyway, we got to talking, and I let it go at that for a minute. But just a minute. We grabbed lunch a few days later, and, when I figured out for sure that she wasn't a Republican, I asked her if she wanted to grab a drink after work. She made it a coffee, and we did that. Met at a Star-yucks in Arlington, then went to see Wreckless Eric play a night or two later. Anyway, that was a good show. Played 'Whole Wide World' and didn't mind doing it. Afterward, we went back to her place, and I spent the night and we were off and running."

"Lovely," Karen said. "When did this little romance begin to involve the FBI?"

"Oh, not till a little later," Hugo said, ignoring Karen's sarcasm. "You know, you need to be with someone at least a month before you get the FBI involved."

"Anyway ..."

"*Anyway*, that was it. For quite a while. She wanted to keep things cool between us because she had been dumped by some jerk before me and because of the whole work situation. It made things easier that I was just a contractor and wasn't going to be in the office with her forever, she said, but still. It wasn't something she was all that relaxed about. Apparently, being the only girl engineer in the office was not always the easiest thing in the world, though I never saw any of those nebbishy guys give her any shit.

"But that was okay with me. She was as into getting laid as I was—I won't tell you how long it'd been since I'd been with anyone—and my overall timeline forward was as hazy for me as anyone else. No reason to saddle anyone else with that in any serious way. Not anytime soon, anyway. When I let a girl know how little interest I have in staying put or getting serious or having a white-picket fence or any of that stuff, that's usually the end of things, and I wasn't in a hurry for that. Not this time."

"Yeah?" I asked. That was a little different for Hugo, who was usually ready to flee the first morning after.

He nodded.

"Turns out I liked her. A lot. I mean, I really liked her. Like her. Still do, that is. She was, uh, really cool."

"How so?" I asked again.

"Just, um ..." Hugo worked at retrieving the right vocabulary, again very uncharacteristically. "She, uh, she was just it. It. I don't know how else to put it. She was an Iggy Pop fan. And a Clash fan. She's from the same place. Mentally, that is. She was a math-and-computers kid, whereas I was anything but, but she was *us*, Ivan. We would've hung out in high-school. Except she's younger. She's pretty, smart, loved great music, and actually funny. Do you believe that? When was the last time you met a girl who was actually funny? Most of them are like Karen, here. All trying too hard, one way or another."

"I'm extremely funny, asshole," Karen insisted. I felt immediately disloyal for having nothing to say in her defense.

"Well, I'll take your word for it," Hugo said. "But she really was. Just the stuff she said, the turns of phrases she had. She had nick-names for all of the guys in her department that were dead-on. Even her political opinions were hilarious. But that was the best part, really. She had it all going on the politics department, too. Her head was in the same place ours is, Ivan, just right on. Despised both the Republicans and Democrats, had really thought through what this country needs to step in a better direction. Had some very interesting ideas about democratic socialism and had read Marx and Gramsci and, really, more than I even have. I learned a few things from her while we sat around drinking more coffee than I even like to drink. But she wasn't a drag about it. She only brought it up if you did. Dude, it didn't take more than a couple of weeks for me to figure out that I was in love with her."

"Woah!" I said.

"I know! It was strange—but great. But strange. Very strange, man, I can't tell you. Now I understand a few things I didn't quite get before. Why people can turn into such morons when lightning strikes. Nothing ever made me question my momentum before, but, suddenly, I was. Did I want to just finish this job and then move on out of DC? I had planned on maybe heading back to Seattle next, to connect with some people there that I hadn't seen since the WTO demonstrations. We were all itching to get that issue back on the front burner again.

"Anyway, I was. I was thinking, maybe Arlington is a pretty nice place and not just Washington, DC's entry-level armpit after all and maybe I could hang around a while, and so on and so on."

"But then?" I prodded him.

"But, then, at dinner one night, she had some wine and a half and told me a little more than she should have about what sort of data it was we were building this software to handle."

He let it rest there for a beat until I nodded at him to continue. He bent forward before speaking, as if we were all bowing into a football huddle, and his voice lowered.

"It's everything," he said. "Everything. About all of us. Emails, telephone-calls, web search histories, travel data. Information about all of us private citizens, culled from all of the databases of every web, internet, telephone, airline, you-name-it company out there. The NSA collects it all, and the corpos just hand it over. They're keeping it forever, and that's what this company's database was designed to handle. An unlimited amount of personal information to be stored infinitely."

"Well, yeah," Karen snorted. "We know that. Everyone knows that now. That guy that ran off to Russia with the backpack full of hard-drives has been broadcasting that all over the place for months."

"Snowden," I said.

"Yeah," Hugo nodded. "Of course. But, at the time, you didn't know that. I didn't know that. Nobody but a few people knew that. But Francine knew. And she told me. She wasn't supposed to, but she did."

"So then what?" I asked him.

"So I finished my wine, leaned back into my chair, and finished having dinner. And then proceeded to quietly freak the fuck out. I didn't sleep for two nights. I dragged my way through work, doing hardly anything, not wanting to get that project any closer to being done. I didn't want to be a part of it. Me. Can you imagine? Holy fucking Christ! Working for NSA goons. The sixteen year-old me would've kicked me in the balls for doing it."

"You didn't know what it was."

"One day I didn't, but, then, the next day I did. Ignorance is a defense only to a point. You need money to pay rent, that's a defense only to a point. You need money to put gas in your pointless SUV, that's no defense. You need money to go on a vacation to Tahiti, that's no defense. I don't need SUVs or trips to Tahiti. I don't have kids to feed. I don't have the shit going on that people do thankless jobs just to fund. I have no defense. I *get* no defense. I've stripped away my need for any kind of lifestyle super-structure on purpose. So that I can do the right thing always, no apologies, and never need to make an excuse. That's all I've wanted out of this life, and that's what I've done."

He was growing red-faced, the color flooding back to his gaunt cheeks, as he fell into his old rant. He looked more like himself, but that old, pontificating Hugo was just the version of himself I knew that Karen least wanted to entertain in her kitchen. She tensed in her chair.

"Can you get to the point?" she sighed.

"I'm doing that, Karen, but it's not a *simple* point."

"Fine."

"So I was freaking out. On a couple of levels. One, I was participating in something horrible and unconstitutional and illegal. Two, worse to me, was that Francine was participating in something horrible—and she knew about it. All along. She pasted a photo of Iggy Pop on her monitor and talked to me about The Clash as if she were actually practicing what she preached. As if she were a real punk rocker."

"*Punk rocker?*" Karen laughed aloud. "Give me a break. How old are you, Hugo? Who says something like that?"

"Oh, now the sense of humor comes out," he said, waving her off. "It remains a useful appellation, if used correctly, in the right environment, where it won't be misunderstood. Ivan gets it. I knew he would. So I used it. I knew you wouldn't, Karen Law School."

"Again with that? Law School and Law, rememberS," she said.

"Yes, yes, we all know. You're a lawyer. Got it. Dime a' dozen in DC."

"You're not in DC," she said.

"And neither are you. So just take my little phrase for what you will and let me get on with it, okay?"

She didn't respond. That was her version of "okay."

"I get it already, Hugo," I chimed in. "Point taken. Francine was not being true to her school, and it rubbed the shine off of her apple for you. You fell for her and then felt a little ripped off, right?"

"Right. Exacti-mundo. I was burned, man. I was trying not to be angry about all kinds of stuff, all at once. But I was doing a shitty job of it over those few days, and she called me on it. At a show at the 9:30 Club we'd already bought tickets to see, screaming at me over the music, she had me up against a wall, wanting to know why I was being an aloof asshole all of a sudden. So I told her why."

"And how did that go?" I asked.

"Not good," he said. "Not at first. It was hard to talk, much less about anything sensitive. I told her I was sorry and asked her if we could have a chat after the show, someplace quieter. I held her hand nice and tight when I said it and gave her the old deep-eye gaze, and she settled down. We watched the show and then headed off to an Indian restaurant for some chicken tikki."

"You said you were sorry about something?" Karen shook her head. "The girl must have gotten to you."

"I said she did, didn't I? Yeah, and I was sorry. It didn't feel right at all, avoiding her at work and missing her texts and emails on purpose. Took everything I had for those couple of days not to just let myself forget about the whole issue so that she and I could just innocently pick things back up. But you can't stuff a genie back into a bottle, right?"

"I guess," she said, unconvinced.

"So we had our chicken—tandoori, not tikki masala, as it turned out—and I 'fessed up. I told her that I had a problem with what was going on and that I wasn't sure what to do about it. What to do about her being involved with it, specifically."

"I'm sure that went over well," I said.

"Right. Francine's no wet noodle. She didn't just fold over and weep or anything."

"I like her better already," Karen said.

"Well, I like that about her, too," Hugo agreed. "She had a good defense, and she hammered me with it."

"What was the defense?" I asked.

"More or less a defense of the software itself, that

it wasn't like building a nuclear bomb or something that has only one specific purpose. She said that it was a general purpose tool that, yes, had been contracted for by the US government for that purpose as an initial matter but which had a lot of general purpose application as a step-forward in large volume database design, or something like that. It's not my field. But she was insistent that the software would be used for a lot of different things and that the NSA data-gathering was just one of them. Maybe the first of them but that more would come and that the government had a legitimate interest in being able to handle large volumes of data of that sort, not just for snooping purposes but to conduct business generally. And also that the software would probably be licensed for other uses and that her company was involved in some talks with the NSA to actually sell licenses for private business use later on, once the proprietary version the NSA wanted was all up and running and—this part I didn't really get—somehow differentiated from the lower-grade version they'd license for private use. Or somehow made to look like it didn't have the initial purpose that it did, for the NSA. Long story short, she was just very into her work and was sort of in love with this Frankenstein's Monster she'd helped to create. A nerd's argument, I'd call it. A wonky argument."

"Not a bad argument," Karen suggested.

"Well, it almost got me," he agreed, "but only because I really, deep down, wanted to find a reason not to be freaked out anymore. I was looking for something to cling to and just make the issue go away for myself—but it wasn't that easy. Not for me. I don't let myself off the hook any more than I let anyone else off the hook."

"Well, if you're going to be sanctimonious, that's the least you can do," Karen said.

"Ignore her," I told him.

"Always do," he shrugged. "Anyway, so I listened, and we talked about that line of reasoning. Talked about some other examples than the one-purpose nuclear bomb, like creating a mutant virus that, on one hand, could cure a single disease but, on the other hand, could destroy all life on earth if it got loose. Like in that movie. Or, more directly, if you could only develop it with a lot of human testing that was sure to kill hundreds of people as it was developed. Or chimps and kittens, even. We went back and forth like that, went through a few other analogies, and, in the end, though we didn't seem to be getting anywhere, I could tell that she was trying really, really hard not to convince me but to convince herself."

"Of what?" I asked.

"Of her own argument. It occurred to me that she'd had that many-uses defense ready awfully quickly, cocked and loaded the minute I told her what was bothering me. That told me that she'd already been using it. But on who? She wasn't allowed to talk about her work with anyone else, so it had to be on herself. The truth was that, no matter what she said, she really wasn't all that comfortable with it, either.

"So I let her talk, finish whatever it was that she was saying at that time, and then I just sipped some tea and told her, 'Everything you say makes a lot of sense, but the bottom-line for me is that being involved in something like this on whatever level and for whatever ancillary purpose is wrong and a betrayal of everything I've ever stood for and that, now that I knew about it, I had to react to it.' I told her that, although we'd only known each other for a short time, she'd already affected me in a way that no one else ever had and that, no matter what happened, I didn't want to fuck that up. But that something had to happen. I talked at her until I was sure I'd put her to sleep about the US Constitution and the limits of the law and scope of Executive authority and blah-blah-blah after that. I wasn't even sure that I was making any sense, really."

"Probably not," Karen said.

"Probably not," Hugo agreed, ignoring her tone of voice yet again. He was being far more patient with her cracks than he ever had been in the past. "Probably, I was being pedantic and dull and everything that I usually am that drives everyone but Ivan away from me after a certain point. I'm sure I was. How could I not have been all of those things? The problem was, though, that even if I was, Francine was actually listening to me. Can you believe that? When was the last time someone besides you listened to anything I said, Ivan?"

"Well, you had all of those people ready to rip that Wall Street bull statute down and throw it into the river that one time."

He chuckled, remembering.

"True," he allowed, "but they didn't do it, did they?"

"Still, they listened. For a minute, at least."

"Well, I got a minute or more out of Francine, much to my surprise. When I finished blathering, she just sat there, not saying a thing."

"Dumbfounded by the wall of idiocy she'd just been presented with, no doubt," Karen suggested.

"Probably," Hugo laughed. "Then, again, I might have actually accidentally made a convincing argument. At least for someone who had in the back of her mind already been thinking the same thing anyway."

"So then what?" I asked, stifling a yawn despite myself. Hugo noted it and winked.

"I'll get to it," he said. "Bear with me. So, then, we went back to her place, fucked like mountain lions, and then got up in the morning and went to work without mentioning it again all day.

"That next night, however, she came up with it. Not me—her. We were sitting watching TV when she crawled up onto my lap and said, 'Let's blow the whistle!' She was all excited and turned on by the idea, seemed like. I asked her what she meant, and she just started kissing me and shit. So we fucked like mountain lions again and then, afterward, finally got down to brass tacks."

"Which were?" I asked. "And how exactly do mountain lions fuck?"

"I'll save that one for another time," he replied, "but, as to the first, the brass tacks were that the type and volume of data the NSA was collecting, and the means by which they were collecting it, was surely illegal and that someone other than the two of us probably ought to know about it. Like *The New York Times* or *Mother Jones* or somebody, although the *Times* is just about as shitty a corporate status quo rag as any of the rest of them. Probably *Mother Jones*, or the foreign press. But, anyway, we were going to blow the whistle. Blow our jobs, sure, and maybe get into a lot of hot water, but do some good in the meantime. Of course, I could have given a shit about the job. I was a temp, anyway. But it was a big thought for her. She hadn't worked anyplace else since college and actually had something to lose. I didn't try to talk her out of it, though. Just told her that I loved her, and that was the end of that for her."

"Oh, I'm sure," Karen sighed, rolling her eyes. "We're all just swooning bimbos in the end."

"Hey, now," Hugo cautioned her. "I meant what I said, and now more than ever. So come on."

"Okay, sure," she said, letting it ride.

"Anyway, so we decided that what we'd have to do to make an impression is to actually hand over a huge volume of the data, especially some chunk with juicy bits in it. But the problem was that Francine couldn't sift through it and run searches for juicy bits without other people catching on. So the only thing we really could do would be just to take as much of it as we could get and increase the odds that we'd get something attention-grabbing on in there. I mean, really, it probably wouldn't take much. Just to let people know that their personal information had all been up for grabs for ages, since just after 9/11. But, if there was something particularly revealing, like, I don't know, confidential information about someone famous in there, all the better."

"Gee, this is sounding awfully familiar," Karen interrupted. "Isn't this exactly what's already happened?"

"*Yes*," Hugo hissed through his teeth, losing his patience. "But, like I said, *we didn't know that at the time*. In fact, that Snowden fucker is the reason we're in this mess now in the first place."

"How do you mean?" I asked.

"I mean that that jerk pulled his little stunt the day before we did," he groaned, rubbing his eyes. "He made off with his ball-sac full of laptops one lousy day before we planned to do more or less the same thing, and, as a result of which, the jig was up before it was on. Overnight, after he got on the plane to Hong Kong, all kinds of new bells and whistles were in the system that even Francine didn't know a goddamn thing about."

"What did you actually do?" Karen asked.

"We went into work a couple of mornings after we'd talked. Same as always. I to my cube in my department, Francine to hers, half a floor away. She had the access, I didn't. So, really, it was all on her. She was pretty fucking brave to even volunteer, in my book. Anyway, she went in with her gym bag in tow, which was not uncommon since she worked out after work at least two or three days a week, normally. Only, along with her gym clothes, she had in the bag, like, ten external hard-drives that could each hold ten bazillion-bytes of data or whatever. She picked them out, I don't know jack-shit about that sort of thing. At some point in the morning, while she was working, she pulled one of them out, plugged it into her USB port, and started downloading. Whatever she could get, I guess. As much as she could get.

"We had prearranged to meet outside at lunchtime, to walk out just as if we were going to lunch or to the gym together or something. We'd started eating lunch together every day at that point, so we didn't think it would look weird for her to hustle out with a temp. So, at around twelve-thirty, I stretched, told my supervisor I was going out for lunch, and I walked out of the room, down the hall, and out the front door. I hovered around a little bench outside, near the shit-can where people smoked, just like I always did, waiting for her.

"I kept my eye on the door, watching for her through the glass. It was sunny out and I could barely see through the reflection, but, eventually, I saw her coming down the hall with her bag over her shoulder. She waved at me, and I started to wave back but, then, the two goons at the security desk got up and intercepted her about five feet from the door. I couldn't hear what they were saying to her, but I saw one of them push her down and pull his gun from his holster.

"And that's when I went berserk. I yanked the door open and launched at the guy and knocked his ass over. His partner wheeled on me, but I ducked his punch and ankle-swept the guy with the gun back onto the floor when he tried to get up. You remember when I took kung fu for a while back in high-school and college, Ivan? It fucking came back just when I needed it. He dropped the gun, and Francine pepper-sprayed the other guard right in the face. I don't even know where she pulled that from, but he went down spitting and gagging. I butted him with my shoulder and knocked him the rest of the way over, and we grabbed the bag and got the hell out of there onto the Orange Line back into DC. It wasn't 'till we were stepping off of the Red Line in Silver Spring that I realized that Francine had grabbed the guard's gun, too."

"What?" Karen gasped.

"Don't worry," Hugo said. "We never used it or anything. But, if they say anything about us being armed and dangerous or some shit, that's probably why."

"Well, I guess so!"

"So how did you get here?" I asked him. "Why is Francine on her own now?"

"That's a longer story," he said, yawning as well now. "The quick version: it made more sense after a point. But what we did was double-back into DC from Silver Spring, cabbing it back to China Town, where we grabbed one of those China Town busses to Manhattan. Francine had the timing all mapped out, and we knew when the bus would leave and all that. As well as you can ever know when they're really going to leave, anyway. So we did that, got to New York, where we hung out for a couple of days, taking it easy in a little hotel in Brooklyn, then decided after all the Snowden hubbub hit the airwaves, to mosey along separately for a bit, re-connecting here. She actually has plenty of cash. Pulled it out of her 401(k) the day before we did all of this. What I've got she gave me. A little has to go a long way for me."

"Why here?" Karen asked. "You had to know you'd only be making trouble for us."

Hugo slumped a bit and closed his eyes.

"Where else?" he said, after a moment. "Who else?"

"That's the opposite reason you should've come here. If Ivan is the only person you have, wouldn't you want to sort of treat that as sacrosanct?"

"Probably," he agreed, "but you're also on the way."

"To where?" I asked him.

"Canada."

"That's a terrible idea," Karen pointed out. "The border here is more uptight than ever since 9/11, and Canada has every kind of extradition treaty with the US."

"We weren't planning on going through here," Hugo said. "Just meeting here. Then heading north to step through at Sault Ste. Marie or some backwoods crossing point in northern Wisconsin or something. The problem is that something's gone wrong. We were supposed to meet up the first time I came by here and saw Ivan. Only she wasn't here yet. We were supposed to move on and up there fast and then buy a plane ticket from Canada to someplace else. Maybe Cuba now that that's all loosening up. From Toronto, maybe? I guess we didn't flesh that part of the plan out too well, but that was the idea. Get the data to someone overseas, like I said. Wiki-Leaks or whatever."

I nodded.

"Anyway, I don't know if it's too late to do that or what, but, until Francine and I re-connect, we can't shift gears very well and come up with a Plan B of any sort. She was just to take one bus this way and I'd take one bus that way, and we'd meet up here at Ivan's place and then proceed from there."

"What happened to the data? Did you even get any?" Karen asked.

"We got it," Hugo nodded. "I have some of the hard drives, she has the others. I've got mine stashed right now."

"Where?" I asked.

"Stashed," he said more firmly. "Let's leave it at that."

"So, then," I said. "You staying the night or what?"

"Don't think so," he said, "as much as I'd love to steal your couch for a while. I really didn't mean to put either of you in the crosshairs, and I don't mean to keep doing it if I have. I've got to see to Francine and try to make all of this hassle worthwhile somehow."

"At least you finally tricked someone into hooking up with you," I said.

"Look who's talking," he laughed. "When was the last time either of you got laid?"

Neither of us responded to that.

"Seriously," he said. "I think it was just my time. I think I needed this. I won't kid you, Ivan: I'm a desperate man. Things are very strange for me right now, but this whole love business has been some kind of silver lining through it all. I've started to think of love as destiny, as dopey and hackneyed as that sounds. Destiny like a swinging wrecking-ball ... When it's your time, you can't avoid it."

"That's a theory, anyway."

"It's more than a theory. It's the truth. You can always smell the truth when you live it."

"Oh, brother," Karen groaned, once again.

He got up from the table and peeked out through the curtains. A wand of moonlight bisected his face.

"Looks pretty quiet out there," he said. "Is it always like this?"

"Pretty much."

"Must be nice," he sighed.

"Yes and no," I said.

"That seems about right. I'd chafe at this whole domestic thing, myself. Maybe."

"Maybe?"

"Maybe," he nodded. "For that couple of weeks drifting in and out of Francine's apartment, I thought I could do it for a little while. I admit that I daydreamed my way right up through romance, marriage, kids, and even divorce. It all seems to follow, you know, that basic pattern.

"I hope not."

"Yeah," he said. "Me, too. For your sake. For me, I guess it's all out of my hands now, personally."

"Nothing to change your priorities like being hunted by the FBI."

"True that."

"Nothing is out of your hands, Hugo," Karen said. "This definitely isn't my area, but you have a choice you can make. You can make a deal to turn the data back over or something. I don't think you need to ruin your lives any more than you already have by running from it. I don't know nearly enough to suggest whether there's any possibility of avoiding some prison time, but my guess is that we aren't actually talking about a life-sentence here."

He thought it over, staring outside, and finally shook his head.

"Yeah," he said. "I figured. But, obviously, I'm not going to do that. You *know* they'll charge us with whatever they want. You make it sound optimistic, but who's to say what will happen now that there's some kind of assault or battery or whatever involved. And a gun. Far as I can see, the only thing to do to make the best of it is to accomplish the original goal. Get the data somewhere useful, bolster the stuff that's already out there. Maybe we even have better stuff than Snowden did, you never know. Help that guy put some nails in the NSA's coffin. I called him a fucker, but he had the same idea we did. Self-sacrifice for the greater good. It doesn't matter who makes the sacrifice once the good is accomplished. That's the end that really feels worthwhile to me, even if there is some duplication of efforts going on. That dude is definitely punk rock."

"It seems pointless at this point," Karen said. "Just turn yourself in and let it sort out somehow. Pepper-spray and a shoving is not murder. Running on is only going to make things worse."

He picked his coat up from the chair.

"Of that," he said, "I have no doubt. Yet that's exactly what I'm going to do."

"Come on, man," I said. "Where will you go? With how much more of Francine's money? Maybe you should just call it a day. Turn yourself in. Tell them that you didn't have anything to do with it, other than defending Francine from the jerk with the gun. She did the actual data theft."

He turned and stared me down hard.

"I'm going to pretend that I didn't hear that. I'm not going to lay Francine down on the tracks."

Karen threw her hands up.

"All I can do is advise you, Hugo, and I've done that. If you want to make things worse for yourself, all you have to do is walk out that door."

"Well, I need to hook up with Francine again anyhow," he said. "I can't make any decision without her."

"Where is she now?" I asked.

"I told her not to tell me," he said. "Just in case either one of us got picked up. All she knew was that she could pick up a letter from me here. And she did, so that's cool."

He winked and smiled, but, when he zipped up his jacket, I thought he might go on zipping until he'd disappeared completely. I walked him to the door, but he held me back as he switched the kitchen lights off before stepping out.

"Don't be dumb, Hugo," Karen said.

"Too late," he said, shrugging. "Thanks for the refreshment."

He tipped an invisible hat and slipped out into the yard, and then out of sight around the corner of the house.

Who was the last person to see Anosov as a free man? Lyudmila? Or some unnamed confederate eating bread and beans with him around a fire? Trotsky himself? There was no record that I'd ever seen of Stalin and Anosov meeting, or even being within one hundred miles of each other. Anosov approached Moscow and Petersburg only near the end, and the approach proved to be a fatal mistake. He had been more or less unrestrained by the over-extended Red Army when he'd been operating in the east, harassing supply lines and berating peasants about their social obligations. Success and a little notoriety proved to be unfortunately inspiring to my hero, encouraging him to certain excesses in his work, to raising his voice a little louder, to reorienting his map constantly so that he remained ever at the center, to moving his small army in the wrong direction, toward a much bigger, better organized one. Toward Trotsky rather than around.

In the end, someone was the last person to shut the door or tighten the blindfold or light the cigarette or take careful aim. When Hugo skipped out of sight that evening, I stood staring at the space he had momentarily occupied in the yard, wondering if that person, in Hugo's case, would turn out to be me.

13.

The next day, after Karen had silently padded past me and out to her car, I buttered my toast, ate it, washed the dishes, frantically searched for the TV remote under couch cushions, and waited for an imaginary U.S. Marine to walk up beside me and whisper, "It's quiet, Sarge—maybe too quiet." I opened the windows, but the streets were next to deserted with the season's first really cold wind and initial peppering of snow rushing through them. No kids shouted, no dogs barked. Even busy Crooks Avenue beyond my familiar tree-line broadcast no sound onto my little plateau. I re-watched several episodes of Ken Burns' World War II documentary on DVD and considered that history would be more successfully taught to American students if Tom Hanks would just flit from high school to high school and read the stuff aloud.

The day proved too long for Ken Burns even to fill, though, and it left me with too much time to think. I stared at the screen and formulated various excuses and apologies for not telling Karen about Francine's visit, but none of them gelled. I wondered if she had slept well the night before, if she had just collapsed onto the mattress and conked out, or if she'd just stared at the moonlight striping the ceiling, fists clenched beneath the blankets. She had always been a good sleeper and had no trouble with noise, light, or motion. I could not picture her falling straightaway to sleep without directing a wasps' nest of silent invective in my direction, down through the mattresses and floorboards to the occupied couch below.

I moved robotically on from Ken Burns to other cable TV re-runs, and, at the same time that Corporal Radar O'Reilly announced to the other denizens of the 4077th mobile army surgical hospital that Lieutenant Colonel Henry Blake's airplane had been shot down over the South China Sea, I concluded that my marriage was finished and that there was likely nothing in the world that I could do about it.

Eventually, by the time she came home, I had worked myself into a fever pitch. When she walked in, I was standing on a chair, screwing a new lightbulb into the ceiling light over the dining-room table. I tightened the bulb into the socket and winced at the sudden glow as she kicked her shoes off. Over the course of an hour, I had changed every lightbulb in the house, whether they needed changing or not, replacing every bulb in every lamp and socket in every room. The house was alive with light, all darkness and shadow obliterated from every corner, and I stared down at her from the chair I stood on with an incandescent halo ringing my skull. I was not unaware of the effect as I stared down at her.

"Jesus," she said. "Bright enough in here? The electric bill is going to be a million dollars."

She was right: the house glowed like a shopping-mall atrium, but it brought focus to details of Karen's appearance that I had missed before: the gray in her bangs, a chipped fingernail, skin hanging a little more loosely than it used to beneath her chin.

"It is now," I said, rubbing my eyes. "100 watts. All of 'em. Every bulb."

"You've lost it."

She shook her head and plodded up the stairs to the bathroom. I listened as she clicked that light on, too.

"Jesus!" she swore again.

I finished screwing new bulbs into the chandelier and followed her upstairs when I was done. The light from the bedroom lit the back end of the hallway. Inside the room, Karen sat on the bed beside an open suitcase, which I would have been surprised not to see. She'd turned the nightstand radio to a classical station broadcasting from across the river in Windsor, Canada, and examined the contents of the suitcase, ignoring me. There were several days' worth of clothes in the suitcase, and her makeup table looked ransacked.

"I'm leaving," she said, without looking up.

"Surprise, surprise," I sighed, nudging the corner of her suitcase with my kneecap as I walked in to stand in front of her.

"What do you mean by that?"

"Nothing," I said. "Just—why wouldn't you?"

"Don't pull that self-effacing shit on me," she said, scooting further back on the bed, away from me. She slid to her feet off of the end of the bed and closed the suitcase with a snap.

"I'm not being self-effacing," I said. "I just expected it. All day."

"It's just for a little while," she said. "Don't get carried away."

"How am I supposed to react? It isn't like you haven't been dropping hints or anything. You've been acting done with me for the past year, at least."

"Me? I have?" she yelled, her buttons pushed. "You mope around the house like a zombie for ten years and then accuse me of detaching? I think I've been saint-like with you."

"Oh, sure. Saint Karen of the Poor in Ambition."

"Oh, that's it, Ivan," she said, shaking her head. "That's fucking *it*."

"You think it's that easy?" I said, following her down the hallway and onto the stairs.

She didn't answer me, so I repeated myself, chasing her through the living-room to the front door.

"Answer me, Karen," I demanded, as she stepped out onto the porch. "You think you can just get pissed at me once and use that as an excuse to flush our entire life down the drain?"

She stopped and looked at me. Her eyes were red, and her lips were pressed tight. The bright light from the dining-room chandelier behind me, my shadow buried her.

"I don't think anything is easy, Ivan," she said. "That's where you and I are different."

I opened my mouth to reply, but then shut it again. The corners of her eyes moistened, and I couldn't think of anything else to say.

"Come on," I groaned, after a moment.

"I'm not doing this out of anger," she whispered. "I'm doing this to force a conclusion."

"To what?"

"You know what I mean."

I did.

I backed away from the door, into the living-room, knowing that she would take the knob in her hand, and push the door closed between us. Up until the last moment, when she bumped her suitcase against the door-frame as it swung shut, parting us, I saw these things happening without really believing that they would. Only inches away, through the closed door, she became just another rustle in the bushes, like Hugo. She was outside; I was inside. As simple as that.

"I'll call you when I feel like it," she said, through the door. "I'll be at my mother's."

I watched through the window as she struggled down the front steps with her suitcase and shoved it into the trunk. Without looking back at me, she slid into her car and, gunning the engine, backed out and away.

14.

    When I heard the crash, it seemed natural that someone else should be in the house making noise. I didn't live alone, and a little noise was normal. I wanted to call out to Karen not to worry about it, that I'd clean it up in the morning, but another loud bump knocked me completely upright, petrified, and aware. I slithered out of bed and felt around for my old Al Kaline signature-embossed Louisville Slugger on the floor beneath the bed. I hefted it up and moonwalked out into the hallway, experimenting with different grips while doing my best to hover above the squeaky floorboards. I momentarily wished for a gun but thought better of it even as I moved toward the stairs, my lungs venting into space with every step. If it turned out to be Karen downstairs, back with a new suitcase full of apologies and regret, I would surely not want to charge in, blazing away with a pistol. Anyway, I might obsess about Anosov, but I knew the difference between the two of us at the necessary and proper level. I could barely manage a baseball bat.

The floorboards in the hallway gave me away at the first step. If anyone else was in the house, they were already waiting at the bottom of the stairs with the pins already pulled on their hand grenades. I took the stairs as quietly as I could down the stairs, one by one, assuring myself with each cautious step that no one was yet in sight. My vision soon acclimated to the dark, and I moved with increasing confidence in the idea that there was nothing to worry about. When had anyone else been in this house? Ever? My knowledge of the household geography was supreme, after all. I knew every nook and cranny of the place; there could be no hiding from me in my own house, even in pitch darkness, and it was not exactly that. The ambient light from the street poured through our flimsy living-room curtains reasonably well.

At the bottom of the stairs, I saw no light streaming from under the kitchen door, and a quick circuit of the living-room proved that all was well in the front end of the house. I padded toward the kitchen, trying to remember where the squeakiest parts of the floor lay. Halfway through the dining-room, I gave it up and kicked the kitchen door open.

Immediately, I skidded into the table and chairs just inside the room, stubbing my bare toes into a tableleg and stumbling. I dropped the baseball bat onto the floor, and the sharp crack of its impact echoed in the corners of the room. My forehead level with the table's surface, I didn't know if anyone else was in the room or not. The back of my neck heated where I expected a fist or blunt instrument to strike first, and I tensed, wondering whether to resist the blow or fall with it. However, nothing happened. My eyes adjusted to the paper-thin light after a beat or two, and I scanned the floor beyond the legs of the table. There were no feet there, no legs, no bodies. I held my breath for another few seconds, and then stood up. The room was empty.

I found my bat on the floor and picked it up again. My toes throbbed where I'd stubbed them, and a tickling warmth between them told me they were bleeding. Somebody or something had made not one but two loud noises, regardless, and I didn't want to stop to deal with stubbed toes until I knew what it was. I had made an amount of noise sufficient to alert the Premier of China of my presence in the kitchen, and what was done was done. I staggered over to peek out through the window in the back door, testing the knob to ensure that the crash had not the door or its small window. It was still locked, however, and the window-glass was intact. The back yard was empty, moreover. I repeated my inspection of the other window with the same results, and then set my sights on the only avenue remaining to me—or anyone else: the basement door. It occurred to me that the piece of wood I'd shoved through the hurricane doors and the other items I'd piled up down there had been the source of the crash.

Whomever had sliced that padlock in half was back.

I moved toward the door, but the odds of someone being behind it seemed so great that I was unable to grasp the knob. The merest turn would reveal all of my embodied childhood fears: a clown with a chainsaw, a blood-spattered dentist, a supernaturally large Doberman pinscher, a vampire of the *Nosferatu* variety—bald, hunched, grasping with curved, evil fingers. It didn't occur to me to run to the phone, or, better yet, a neighbor's phone, and call the police. I sucked in my breath, adjusted my grip on the baseball bat, and swung the basement door open.

A groan from inside rose up to greet me. It spiraled up the staircase, a long, mournful sort of howl, followed by a loud snap, the sound of a bare hand slapping the concrete floor. Someone was definitely down there. It was no longer theoretical, and, although the groan was not an intimidating sort of sound, it was a sound. From a human being. In my house. And that was enough to paralyze me again. I stood at the top of the stairs, a perfect target, staring down into nothing, slack-jawed and stupid.

"Who's there?" I whispered after a very long, hanging second.

The sound of my voice echoed back, but my breathless croak made no impact below. The groan repeated, more faintly, and then truncated. I took a step down, testing the stair, attempting to jar myself into action of any sort.

"Who's there?" I yelled, doing my best to sound mean.

At first, there was no response. But then the groan rose up again, coalescing into what sounded like my name.

"Ivan?" the darkness moaned.

I recognized the voice instantly.

Switching on the lights, I descended. When I reached the floor below, Hugo threw me a halfhearted salute from the floor at the bottom of the hurricane-door steps. His foot was cocked to the left in a way it shouldn't have been, stretched across my fallen wood plank.

"Expecting Kirk Gibson were you?" he said.

I lowered the bat, but I was too keyed up to lay it down completely. I strode over and loomed over him with it, laying it across my shoulder like a rifleman on parade.

"What the fuck are you doing here?" I asked him.

"I had nowhere else to go," he said, shading his eyes. "Put that thing down, will you?"

I lowered the bat but continued to hold it.

"I thought you were going to meet up with Francine."

He struggled to sit up, pushing himself upright against the bottom step.

"Dude, I've been down here a while," he said.

"But you left!"

"Yeah, well, I came right back," he said. "Goddamn, I can't believe I tripped. I must have been in and out of that door fifty times."

"I had a piece of wood through the handles, though."

"It fell out the minute I jiggered the door. Weak, Ivan."

"You were the one that clipped my padlock on those doors?"

"Yeah," he admitted. "Sorry."

"Why?"

"I told you, man ... I had nowhere else to go."

"So why were you out? Why leave and come back and make all this fucking noise in the middle of the night?"

He groaned again and rubbed at his ankle, twisting it around.

"You think you could give me a minute on that? Maybe you haven't noticed, but I'm pretty fucked up here ..."

"If you can move it like that, it isn't broken," I told him, not moving.

"True," he said, wincing as he tested it.

He grimaced as he struggled up and tried to lean some weight onto the foot.

"Damn," he said. "I just wanted some fresh air now that it was dark outside again ..."

He sat back down, breathing hard.

"Let me take a look," I said, setting the bat down and stepping over to make sure the hurricane doors were fully closed.

I crouched down beside him and carefully unlaced his boot. He sucked air when I yanked the string free and slid it off of his heel. Beneath the boot, he wore a tattered, filthy excuse for a sock that appeared to be both damp and crusty where it wasn't worn entirely through.

"Lovely," I said.

Hugo laughed and tried again, without success, to bend his ankle properly.

"What are you going to do?" he said. "Socks are the last you think of when you're fleeing the law."

"Well, your penance for home invasion is to pull that thing off yourself," I said, backing away. "There's no way I'm touching it."

He bent over and tried to inch the sock off without actually bending his leg, but he couldn't quite reach. He managed to ease most of it off, but I ended up giving it the final yank after all, flinging it across the room like a piece of roadkill. I lifted the leg of his jeans up to examine his ankle. It was swollen and a little bruised, but he could bend it.

"It's just sprained or something," I said.

"Damn," he said again.

He looked miserable, curled up against the steps with his dirty foot splayed out on the cold floor.

"Do you think you can walk?" I asked him.

He tried to stand, but he winced and danced back down. I lifted his arm over my shoulder and propped him up on his good foot.

"Let's at least get you away from these doors," I said, noting the cold air seeping through. "Can you make it to the other side of the basement?"

"I think so," he said, gritting his teeth.

Slowly, we made our way to the other side of the room, closer to the stairs and the water-heater.

"My stuff?" he said, pointing behind me.

There, tucked behind the water heater, I found his jacket and denim backpack. It was a terrible spot to hide, cramped and probably either too warm or too damp, depending on the ever fluctuating integrity of the aging heater. However, it was out of the line-of-sight from the stairs and washer and dryer, and I could easily see how, if he curled up and lay still enough, he would never be noticed by either Karen or myself entering the room for casual utilitarian purposes.

As I'd thought before, it was the only place to hide in the room—and he'd found it.

His backpack was a shapeless mass bound by a ratty piece of twine. I considered opening it up and dumping it out for inventorying, but the manner in which it had been bound up and secured was too elaborate for me to deal with. Instead, while Hugo was bent over, massaging his ankle, I quickly squeezed it, running my hands over its corners and contours like a 19th century phrenologist looking for evidence of criminal intent on the skull of a convict. Parts of the bag were soft and pliable, and I pressed at them with my fingertips, testing their give. Other protuberances were more easily defined, and I identified them as best I could—a can of soup or Dinty Moore beef stew or somesuch, a tennis or stress ball, a hardcover book, and something else. That object was like a large letter "L," sharp even through the canvas, and heavy. I traced its outline and stubbed my fingernail on it. A gun. Presumably the one that he and Francine had taken from the security guard. I set the bag down on his jacket delicately. Why did he still have it? Hadn't he said that Francine had it? He'd be an idiot to be caught with it, but who knew?

I arranged his gear in the little area a little more neatly for him, making sure to set the bag a little further out of arm's reach of his nest than he might have preferred.

"I can't believe you've been down here all this time," I said when he was comfortably slumped against the wall. "You're unbelievable."

"That's what she said," he laughed.

I wasn't amused.

"What happened to your other friends?" I asked him. "Don't you have some extensive underground network of shady contacts who can smuggle you to Mexico or something?"

"You run out of friends fast in a situation like this. And, also, no, of course I don't."

"I wonder why."

He yawned and reached down to massage his wounded leg.

"You're it, Ivan. You're my friend. You're my *only* friend. But I'll leave if you can't help me out. I'll understand."

He didn't mean it. We stared each other down, and, eventually, I scored a rare victory against him. He leaned back and closed his eyes.

"You know that Karen left?" I asked him.

"I heard," he said. "Not all the details, but you'd be surprised how much you can pick up through ductwork."

"It doesn't break your heart, I presume," I said.

"Well, I'm sorry for you, man. I really am. But it does make things easier for me, here. You understand."

"Not really."

"Well, clearly, I'm not going anywhere right now," he said, nodding at his ankle.

"We'll see about that," I said. "But you couldn't have picked a worse place to hide. The FBI has been here once already. Karen could come back anytime. Why don't you just do what she told you to? Turn yourself in. I'll go with you, make sure they don't fuck you over or anything."

"It's a bad idea," he sighed. "That's what cops do, you know: fuck people over."

"But they usually pick on those who can't fight back. Not people with lawyers."

"What I should have done was leave some sort of clue behind to totally throw them off. Some bit of evidence that I was heading for Alaska or someplace completely out of the way. But I was really in a bad state that first night I stopped by, you know. Not sleeping for days on end will mess with your ability to reason and plan."

"I'll bet."

"It's true. You see movies about things like this, and it seems exciting or romantic or something. But it isn't. It just sucks. Even when you think you're safe for a while. You get yourself free and clear, somehow, if you're lucky, living with a new name, new job, even a new family … But you still wonder. It's still a monkey on your back. It's like a mosquito buzzing in your ear constantly. It can drive you *insane*. Believe me, I'm not going to move in and drive you out. I want the best for you, and, believe it or not, for Karen, too. But tonight I'm tired. Really fucking tired. I can't walk, and I can't move on. At least not tonight. You're stuck with me, so it's up to you to decide to turn me in or not. I've already made my mind up."

My first thought was that Karen would kill me if I did anything other than kick him and call the cops. There was no Karen at the moment, however. She was gone, and I didn't know when she'd be back. If she'd simply been furious, if she'd simply exploded at me out of a flash of red anger, she would be back as quickly as she cooled. Deciding to pack a suitcase and leave as the result of a reasoned and rational thought process, though: that was different. She was gone for a few days at least. Maybe a week. Maybe longer. I'd have to convince her that she'd made the wrong decision at some point, and that wasn't an easy thing to do with a lawyer. Here, now, I remembered how little I'd liked watching Hugo vanish through our back door, apparently never to return. I found that I was, in the alternative, simply relieved just to see him again.

"I won't turn you in," I told Hugo. "Not tonight, anyway."

"Groovy," he said, giving me a thumbs-up.

"Don't get comfortable," I said. "Your ankle doesn't look that bad. It should be fine tomorrow-ish. Just leave the same way you came when you go, and we won't have any problems. From anyone. If you get caught, I didn't know you were down here."

"Understood. I wouldn't have it any other way. Can I have something to eat? And maybe a blanket?"

I left him alone while I fetched him some provisions upstairs. He was half-asleep by the time I returned with a sleeping bag, pillow, and a bologna sandwich, but he snapped alert at the sight of the food. I made another trip for some beer and an extra blanket or two, and he ate while I set it all up as best I could. The motion of laying a sleeping bag out for him triggered my manual memory. Despite the circumstances, it felt like old times all of a sudden. In high school, we'd sat up late playing records, watching television, and shooting the shit on almost a weekly basis. I was forever making up couches and spots on the floor for him to sleep on back then. I brought him a change of clothes, one of my t-shirts and a pair of sweatpants, and, when he put them on, he almost looked like that kid again, the one who, despite all of his intellectual and political braggadocio, still laughed himself sick over Bugs Bunny cartoons and Bill Murray movies.

He steadied his leg and settled into his makeshift bed on the floor.

"Man, this is like a cloud," he sighed.

"Just don't get too comfortable."

"Me? Get comfortable? I'm my own worst enemy in that department."

"I guess that's true," I laughed.

It felt good to laugh, and to laugh with Hugo. Just like old times.

15.

The crows had been at Piorotkin when Anosov found him, wrote Piroshev and Millar. Anosov supposed that it wasn't that unusual to find corpses like around this particular forest, given everything happening in the wider world around it, but this corpse should not have been in this place. It should not have been a corpse. It should have been a man, walking in a very different direction on two intact legs, neither of which had been shattered by a bullet. Yet here it was … Here he was. How could have been gotten so turned around? It was a simple thing, to walk a straight path in a single direction, to simply fail to waver, to just not stop, lean back on one's heel, and turn around. And yet here he was.

What had happened? Had the path itself circled back on itself? Had he come running back after Anosov upon running into the Bolsheviks, who Anosov presumed to be responsible for the lodging the bullets in Piorotkin's thigh, knee, and breast? If so, how did he end up further along the path than Anosov himself? And for long enough for the crows to rend him to the extent that they had? It didn't make any sense, but, then, Anosov was lost himself. His end of the path had not reached any termination. He had been walking so long that he no longer fully remembered where he hoped he might end up. There had been no forks, no turns, no circling back of his path; it just went on and on and on. Three nights had come and gone since he'd parted with Piorotkin, and he had never felt so desolately alone. He had laughed a few times, his voice echoing off of the trees, thinking of Piorotkin in the same situation, bitching with every further, aching step taken, as he was wont to do. At other times, the certainty that his friend had found warm and dry shelter had given him comfort. Was it not logical to assume that, if Anosov had taken the wrong turn, Piorotkin had taken the right one? The one that led to a fire with a spitted rabbit roasting over it? And a fat serf woman with loose skirts turning that spit? It seemed logical to him.

So much for logic.

Who was this thing in front of him? Not his friend, not any longer. Not one of the nameless corpses he'd stepped over on the battlefield, either. Something in between: a dead man with a name. A body in need of both burying and forgetting. He clasped the former Piorotkin's shoulder, as he had done many times in the past, the last upon parting here in the woods. It was not Piorotkin's thickly muscled knob of a shoulder any longer but a gnarled tree root, a stone in the ground. If he had tripped on it, he would simply have kicked it aside. His friend's limbs were the same, all stiffened now with rigor mortis. Anosov pushed at Piorotkin's jaw, frozen open, but it did not budge easily. He would have had to break it to close it. The man's famously yellow and broken teeth were on display now for all to see. He had usually only revealed them when laughing his deepest guffaw, the one that rumbled up from his belly and made its way to his mouth only over the course of several long seconds, during which Piorotkin's face would redden, his cheeks bulge as he attempted to stifle the laugh back down, and his eyes begin watering. It defied logic once more that Anosov would never again hear—and see—that laugh.

When had been the last time he had heard it? Not for a long time. There had not been a lot to laugh about over the past several months. The campaign had gone so badly that their men, he knew, had not been all that broken up over being forced to zig when he had zagged into the forest. There were a couple of good brains among them; they were fine without him and knew it. Those fellows were with that peasant woman and her spit at that moment, he was sure. And he was here with Piorotkin, who the men had liked better than Anosov. Everyone liked Piorotkin better than anyone else, he didn't take it personally. He liked Piorotkin better than everyone else as well.

Had liked.

When he and Piorotkin were young, standing on either side of his father's mule, nothing had existed in the past-tense. Even the very idea of a past tense was something he had yet to learn of, something he would not have ever considered no matter how many times he might have utilized in his speech, had it not been for the old Jew and his books. That was yet to come. Future tense. Old Simkin had taught him that one, too. The sky lay out there, on the edge of the forest, and so did everything else.

"What would you do with a hundred roubles, Sasha?" Piorotkin was fond of asking over the back of the mule, usually while pretending to help with the plow's harness.

Anosov never had an answer for that. It was irrelevant whether he had a hundred roubles or not because he would still be a serf. He would probably just be a very drunk serf with that much money. Piorotkin, on the other hand, had many answers for that question, which was the reason why he always asked it, nearly every day. The first of them was always that he would get very, very drunk. That was the obvious answer for anyone either of them knew, and the last answer for most of them. His friend had at least a hundred other answers, one for every rouble.

So what was the answer for this, Piorotkin? Was it the fat woman and the spit? If not the roubles, that was usually the conclusion his friend would come to when put to it. Neither would do him much good now. Neither would bring his friend back from the dark place to march and sing and laugh beside him. The question, in fact, was itself unclear. Whatever it was always was the question for men of war, in any case, though there was always someone in addition to yourself that you hoped it would not be asked of. Piorotkin was Anosov's exception to the rule that, when you picked up a rifle, you yourself were likely to be shot. He had not imagined that there might be a time when the two of them were not alive on this planet together. Despite circumstances, the idea had never occurred to him. There were so many times when either or both of them could have been killed but had not even been wounded that the possibility was less than remote as far as he was concerned. Tambov, that corn field outside Novorossiysk after Deniken's failure, more fights with knives and broken bottles in taverns than he could count. Piorotkin excelled at getting himself out of the latter sort of scrape, usually leaving several or even a dozen very unfortunate souls behind him with every ugly exit.

And now who was making the ugly exit? Anosov

supposed excelling in assisting others with such exits inevitably resulted in one's own, but that didn't seem fair to Piorotkin, who had not asked to be shot other than by agreeing to follow Anosov out of their village so very long ago. He laid his hands on his friend's shredded chest and bowed his head over him. No breath, no hissing, no sharp rebukes, no intoxicated slurring, no halitosis, no nothing. The open mouth had nothing to tell him, not any longer.

"Be at peace, my brother," he whispered, closing Piorotkin's eyelids over his ruined sockets with a gentle stroke of his hand, but it seemed like a stock platitude, the sort of thing people say because they feel that they ought to. It brought Anosov no comfort to say it, and he knew it did less than nothing for Piorotkin, who was now beyond the need for platitudes and social grace. Anosov felt a little stupid saying anything at all. What he wanted to do was cry, but he realized he would be crying only for himself, which was pointless, and, in any case, he had forgotten how.

Instead, lacking a shovel or pick-axe with which to penetrate the frozen earth beneath them, he looked around for stones and branches and leaves, anything he might use to cover his friend. Plenty of all of these lie around them, so Anosov gathered and fashioned them into a sort of burial tent for Piorotkin, constructing first the frame of a rough lean-to around the body, ringing that with the largest stones he could find, and then thatching it over with branches and dried leaves and pine needles. It was a sturdy enough shelter by the time he finished.

"If I couldn't save you or die with you, Mitya, at least I will keep those fucking birds off of you," Anosov boomed, his voice echoing from tree to tree, scaring away every bird for a hectare, he hoped.

The forest would no doubt have its way with his friend. Nothing Anosov could do about it but what he had done, and whomever had killed him might still be lurking. He stared at the lean-to for another long minute or two, muttered a quiet prayer and asked God to accept his troublemaker of a friend despite his flaws and petty crimes, and then, finally, turned away.

Whatever lay at the end of his path remained.

16.

Hugo was still sleeping when I pulled the blanket off of him in the morning.

"Rise and shine," I said.

He stretched upright, yawning.

"What time is it?" he asked.

"What do you care? Going to be late for work, are you?"

"Just tell me."

I told him, and he ground into motion with mechanical precision, stretching his arms and back, cracking his neck, yawning.

"How's that ankle feel?" I asked him.

"Dunno," he said.

Carefully, he pushed himself upright with his good leg.

"So far, so good," he said.

He hovered over his sore foot and gingerly applied weight. At first contact with the floor, he gasped, and then he was down again a second later, panting, his chest rising and falling as if he'd just completed a marathon. His face was bright red, and the corners of his eyes were moist.

"Damn," he said. "It hurts more than it did last night."

I believed him. The bruise on his ankle now wrapped around his foot like a manacle. A dark streak rose upward along the back of his lower leg, and I guessed that he'd badly wrenched his Achilles tendon, although I knew far more about the mythical Achilles than I did any tendon.

"Damn," we both said.

He recovered his breath and managed to sit upright again.

"I'm sorry, man," he said.

"Well, what're you going to do?" I replied, shrugging. "You probably wouldn't have wanted to leave here until nightfall anyway, right?"

"True," he said.

I retreated upstairs to cook up a pan of scrambled eggs and fill a pot of coffee for him. He couldn't possibly eat a hearty breakfast without having to get upstairs to the bathroom eventually, and I figured that would keep him testing his ankle, keep him from growing complacent. Either that or doing something so awful to my basement floor that I didn't even want to think about it. I dressed up one of my parents' old aluminum television trays as nicely as I could, arranging sliced oranges and buttered toast symmetrically on either side of the plate of eggs.

When I finished, I found that, despite my ulterior motive, I was happy to have someone here in Karen's absence and that it was fun to host someone again. It had been a very long time since I'd had occasion to do so. I carried the tray downstairs, and Hugo's wide eyes and pie-swallowing grin were all the reward I needed.

"Wow," he said.

He was too hungry to talk much while eating, but I sat down and finished the food off with him. It was very odd to be eating in my basement. I wished we could just relax at the dining-room table with the morning sunlight pouring in over us. I had a tough time making myself comfortable on the floor, but Hugo didn't seem to share that concern.

"I can see how you'd get used to this," he said, sipping the coffee.

"What's that?"

"The lifestyle. The house, the coffee in the morning, bathrooms, garages, the luxury of it all."

"This is hardly the Palace of Versailles."

"Hey, I'm not used to the lap of luxury, you know. I'm like Pocahontas visiting Buckingham Palace."

"Yeah, well, Pocahontas died at 22."

"That's why you don't have to worry about me hanging around—I don't want to catch your white man's disease."

I scooped the last of the eggs out onto his plate, and he devoured them with gusto.

"Anything else you want?" I asked him.

"Nah, this is cool," he said. "I haven't eaten so much in weeks."

He belched and reached toward the wall for one of the beers I'd brought him down the previous night. Twisting the cap off, he washed down his eggs with a heavy mouthful.

"Little early, isn't it?"

"What else am I going to do in the basement all day?"

"True," I said.

"I'll get trashed here all day, sleep it off, wake up

sober and healthy, then—like the mighty bat—unfold my leathery wings and glide into the midnight sky."

"Sounds like a plan," I said.

He picked up another bottle and offered it to me. I couldn't see any reason why not, so I accepted it. I tried to twist the cap off as he had, but it turned out that it wasn't that kind of bottle. Grunting, I handed it back to him.

"It's not a twist-off," he said. "You've got to put some muscle into it."

He held the cap with one hand and twisted the bottle with the other. It popped open, and he handed it back. I drank it dry in a few swallows, enjoying the way it coated the eggs inside me.

"Well, I'm not going to sit down here all day," I said, looking pipes in the ceiling. "You want something to read?"

"Yeah, man, that'd be great," he said. "I've been carrying the same paperback around for months. I've read it four times."

"Let me guess: Marx?"

He laughed and opened another beer.

"What do you think I am? Some kind of fanatic? It's a sci-fi novel, I'll have you know. Pretty good one, too, but once was plenty."

"I stand corrected. I'll run up and grab something for you, if you want."

He sipped at the beer and nodded. I picked up the tray and dishes and carried them upstirs and washed them quickly, before I forgot entirely and some friendly FBI agent with a bulldog's neck burst in to see that I had more than one person's worth of dirty dishes in my sink. It took a few minutes to do that, and Hugo began to sing under the floor, his subtle hint that I was taking too long. Under the influence of a few beers, he had always been the sort to leap onto a table and improvise a microphone out of a lampshade or some woman's shoe. Karaoke hadn't made the rounds in America yet when we were in college, but I imagined that it was probably something he enjoyed now, or might enjoy if he were normal, at the very least, as a means of forcing people to stop doing other things and to pay attention to him. I got the message, though, and hurried upstairs to my study to collect an armful of books. When I dropped them on the floor in front of him, he was just completing a verse of Harry Nilsson's "Coconut," a song I loved—so long as nobody but Harry Nilsson or The Muppets were singing it. Hugo looked over the array of history books I'd delivered to him with disdain.

"Don't you have anything fun to read?" he asked.

"I don't read sci-fi anymore," I said. "Life's too short."

"Life is short," he agreed, "but I still like sci-fi. The good stuff, that is. Why read all this garbage about the past when you can consider the future? Look how much of what people like Arthur C. Clarke and Isaac Asimov and even that right-wing fuck Orson Scott Card wrote has come to pass. History is just *history*."

"'History is the only laboratory we have in which to test the consequences of thought.' Etienne Gilson," I quoted.

"'History does nothing; it does not possess immense riches, it does not fight battles. It is men, real, living, who do all this.' Karl Marx," he riposted.

I laughed, and he picked out the same Bruce Lincoln book I had hidden his letter to Francine in.

"Nevertheless," he said, "this book has a nice, flashy cover, so I'll bite."

He flipped it open to the middle of the book, and I went upstairs to take a shower. While I washed,

I planned a nice afternoon of waiting for Karen to call. I would eat some lunch, do some reading of my own, and watch television. My usual routine. All while not thinking of the fugitive from justice in my basement. It seemed like a nice idea, until Hugo began to sing again. His voice burbled up through the plumbing like swamp water.

I was sitting downstairs with Hugo later that afternoon, talking about his parents, who likely had been visited by the FBI as well, and the fact that Hugo had not spoken with them in years when the doorbell upstairs rang. I panicked, but Hugo was nonplussed.

"Probably just Jehovah's Witnesses," he shrugged.

"I'd rather it have the FBI."

As it turned out, it was worse than either option: it was a teenager.

I was panting after sprinting upstairs to swing the door open to find Eileen's son Leonard standing there, hands in pockets.

"Oh, hey, Leonard," I gasped. "What's up?"

"My mother's got a boyfriend," Leonard said.

"Oh?" I said. "That's ... good."

I tried to answer as if puzzled by the question, but my I knew that my reddening face gave my darkest thoughts about his mother away. This was not desirable as the polite, little four-year-old who had greeted us in our driveway the day we'd moved into the house was now larger than I was and with a chip on his should to match.

"So what's up?" I asked again.

He sucked in his breath, expanding himself under his winter coat. The kid obviously worked out, whereas I very plainly did not, but his baby face made it impossible to feel intimidated.

"My mom wants to know if you have a handsaw

she can borrow."

"Wait here," I told him, closing the door in his face and breathing again only afterward, as I hurried through the kitchen to the basement and my dusty workbench.

"Handsaw's hanging there," Hugo said, nodding at the bench.

"Shut up," I told him. "Just how much can you hear down here, anyway?"

"Pretty much everything."

"Peachy."

I hustled the saw back upstairs and handed the saw to Leonard, who, normally, would not have been left waiting on the porch in cold weather.

"Here you go," I told him. "Let me know if this isn't what she wants."

He glanced down at it the pristine metal, squinting as a gust of wind blew across him.

"Looks brand new," he said.

"I used it once," I insisted. "Maybe."

I shut the door without waiting for any further comment and listened for his footsteps down off of the porch on the other side of it. When he finally clomped back down onto the sidewalk, I went into the kitchen and poured myself a glass of water and drank it slowly beside the sink, staring out of the window at the spot I had incorrectly thought might be the last place I would ever see Hugo. I opened the basement door and hissed down at Hugo that everything was alright, and he replied with a loud fart that echoed up the stairwell. Closing the basement door again, I climbed up to my study and looked out of the window overlooking the street out front, pressing my overheated forehead against the cold glass.

Strangely, Leonard still stood on the sidewalk out

front, staring at my front door. If he had turned to look straight up into my eyes through my curtain, I would have phoned a Catholic priest in a hurry. I waited to watch him shamble back across the yard to his own house.

It took a while.

I settled down against the wall opposite Hugo in the basement, later, and told him about Leonard. He laughed and set his book aside.

"Kids can see through bullshit," he said. "Remember? We did, too, once upon a time. Coach T., running through the hallway high-fiving kids? Remember how we used to just roast him alive?"

"Behind his back, anyway."

"And in front!" Hugo shouted. "Remember, you were the one who whacked Mr. Ronson with the Coke can!"

"I didn't do that ..."

"Like hell you didn't, Ivan! I remember it like it was yesterday! We were eating lunch in the cafeteria, and in comes Ronson in his Hawaiian shirt, bending over the tables, flirting with girls twenty years younger than his flabby ass, shaking hands, pumping his stupid fist in the air like he'd just won the Olympics or something. Asshole. I still hate that motherfucker. When he got closer to us, you picked up your half-empty can of Coke and whipped it. Got him right in the head, sprayed the hell out of all of the rest of us, too."

"No, that was *you!*" I insisted, not really remembering the incident very clearly. "You were the one who did shit like that!"

"No," he insisted, shaking his head. "You did it, Ivan. You did. We'll get on the phone right now to Ugly Nora if you don't believe me. She was sitting right there. You got pop all over her bologna sandwich, and she was really pissed. We can call her right now."

"No ..." I said again, but it was coming back to me, inch-by-inch.

I *had* thrown the can at Ronson. Maybe. I remembered the incident well enough, but I had remembered Hugo pitching the Coke all these years. Even as I focused now, it was a strain to superimpose myself over Hugo's image in my memory. I had done a fairly complete job of editing, it seemed, even going so far as to draw a fierce sort of expression on his face as he lobbed the can. Had I looked like that? Truly angry, moving with a viciousness that nearly tore the humor away from the sight of Ronson stopping dead in mid-flirt, double-taking, and rubbing the red spot on his forehead. That was the sort of thing I associated with Hugo, but I guess we'd been birds of a feather in more ways than one. I didn't remember being angry enough to throw a can of Coke at a teacher, but had I been?

"Wow," I said.

"You were a tiger, man. Funniest kid in school, I swear to god."

"Whatever happened to Ugly Nora?" I asked, trying to change the subject.

"Hot," Hugo answered, wide-eyed with respect. "Extremely hot."

"Huh, what do you know?" I said, trying to picture it.

He stood up and stretched his leg out in front of him, rotating his ankle tenderly.

"Ivan, I don't think I'm going to be able to take off tonight. I'm just not up to it," he said.

"Let me see you try," I said.

He struggled to stand again, as he had that morning, but with the same result. I examined his face for any sign that he was exaggerating, but Hugo was no actor. I'd pulled tendons the same way before and been laid up for days and days on end. I hoped this wasn't the case now. I didn't want to send Hugo hobbling out through the hurricane doors, but I wouldn't avoid it at the expense of the very proud fact that I had never been sentenced to prison, or been divorced. He collapsed onto his sleeping back and did his best to look pathetic. It wasn't a stretch, but he stretched it anyway.

"And the Oscar goes to ..." I intoned.

"I just need a few more days to recuperate. I just can't hit the pavement again quite yet," he said.

"Hugo ..." I sighed, without any real intention of tossing him out.

"I know, Ivan. But you don't know what it's like. You don't."

He settled back against the wall and rubbed his red eyes.

"I always considered myself a bit of a rolling stone," he said. "But this is too much. Even for me."

He curled up on his blankets, hugging his pillow the way a child hugs a teddy-bear.

"Okay," I shrugged. "What's another night at this point?"

"Thanks," he whispered, his face still buried.

"But this has to come to an end, don't you see?" I said. "Karen's right. You can't keep going like this."

He didn't respond, and his breathing evened. He was either asleep or pretending to sleep, but, if he had at least retained that much of himself from childhood, they amounted to same thing. When he had forced me to tip-toe around him after our high-school all-nighters, I'd never really known if he was really out cold or not—but I'd gotten the point either way and had left him alone. I did the same thing now. Kicking his other blanket over him, I crept back up the stairs and turned the lights off

172

for him. I listened through for sounds of movement, but only the sound of the sump-pump kicking in pushed back.

17.

  I was in bed, half-awake, when Karen called. Her voice over the phone was both familiar and wrong. It was like hearing a Muzak version of a song I really loved and not being able to quite name the tune. The full body of her person remained across town, at her mother's house, and yet here she was: speaking beside me. I didn't know what to say after her initial greeting.
  "Ivan?" she said again, after her initial hello.
  I nearly hung up. This was not what marriage was supposed to sound like.
  "Ivan, are you there?" she demanded, and I finally admitted that I was.
  "I just called to check in," she said. "How are you doing?"
  I sighed.
  "What do you think?" I said. "Come home."
  I didn't know what else to say. All that I felt at that moment was that Karen ought to be beside me, whether speaking to me or not, cold and distant perhaps,

but here. Marriages across the world hung together at the corners. Ours was no different.

"I wish I could," she said.

"What's stopping you?" I asked her.

"It won't have meant anything if I just come home now," she said. "Nothing will have changed."

A television blared behind Karen's breathing. Her mother suffered from terrible insomnia and watched television night and day. The volume increased as we spoke, the old woman becoming irritated, I guessed, at having to listen through Karen's conversation. It was loud enough I was able to pinpoint the exact episode of *Three's Company* that the old woman was watching: the episode where bartender Larry's family comes to visit, and he reveals at last, to everyone's delight, that he is Greek and that his full last-name is "Dalliapoulous" rather than "Dallas."

"Would it help if I apologized?" I asked.

"It might," she said, "but I can't guarantee it."

"Well, I apologize," I said. "I really do."

"That's nice, Ivan," she said. "Thank you. But the problem is, I don't think either of us knows what you're apologizing for."

"I'm apologizing for not telling you about, um, those certain people being here before," I said, not wanting to name names on the phone and choking on the fact that I was at the same time not telling her that Hugo was in the basement.

"That's a start."

"A start?"

"Maybe," she said. "I don't know. The problem is, I'm not mad. I left as a matter of principle. It's easier to just accept an apology and be done with it if the only thing involved is emotion. I thought that was a good thing when I left, but now I realize that it doesn't leave us with an easy point of resolution. If I were mad, I'd just come back when I wasn't anymore. Now, when is everything better? When have things actually changed enough?"

"I don't know," I answered, not sure she was actually asking me a question. "I'm guessing we have different ideas about what needs to change."

I wandered over to the study window and looked out over the street. Would Leonard be there again, gazing up with glowing, green eyes?

Two of the streetlights visible from my vantage point were broken and dark, and the remaining few cast a shoddy light over the sidewalk that accentuated the cracks and flaws in the pavement. Dry leaves tumbled across the illuminated band of lawn in a strong wind.

"If I came home, would we talk about that, or would you want to just sweep this under the carpet and try to move forward?"

"Well, if I had my choice," I laughed, "I'd meet you at the door in a loincloth made of flowers, and we'd live the rest of our days together in a cottage beside an enchanted wood, no questions asked."

She laughed with me, but then stopped abruptly. "That's what I thought you'd say."

"Why don't you just come home?" I said. "We'll talk about it. You know I'm not afraid of that. I'm half Irish, aren't I? Gab is in my blood."

"When it works for you, it is."

"What do you mean?"

Somebody coughed. Behind me. Followed by the off-center creak of a limping person descending wooden stairs.

"What was that?" Karen demanded, her voice hardening. "Is someone else there?"

Clearly, then, behind her voice and the sound of my own breathing and her mother's television, there was someone else. An exhalation and brief, surprised choke. Then a click.

"Who's there, Ivan?" Karen demanded.

I stammered but didn't manage to answer her properly.

"Ivan?" she repeated.

My breath caught in the thorn bush inside my throat as I panicked.

"Goddamn it," she said.

She hung up, clicking off.

I tore down the stairs to the basement and kicked Hugo's backpack into the wall without any regard as to what was inside it. He rolled aside, feigning surprise, his eyes wide and mouth gaping. He was less than subtle in the way he coaxed his bag back toward him with the edge of his good foot.

"What the hell were you doing?" I demanded. "Eavesdropping?"

"I don't know what you're talking about, dude," he said. "I've been sleeping like a rock on this fucking floor ..."

"Oh, bullshit," I spat.

I was too furious to react properly, so I ran back upstairs and to compose myself. I peeked out of my living-room window at the empty street in front of my house and tried to breathe rhythmically, calmly. I focused on the dark windows of the house across the street, centering my field of vision on the front-room window there, curtains closed behind it. Jerry's house. And formerly Mary's. She'd died a few years back, and the old guy was there by himself now, along with his old dog, Marty, a slow-moving, increasingly gray-haired beagle, the sight of which at the end of his limp leash on his daily afternoon walks always made me unbearably sad. Jerry had lost the spring in his step, too. I thought about how Mary, who had been hard of hearing, had never been able to tell in her last bunch of years whether Jerry was yelling "Mary" or "Marty" from inside the house while she tended the flower beds out front. I thought about them for a while until I wasn't thinking about Hugo any longer.

Eventually, I turned away and returned to the basement, keeping Jerry in mind, resolving to take the time to offer to lend him a hand or two with his yardwork if he needed one and to get my ow Mary back as soon as possible.

"Why were you eavesdropping?" I asked Hugo again, from the middle of the basement stairs.

"I didn't," he growled at me.

"You're a terrible criminal," I said. "You make enough noise to wake the dead."

"Could've been anybody," he said, waving me off.

"There's nobody else coughing in my bedroom, Hugo. How have you avoided the FBI this long? That's just pathetic."

He stared at me for a moment with his lips pursed and eyebrows furrowed then burst into laughter.

"Fine," he said. "You got me. Whatever."

"Uh-huh."

"I'm sorry," he said. "I really am. Didn't mean for her to hear me. I held my breath through most of it, but I started to sneeze and couldn't quite stifle it. Couldn't be helped."

"Did you ever consider *not* eavesdropping on my personal conversations?" I asked, stepping over and tapping my foot beside him.

"I'm sorry," he said again. "I just had to be sure it was a personal conversation, you know."

"What do you mean by that?"

"Nothing. I don't mean anything. Really."

He flipped over on his side to face the wall, and I was very tempted to continue the conversation with a firm boot in his ass.

"If I wanted to turn you in, I'd have done it already," I said. "Honestly, I'm insulted. It's *me*, here."

"I know," he muttered, pretending to be drowsy. "I know."

"You need to get out of here tomorrow," I insisted. "Karen was on the verge of coming back until she heard you."

"That's not the way I read it," Hugo said, turning around again. "Sounded to me like she was just fishing for the right kind of apology. You need a serious self-respect injection."

"I don't need anything but some peace and quiet," I said.

"That's your problem, Ivan. That's most people's problem. You're all turtles tucking your heads into your shells. Why do you think all of this data-gathering can continue to snowball, all of these encroachments upon the space around us? Because no one pays attention, no one wants to emerge from their shell to push back at it. There's no peace and quiet to be had in a world where the water we drink is being privatized. There isn't any peace and quiet when the local police are driving around in fucking tanks left over from the Iraq invasion. It's only going to get noisier from here on out, and the only people who don't realize that are people like you, I'm sorry to say. You're all about the illusion, the idea of peace and quiet and living comfortably in your own little nooks and corners. It's just icing, all of this around you."

"I'll be satisfied with peace and quiet in this house."

"Yeah, man, that's your problem," Hugo said, lying down again and closing his eyes. "You always were."

"So you're going to throw your stone and then pretend to sleep?" I asked. He rolled over, directing his ass at me, unplugging from the conversation. I wasn't in the mood to pull him back in. That we both probably wanted this particular conversation to end was good enough, although it was, as usual, ending on his terms and without my getting any satisfaction.

I slunk upstairs, annoyed by Hugo's perpetual upper hand and my own inability to ever talk my way around anyone else's argument. Between Hugo and Karen, I had surrounded myself with people who were very good at that sort of thing. I wondered if I'd done it on purpose for some deep, psychological, masochistic reason. Passive aggressiveness being my usual defense, I considered leaving the basement light on at the top of the stairs, just to fuck with Hugo's phony attempt at sleep, but the thought of roving FBI agents being attracted by the unnatural illumination from my basement windows changed my mind. I clicked the light off and shut the door and realized, as I returned to bed, that I had wasted my opportunity to call Karen back by spending time arguing with Hugo. Strange minutes had been lost since she'd hung up the phone, and that window was probably now closed.

Upstairs, I tried to stop thinking long enough to fall asleep and saw through the curtains that the full moon had only waned a little. There was plenty of werewolf magic still hanging around to bring out the beast in Hugo.

In the morning, I awoke and, upon first sight of the ceiling over my bed, I knew I had to get the hell out of the house. Fresh air was needed. I showered and dressed and left without speaking to Hugo. I got into my old car and felt something vaguely resembling an adrenalin rush when I turned the key. This was what other people did in the morning. I backed out of my driveway, for the first time in a couple of years wishing that I shared this routine with everyone else on my block. This was why they called it rush hour, I figured. The traffic didn't seem as awful as I remembered, though, and I wondered if the terrible employment rate in Michigan had something to do with it. Nobody working, nobody driving to work. Whatever. I would have appreciated the I-75 artery like no one else probably was regardless of whether it was congested or not.

Now where to go?

I had succeeded in getting *out*. Mission accomplished there. I was out of my house, away from Hugo, away from the telephone, away from the lawns and the fences. I sensed that, sooner or later, I would head toward Karen's office to try and talk to her face-to-face. The telephone wasn't a proper medium for married people. I would interrupt her and tell her to come home, in no uncertain way. She would resist, irritated that I had burst in to make waves in her safe harbor, and she would argue. I would persist, however, and, impressed with my insistence, she would cave in, wrapping her arms around my waist, pressing her lips to the side of my neck, whispering that she was sorry and that she wanted to come home. The light from her tinted office window illuminating me, I would gently lift her chin and kiss her. She would tell her boss that she was leaving early, we'd head home together, where we would find Hugo packed and ready to give himself up to the authorities. We would call our two friends at the FBI, give them the good news, they would give us some kind of cash-based commendation, and Hugo would be quickly exonerated and would eventually attend graduate school. He would come to visit us at Christmas, Francine and their new baby in tow, and Karen, over egg nog, would announce that she was quitting her job to teach German to needy mono-lingual children.

Seemed like a plan, anyway. It was amazing what one could accomplish simply by leaving the house. I slipped off of I-75 at West Grand and took Woodward Avenue southward into downtown Detroit, passing pieces of Wayne State University's campus and the Detroit Institute of Arts as I eased through the New Center area of town, over Warren Avenue, closing in on the tall buildings on Jefferson across from the river where Karen nested most of the day.

Woodward was nearly as crowded as the expressway, and I was forced to putter my way south in the parking-lane on the side of the road. Occasional busses, abandoned cars, and shuffling old men in no hurry to be anywhere forced me to press back into the mob in the proper driving lanes. I wasn't sure where I was going or what I was doing other than following Petula Clark's general directive that, when alone and lonely, one must go downtown. I took my time but pressed forward, amused at the immediate instinct to rush and hurry and swerve and run yellow lights. Where had that come from? Was I going to be late for work somewhere? No. The city both brought it out in me and then forced me to ease it back in the face of the general impossibility of getting anywhere all that quickly. After traveling a few miles down Woodward, I stopped pressing at all. I just flowed off of the big artery, westward to Cass and onward through a neighborhood that was once feared by suburbanites like myself but which now seemed to be ripening with small shops and restaurants and coffee houses stretching out from the south end of Wayne State's campus.

When I turned right onto Lafayette and passed the Detroit News building, I realized that I knew that I was heading toward John King Books, a dusty, four-story palace of a used and antiquarian bookstore just over the Lodge Freeway, at the very edge of Corktown, and the best thing about Detroit as far as I was concerned. The building had once been painted bright blue, but, now, it was a peeling and faded non-color, easy to miss against the flint gray sky. I crossed the freeway and turned a sharp left into the uncomfortably small, fenced-in parking-lot behind the place. It was a little early, so I sat in the car, listening to the morning DJ on WCSX playing a Bad Company song that I really, sincerely never needed to hear again in my life, and waiting for the store to open. Eventually, when the back-door chain fell away as an older mustached man that I remembered from my last visit, quite some time ago, pushed the door open from the inside and flipped the *Closed* sign hanging behind the chicken-wired door-glass over to the *Open* side.

    The place had not changed one iota in all the years I'd been in Detroit, at least not in any way I could see, not having been in the place for a year or more. The blonde woman in the horn-rimmed glasses who had ever been behind the counter when I visited sported more gray hair than in prior years and no longer dressed in the black Riot Grrl dress uniform she once had. From the depths of a peach cardigan, she tossed me a cursory glance and then got back to work sorting through a pile of books beside the cash register. I pushed onward into the store, toward the history section and my beloved Russian history aisle, where I would, as always, mosey its length to the very end.

    Per custom, no one else crowded that space. Crouching and squinting at the first book in the front of the lowest shelf, I methodically dragged my fingertip over its spine, determined it to be of no interest, then moved on to the next one, and then the next one. When

I'd completed the shelf and had found nothing to grab my attention, I started in on the next shelf up.

In this way, I made my way down the aisle, moving slowly, missing nothing, pausing as I wished to disdain books that were either badly written or badly researched, or both, and pausing again to leaf through books I hadn't read or admire those that I had and enjoyed. I loved the feel of the books, even the ones I didn't care for or had read before, and I loved the clothbound smell of the store, that particular scent of old and undisturbed hardcover books. There was a leathery quality to it. The air it passed so slowly through felt as heavy and old as the desert atmosphere of some newly discovered cavern chamber, and the half-measure of sunlight passing through the store's dirty, chicken wire-covered windows was like the first morning sunlight falling over the cracked asphalt of a prison yard. There was an air of confinement in the aisles, in other words, a sense of forced but not ungrateful solitude. This was maybe the one oasis of stillness in all of Detroit that did not also suffer from the curse of abandonment or loss. Nothing else moved in the store at this early weekday hour; no floorboards squeaked in the aisles or on the floors above me. I slid my fingertips over the titles embossed in the fraying bindings lined up before me, and I forgot that I hadn't eaten breakfast, and I forgot Hugo, Karen, and every other living soul on the planet earth likewise.

This was where I belonged, in a monk's cell, alone with everything worthwhile that had ever been written down, away from the noise and distraction of pointless chatter, unrestrained emotions, and the needs and desires of anyone else at all. Even my own. Ellen? Ellen who?

Time passed, and I had no sense of it. Whatever the amount of it was, it was irrelevant. Why must this store ever close? Why could not I not keep a blanket and pillow at the end of the even more rarely visited Philosophy aisle and live like Hugo, curled into an unresponsive bundle on a spare piece of floor? I moved from book to book and dreaded the end of the shelf. There were others, and I would move on as needed to the history volumes, then to political science, and, eventually, upstairs to science fiction for Hugo. This was what I loved best. Everything else in my life was a layer of frosting over this exploration and gathering. I felt like myself crouching and then standing between the shelves, like the kid I'd once been, before high-school and girls and music and all of the clutter of everything since, when every Saturday had been the same: a morning walk to the library with perhaps a slight veering off toward the bakery across the street, and then an afternoon spent between shelves, reading and only reading.

With some amount of guilt toward the image of Karen, not really at all escaping the back of my mind, I considered that to retrieve that for myself now was all that I really wanted. From life, in general, at all, ever. The thought disturbed and unsettled me—but also excited me in some way that I couldn't quite harness. My finger shook a little as it passed over the books' spines in front of me.

It only stopped when, out of nowhere, a certain grainy, black-and-white face stared back at me from the spine of an unpleasantly pea-colored volume. I had seen the woman's face before, if not the photo, set unusually into the book's spine as if to slap me directly in the face. The font spelling out the title of the book was a sort of squared-off Eastern Bloc style, faded into a dull, dark red that must have clashed terribly with the pea-green background cover when the book was brighter and newer. I slid the volume from the shelf and looked again at the photograph, reproduced much larger on the front cover.

The woman was beautiful in a hard and weathered sort of way, with a penetrating stare that belied the peasant quaintness of her flowered babushka. The title of the book was *The Devil's Mistress*, but I stopped breathing entirely when I read the subtitle: *Lyudmila Miroshin and the Downfall of Aleksandr Anosov.*

  I was stunned. Was this real? How could such a book exist? I had never seen it before, never even *heard* of it before. The author, one H. William Ritter, was completely unknown to me. I carefully opened the cover and looked for more information about him. There was no copyright date on the title page, but I guessed that the book had been published anytime from the 1940s to the 1950s. I was not an expert in book-binding or antique valuation by any stretch, but anything earlier than that would have been too close in time to Anosov's execution to have generated such a volume, given that the event hadn't been exactly well-publicized, nor had anyone at large outside the new Soviet Union even heard of Anosov with any particular detail at that time. Even now, what I knew about Lyudmila as anything other than a mostly maligned accessory to Anosov's life I could fit into my pocket. I had never seen this book referenced, footnoted, quoted, used, or misused in any bibliography, nor had Ritter, its author, written anything else that I was aware of. The book contained no author biography in the front or back, no introduction, no forward, no epilogue, not even a dedication page. The publisher's imprint was even unfamiliar to me, although it listed Brooklyn, New York, as its place of business. At a loss, I opened the book to the first page and began reading.

> *In the third year of the new century, in the small village of ——, Evgeni Miroshin was once again disappointed by the appearance of*

a new daughter. Three times before, his wife had borne him a daughter, and, three times before, the daughter had fallen ill and died before her fifth year. This time, he resolved, he would keep the child safe and warm, and he would see that no disease enter their cottage. The pigs would sleep outside.

"Lyudmila Evgenovicha Miroshina," he whispered to the child. "You, of all people, will live."

Still, a son would have been preferred.

I snapped the book closed. How could Ritter have obtained this information? There was nothing on paper about Lyudmila, except via Piroshev and Millar's probably manufactured recounting. Absolutely nothing. To the best of my knowledge, she had been illiterate, a woman of wile and wit but without education. There did not seem to be any possibility that the book could be genuine, but who would bother to forge such a thing? Who, even in the 1940s or 50s, would care? Regardless, here it was. Nervously, I searched for the price on the inside front-cover and was relieved to find the number twenty penciled there. As usual for the store, too expensive for a nondescript volume. Nothing in the bookstore ever seemed to cost less than twenty dollars, but, in this case, a bargain. I hustled the book up to the counter where the woman manning the station frowned at the sight of the thing, which must have seemed a perplexingly random emergence from the far corners of the store. I handed her my authorized user duplicate of Karen's credit card and paid for the book with a shaking hand before hurrying out to my car with my treasure.

The possible contents of my new book wound through my mind like four movies playing simultaneously against the same white wall as I sat and watched my wife through the glass front doors of her office lobby as she leaned against the receptionist's desk, her knuckles curled around the laminate edge, the receptionist mouthing something to her at great and tedious length. Karen's eyes were wide, her jaw hanging slack as she listened, her knuckles whitening, all her usual signs of growing impatience and exasperation blossoming as I looked on. Finally, Karen waved at the woman to stop and glanced up to see me standing there. I waved, but her displeasure at whatever the receptionist had been telling her was not visibly mitigated by my presence. I pulled the heavy door open and walked in as she turned back to the receptionist and barked out a serious of orders, none of made any sense to me except for the final "... and print that all out!" instruction. The receptionist now looked more flustered than Karen, and, when an incoming call lit her switchboard up, she answered it gratefully, smiling momentarily at me, recognizing along with my entrance her big opportunity to get away from my wife.

"What's going on?" I whispered to Karen, but, rather than answering, she nodded at me to follow her inside to her office, and she remained silent until we'd reached it and she'd shut the door behind us.

"What's up?" she said, folding her arms across her chest and standing firmly between me and any chair I might sit and make myself comfortable in.

"Karen, I don't want any of this to happen the way it is," I said. "I just thought maybe we could take ten seconds and talk in person like civilized people."

I listened to myself speak as if hovering out-of-body. Did Anosov find it necessary to have such conversations with Lyudmila? Did he find that she required regular placation in order to be bearable? Or did he love her without qualification to the point where he would not have noticed such things? Was her happiness more valuable to him than his own drive to push the Bolsheviks back out of power? As much as I loved Karen and loved our years together and wanted to explain the mysterious coughing she'd heard, I felt that I was at that moment engaging in some level of pantomime. Was her happiness more important to me than the feeling I'd just had in the bookstore? Why was I here now? Simply because it seemed necessary? Was that a good enough reason?

All I wanted was to sit somewhere quiet with my book open in front of me.

Karen gave me only the time-span of her frown to consider these things.

"I really have a very busy morning going here now," she said on the back end of a long sigh. "I really can't clutter it up right now."

"Clutter?" I said. "What is that supposed to mean?"

"It means I have work to do, Ivan, and I don't appreciate your popping in like this. You know how it is for me here."

She swiveled around me and re-opened her door, stepping back out into the hallway, forcing me to follow her out and back into the lobby.

"You're ushering me out? Really?"

"Keep your voice down," she growled, steering me away from the receptionist with a firm hand on my shoulder. "People are *working* here. You remember what that's like, or don't you?"

"Don't condescend to me," I said, my voice rising. "I came here with good intentions."

Again, the pantomime.

"This is a place of business."

"Karen, please, that's just an excuse," I said. "Let's just sit and talk for a minute. Let me buy you a cup of coffee."

She opened the glass front door with surprising one-armed ease.

"With my money?" she snapped, drawing a quiet whistle from the receptionist and a deep blush from me.

"Uncalled for," I whispered. "Very uncalled for."

"Later," she said, her voice softening to something like a plea. "Please?"

She let the glass door swing slowly shut and then turned and walked back to her office, leaving me standing there, embarrassed, without a shred of Anosov within me. No matter: I had tried, and Karen had just freed me from caring for a little while.

18.

I wound my way through my living-room and into the dining room, trying not to count down the number of hours it had been since I'd left Hugo alone downstairs. The sky was overcast outside, and the house was dark. This suited me fine. I was feeling dark myself and the thought of electrifying the empty rooms with the high-wattage light-bulbs I'd foolishly installed gave me no comfort. I stopped beside the dining-room table and listened for any movement downstairs, but I couldn't hear a thing. I pushed through the door into the kitchen and found Hugo seated at the table, hunched over and scowling.

"Where've you been?" he whined like a child confused and lost in the produce section of a supermarket.

I flipped the lights on rather than answering. He shaded his eyes, and I forced myself not to do the same.

"Hither and yon," I said. "I went to the bookstore and to see Karen."

"You could've said something before just ditching

me. Got my sci fi?"

"No. I forgot. I need to report to you now?"

He shrugged and leaned his chair back on two legs.

"It just would've been polite, that's all," he replied.

"You should have stayed in the basement."

"I got sick of sitting in the basement. I had to go to the bathroom."

"You managed the stairs again?"

"I managed," he nodded, "but not very well. I wasn't about to try to go back down there yet."

"Well, you'd better."

He rapped his knuckles on the table and stretched, cracking his neck. He smiled weakly, and his eyes darted back and forth between me and the basement door. It was maybe the first time ever that I'd made him nervous and not the other way around. It appeared to me that he wanted to say something but was holding back for the right moment, so I stayed quiet and waited. He nodded at the book under my arm and cocked his head sideways to read the spine.

"*The Devil's Mistress?*" he said. "Sounds lurid."

"It's a biography, that's all."

"Of whom?"

"The devil's mistress, of course."

"I can't believe you left me alone here to go book-shopping."

"And to see Karen," I added.

"Patch everything up?"

"Not exactly," I said. There was no reason to get into further detail. He would only say, "Ah, fuck her!" because it was in his best interest that Karen be away from the house at the moment.

"Let me to help you back downstairs," I offered instead.

He sighed.

"Okay. Can't say I'm in a hurry, but this chair is killing my back. How old is this furniture? It's not exactly the ergonomic latest, is it?"

"We bought it at the resale shop in downtown Ferndale just last year," I told him.

"It has that *Leave it to Beaver* look about it," he said. "Why did you feel like you should buy a 1950s table? Were you going for some look in here? This whole phony retro thing really drives me fucking batty. These guys with their horn-rimmed glasses and prissy, little beards walking around. All fucking bank tellers during the day, aren't they? Just cubicle monkeys working for fucking Bank of America or something. But they got the right glasses and the right kitchen table, and now they're so fucking *hip*."

He rubbed at the laminate surface of the table with his thumb as though he expected the veneer to come off. I walked behind him and offered my arm, leaning over. He slung one arm over my shoulders and we made our way to the basement door, step by step, sliding more than walking.

"I'll go first," I said. "That way, if you fall, you'll just hit me."

"And *you're* going to stop me from tumbling down?" he laughed. "Dude, you're nothing but a pile of twigs and baling twine."

"Well, that guidance counselor back in highschool always did say I'd make an excellent mattress someday."

"Brilliant woman—what was her name?"

"Maloney?"

"Mooney."

"Something like that."

We made our way back down the stairs, each of

us clinging to a handrail. Once or twice, I noticed Hugo's allegedly bad foot resting firmly on a step without causing him any apparent discomfort. For all I knew, he'd been leaping from the living-room furniture all day long. When we reached the floor and I helped him down onto the sleeping-bag again, though, he was red-faced and panting.

"I don't think this foot is getting any better," he said when he'd caught his breath. "What'll we do if there's really something wrong with it?"

He reached down and rubbed his ankle. I didn't know the answer to his question, however, and wondered the same thing. If he really needed medical attention, what to do? He clearly couldn't stay down here *ad infinitum* regardless, but what to do? A hospital? In the movies, everyone seemed to know a corrupt after-hours veterinarian that an on-the-run fugitive could be taken to on such occasions. I didn't know any veterinarians, corrupt or otherwise. The only realistic answer was the obvious and true one: that he should turn himself in. Was he giving me an opening to repeat it because it was the logical step at this point and he needed to be told?

Before I could do that, he changed the subject anyway.

"Probably should have just stayed upstairs," he panted. "Later on, I need you to drive me somewhere."

"Yeah, right," I said.

"I'm not joking."

I waved him off and headed back up the stairs.

"I'm serious!" he shouted after me. I stopped and looked back at him. He had propped himself up against the wall, shivering slightly. I noticed how cold it was in the room for the first time. The temperature was dropping outside, and the basement was quickly becoming too uncomfortable for full-time habitation by the day.

"Fine, I'll bite," I said. "Where do we need to go?"
"Not far."
"Like how not far?"
"Not far."
"And that would be about as far as—?"
"The train station. Downtown. Later on. When it's dark out."
"Really? You're leaving?"
I couldn't help smiling.
"I didn't say that," he said. "Is that what you want?"
"What do you think?"
He didn't answer, so I asked him if he was hungry.
"What do you think?" he answered.

I flipped him off and went upstairs to make him some lunch with the last of the bread and bologna. I was running out of groceries rather quickly. Would Karen cut off her credit card if she noticed a weirdly large grocery store visit on the statement? I settled Hugo with his plate and an extra blanket and then fled the basement for the recliner in my study. There, I cranked the chair back into a nearly full recline and opened *The Devil's Mistress* to page one, picking up where I'd left off in the bookstore.

... Still, a son would have been preferred. Evegeni was not to have a son, however, or any other child than Lyudmila. His wife died in childbirth, and he was not to marry again. The daughter left to him became both his focus and his burden.

This is as apt a description of the effect Lyudmila Miroshin was to have on others, most notably Alexsandr Anosov. The focus and the burden of Anosov; it is not the happiest descriptor of a unique life, but it at least enun-

ciates the role history might assign this interesting woman, if only it takes the trouble to remember her.

Some people, like astronomical bodies, are most identifiable and recognizable only by their gravitational effect upon the other bodies that they orbit. Such was Lyudmila, but recognizing this fact—that her most profound accomplishment in her short life was to truncate the life and therefore the military effect of a man who, given time, might have provided some level of bulwark to the sweep of the Bolsheviks through the post-Revolutionary Soviet Union (though it would be a weighty overstatement to consider the possibility that Anosov and the other Whites would ever have prevailed completely in their efforts given the Red zeitgeist)—frees us to discuss that effect frankly and with some level of empirical analysis.

Who was she, and what is it exactly that she did that is worth remembering?

The first answer to this question as regards any historical figure must always be that she was a person, foremost, with hopes, ambitions, fears, and loves, like each of us. History is best examined, after all, through the prism of human nature rather than a topographical review of macro-events. What good is knowing when a war started if one is left ignorant of the ambitions of those who started it?

> *We each of us have within us the possibility of creating a ripple through history, for better or worse, if only we act on our ambitions at the right place and in the right time.*

What a pontificator, I thought, but couldn't help also considering Hugo in this light. He was acting, there was no doubt about that. Historically significant? Hardly. Then again, who could say? It depended on what he did from here and what he did with these mysterious laptops he claimed to have between himself and Francine.

It went on pontificating for a little while longer, but then got back to Lyudmila after a couple of pages, again in a strangely detailed way. Who was this guy? What was his source? There were no footnotes or end notes in the book. No Acknowledgements page. Nothing. He wrote about Lyudmila's childhood as if he'd been her schoolmate, growing up right next door, peering through the window of her cottage as her father alternatively adored and resented her. Whatever. I ate it up.

Lyudmila was precocious as a child, I read, curious and not shy about exploring her little home in the backest backwater of Russia. Few were educated in any way there, even as young as five, she was drawn to those few and notably to the housekeeper of the village's Orthodox priest. This woman was unmarried and childless and had been taught to read by the priest as an idle past-time between the two. She became fond of the little, blonde girl carrying tinder sticks and firewood into the village from the forest at such an early age and passed on the priest's idle interest in propagating literacy. She taught Lyudmila to read and write by scratching out words in the dirt behind the church with one of Lyudmila's sticks, and the little girl was a quick study, impressing both the housekeeper and the priest, once he got wind of it. The two of them did what they could to lure young Lyudmila away from the exotic world of woodcutting to the small ecclesial community that had taken root among the peasants in the little village after the upheavals of 1905, in which the priest and villages felt free to indulge in spiritualist and ethical literature and explore the boundaries of their own religion enforced only by their own creativity. They filled Lyudmila with stories of demons and spirits and the walking-dead and described to her the pilgrimages to far-off places to visit and pray before powerful icons. The old housekeeper had never set foot outside of the village, but Lyudmila absorbed her stories and walked home from her lessons and conversations thinking of nothing else than wandering the steppes or getting lost in a Moscow alleyway.

Nothing of the sort was to be, though, not until Anosov wandered in from the woods. The story of the first meeting, in Lyudmila's village, mostly mirrored what I'd already read elsewhere, with the adjustment downward of Lyudmila's age from "not mentioned" to only thirteen. This book was very specific about that, referring to her repeatedly as "young Lyudmila" and "precocious child." The lost, beleaguered Anosov sheltered in her little church, and she tasked herself with attending to his meals and clothing. She sat beside the priest when he grilled Anosov about current events beyond the pine forest around their little village, joining in to explain to Anosov her theories about the origin of lightning and what the stars were. My Twenty-First Century mind could not comprehend how the babblings of a child could transmogrify into a magnetic source of attraction, how mere months later, Anosov could sweep this naïve girl up onto a saddle and ride her out into a dangerous world, let alone all of the other things one must assume happened between their first meeting in the village and her last visit to him in that jail cell.

Well, things were different then. The usual excuse.

Or that's what I told myself. Truthfully, I simply allowed myself to classify this mythic figure a child. I'd created a different picture in my mind over the years that was too embedded to displace without a proper source citation. Lyudmila was too young to be very worldly upon meeting Anosov, one could presume, but a child? Anosov himself, although older, appeared to have been a sort of single-minded fellow with maybe not a full bindle of life experience other than fighting and politics over his own shoulder in any case. A woman could make an idiot out of a man at nearly any age. Karen had always made me an idiot. Once, in high-school, my English teacher, Ms. Jensen, had asked me how I'd become so eloquent. Enter Karen, and so much for that. I hadn't articulated anything meaningful in the couple of decades since.

So they went off, the two of them, older and younger, naïve or not, idiot or otherwise, and that was the beginning. Lyudmila with her ghosts, spirits, and *baba yagas*, and Anosov with his convictions. A strange coupling by various definitions. Political and military ambition fueled by supernatural inspiration rarely worked out well. Anosov would be no exception.

Hugo waited for me beside the back door, whistling softly, as I shut the lights off and locked the house back up. When I returned, I mused, I would be alone and the house would be open again, concealing nothing other than the same marital bullshit that every other house on the block probably concealed. Simplify, simplify ... I could see no downside to getting rid of my old pal. For him, it was another matter, entirely, but even old friends can walk only in tandem to certain points. I'd done my duty, and, now, he had apparently decided the same, thank god. I'd been a good enough egg; we would part as we always did, our history intact.

I left him in the shadows while I unlocked my Tercel. It was old, and it needed to warm up. The windows were frosted over, and I needed to the usual Michigan amount of scraping time before we could go anywhere. I turned the car's engine on and a loud burst of music split the quiet: I'd left the radio on, full-blast on my previous trip. I slapped it off and froze, glancing at my neighbors' doors and windows across the street. When nothing moved or flickered on, I relaxed and got back out, leaving the engine to rumble as I rummaged in the trunk for the ice scraper.

"Hurry up!" Hugo hissed.

I glared back at him, yanking the scraper free and slamming the trunk again. I cleared off the car windows, but the frost was thicker than it looked, requiring that I put actual muscle into the job. My breathing seemed to roll and echo down the street and back. We could not have managed to be less discreet. By the time I had the glass clean, Hugo was tapping his feet and muttering, "Motherfucker, motherfucker, motherfucker …" behind me. I considered just driving myself away and leaving him to hoof it wherever the hell he wanted to go.

Then, the frost on the rear window glowed as a car pulled into the driveway behind me, its headlights shining over me. Instinctively angling the ice-scraper out from my chest in a defensive position, I stepped back out of the light, away from both cars. I couldn't hear Hugo's muttering beneath the noise of two cars' engines, but I hoped he'd had the good sense to shrink back out of sight and be quiet. The door of the car whipped open, and a lean silhouette stepped out.

"Late night beer run?" Agent Khurram asked,

stepping out of his car.

I squinted through the glare and didn't see Agent Carl waiting inside the vehicle with Khurram.

"It's not that late," I said, trying my best to sound amused by the question rather than intimidated.

"I was just passing by, and it looked like you might need a hand. Thought there might be a problem. Something I could help you with."

"No problem," I said.

"Where you headed?"

I thought fast.

"Ran out of toilet-paper," I said. "And beer."

"Oh," he chuckled. "You're probably in a hurry, then?"

He laughed aloud, but it wasn't the self-effacing laugh he'd used in our living-room. This one reminded me of the growing numbness in my fingertips.

"You might say that."

"I should probably move my car so you can go and get that toilet paper."

"That would be great."

I considered crossing my legs for comic-effect but then thought better of it.

"Sure there's nothing else I can help you with?" he asked, not moving to actually move the car.

Even through the light he'd probably cast over me very purposefully with his car, I could see that he was giving the area the once-over. He stretched his neck to stare into my car and took a few steps toward it so that he could see into the back seat a little better. He glanced around at the yard and at the windows of the house, scanning and cataloguing every detail.

"I'm fine," I answered him. "Thanks, though."

"Hey, to serve and protect, right?" he said.

"I thought that was local police."

"Is any less expected of the Federal Bureau of Investigation?" he asked.

I forced a laugh. He waved and sat back down in his car, closed his door, and reversed carefully back out of my driveway. I stood still and watched him drive off, very slowly. He paused much, much longer than was required at the next corner up before turning around and disappearing.

Hugo wasted no time diving into the back seat of the car headfirst after Khurram's car was out of sight. He slid down below window-level, as close to the floor as he could stuff himself.

"Shit," he said, after I climbed in after him. "That was pretty fucking close, huh? Are they just circling around or what? Better drive to a drug-store or something in case he's got a partner in another car."

"Wouldn't the partner just have seen you dive into the car?"

"Maybe," he admitted.

"He does have a partner," I added. "A really big guy named Carl."

"Oh, fantastic," Hugo sighed. "Just drive to the most logical place you'd go at this hour to get some T.P., and we'll take it from there."

I didn't say anything. I was paralyzed with fear and could only imagine that Khurram still lurked out there in the darkness, his banal smile still hanging over his jaw like a stage-curtain. For some reason, I didn't think Carl was tailing us. It seemed like something he would not volunteer to do at his age. Or he was sleeping one off somewhere while his partner did all of the real work. Khurram was on the job, tirelessly, day or night, with something to prove, career-wise, but Carl—he reminded me a little of Danny Glover in *Lethal Weapon*, just waiting to retire.

Either way, Hugo needed to vanish from my house and from my car, much more fervently than before. As cold as I was, I sweated as I backed the car out of the driveway, while Hugo whooped in the backseat as though we'd just sat down in a roller-coaster. I tried to pretend that I couldn't hear him at all.

My passenger still crouching on the floor, I drove to the Walgreen's drug-store up on Woodward, a busy enough thoroughfare at any hour of the night that I hoped, if Carl or anyone else were following us at a discreet distance, we might get lost in the mix of headlights. I parked for a moment, long enough to watch as many passing cars as I could in the rearview mirror, as well as the few others pulling into the same parking-lot, to inexpertly determine that no one around looked like an FBI tail.

"I think we're good," I whispered to Hugo, who responded only by asking me why I was whispering.

"Fine, then," I yelled. "Let's go."

I spiraled out of the lot and back onto Woodward, heading back south again, toward downtown Detroit and the Amtrak station.

The drive down Woodward to the bus station only took about fifteen minutes. We passed through Royal Oak and hopping downtown Ferndale and into Highland Park and Detroit, passed the disused Michigan State Fairgrounds, and then crossed the Six Mile Road intersection with juxtaposed strip club and fancy Italian restaurant. I hit the gas a bit at that point, speeding along the quiet stretch between the Lodge Freeway and Wayne State University, slowing along to pass the odd police car or two that might have noticed my paranoid and guilt-stricken grimace in their headlights if they'd looked up at the right moment. But no. They puttered by as always. I pulled the car into the Amtrak parking lot at last and straight up to the front door of the small station. Turning in my seat, I extended my palm for Hugo to shake.

"Well, this is it, eh?" I said.

He shook my hand but didn't budge.

We stared at each other over the back of my seat for a while.

"Dude, I think you have the wrong idea," he finally said.

"About what?" I asked, my spine tensing.

"I'm not leaving," he said. "Not yet, anyway."

"You're not?"

"No, man. We're here to pick up Francine. You've got to go in and get her."

"I have to go in and get Francine?" I asked, the words and the idea behind them an ill-fit in my mouth.

"I can't go in there," he said. "You remember what she looks like, don't you?"

"Hugo ..."

He stopped me, holding his hand up.

"I know what you're going to say, Ivan, but it's not like that. Thi was the plan all along, see? This was what I was waiting for. That's what was in the note to Francine. A train ticket. I sent her away, but now she's back. And then we'll both be off together. I couldn't leave without her, man."

I tried to spit out the word "No," but it wouldn't come. My mouth simply hung open.

"We'll be gone by Friday," he said, clamping his hand over my shoulder. "And that's it. We just needed a place to rendezvous. Split up and then reconvene. It was the best idea for us. Can you go in and get her, man? She must be here by now. Can you?"

"For fuck's sake," I said. "Friday? Really?"

"Friday," he said. "That's it. Just a few days to get our shit together. Friday."

"Goddamn it, Hugo …"

A woman in a dark coat appeared at the station door, pressing her face against the glass, looking out. For us. It was Francine, looking much the same as she had on Halloween, wearing the same outfit.

"Fuck!" Hugo yelled, slapping me. "There she is!"

Fuck indeed. I honked the horn and waved her out.

19.

Of course, Friday passed, and Hugo and Francine remained in the basement, whispering and commiserating, lurching into sudden silence each time I stepped down until I felt like a third-wheel tagging along on someone else's big date. Francine sometimes emerged from the basement to sit with me in my living-room behind drawn curtains without saying much of anything. She sat on the opposite of my sofa with her thin legs curled beneath her, flipping the channels between bad talk-shows and the Animal Channel. I didn't like her upstairs, but I preferred it, I found, to wondering what she and Hugo might be planning when they were together downstairs. In any case, in the evenings, she disappeared, leaving me for Hugo again, who never came upstairs, still claiming a lame hoof.

    I tried hard to see something of the allure Hugo had described in her as we moved through the same space day after day, but I could not. Where Hugo apparently found an undercurrent of punky hipness, cleverness, wit, non-conformity, or whatever it was about her that had made him think that she was enough like him to be acceptable, I found only a dry riverbed. When she did speak, it was because something on television sparked a necessary exposition on the topics of celebrity gossip or the good or bad value of something or other advertised in a commercial.

It was cubicle talk. I remembered it from my job at the library. The things people who had nothing to talk about with one another talked about.

Perhaps it had simply been time for Hugo to fall in love and experience the feeling of being smitten the way the rest of us had when we were fifteen or sixteen. At forty-five, how many of us would go choose the same object of our first crushes as partners now? Perhaps it had been a while, despite all of his bluster, since a woman had paid real attention to Hugo. Who could say? I wasn't going to ask, but, the more frequently Francine visited me in my living-room, the less certainty I had that theirs was a star-crossed romance of destiny. For her to be in this position with him, at this point in her life, certainly implied that she had a screw or two loose. Who grabs a gun and runs through a security cordon? No one who really has it together, but one expected slightly better from an engineer sitting in a cubicle than from a sidewalk meth-head or escaped convict. As pedestrian as she seemed nodding sagely at infomercials, she was off. If not for Hugo, the feeling I had was that this girl's next step in life might have been a workplace shooting.

Karen only called twice. Our conversations were stilted, both of us hesitating, neither of us wanting to admit anything about what was really going on to the other. She did not ask again about the coughing on the phone she had heard and surely recognized as Hugo's.

The last time we spoke, at the end of the first

week of November, she'd simply called to ask if I needed money, and I'd swallowed my pride and told her that I did. She texted me a few seconds later to let me know that she'd moved some money over from her checking account into mine. I wondered if that sort of message was going to be what all of our years of exchanging everything between us would be reduced to, until she left and faded out completely. I wanted to text back that I'd logged onto our online banking account and transferred her money back, that all I needed was her—but Hugo and Francine were eating the cupboards bare and so I just held onto the funds, foreseeing an urgent and imminent need for groceries. I tried reading, alone, upstairs, beside the window in the study looking out onto my little street, trying my best to re-reduce my world to what it had been before Hugo had popped out of my shrubbery, but it didn't work. They were in the basement. I knew they were in the basement. I did not know how or when they would exit the basement. I couldn't pretend otherwise and focus on anything else. All I could do, until some more assertive option fell from the sky, was join them from time to time.

"Me neither," Hugo was saying to Francine, as I descended the stairs one afternoon. "You've got to understand that all reporters can do is spurt out whatever oblique, blunt message that has been drafted for them in keeping with the profit-margin status quo. Everything has to be an advertising jingle, ultimately. A person's entire *raison d'être* should be summed up in some asinine mission statement. They don't think we understand, don't think we care ... And they're right, they're right ... Americans don't know anything and don't really care about anything. All of these kids shooting up their schools probably think they have a million and ten good reasons, but there isn't time to air that many on the evening news, see? All they can say is 'The murderers wore black trench coats and were bullied' or whatever. It can't really be about something deeper that's wrong with this country socially or politically. It can't be about our utter lack of a social safety net or a real health-care system that doesn't just garnish the paychecks of poor people who can't pay for psychological treatment."

"Yeah," Francine said.

Her brow furrowed as he wrapped up his rant. *Oh, shut up*, she seemed to be thinking. Or she might be thinking about eating a burrito. Who could tell? Instead of saying anything, in any case, she suddenly reached out and dragged a nail across the back of Hugo's hand, drawing blood as she did so.

"Jesus!" Hugo said, jerking his hand back. "Ow!"

I was startle but said nothing as he stuffed his hand into the sleeve of his shirt and glanced up the stairs at me, blushing. I pretended not to have noticed and sat down beside their open bag of my potato chips, reaching in for one. One of the chips fell out onto the floor, and Francine covered it with her foot, crushing it.

"Sorry," she said.

I pulled another chip from the bag and tossed it onto the floor. Hugo leaped up and stomped on it.

"Now it's mine!" he shouted, rattling the water pipes.

Francine giggled.

"It's all yours," I said, sighing.

Why had I bothered? They were becoming stranger and stranger. Or were they like this all of the time, together? Certain couples became like inbred children after a while, I had always thought, though it had been a while since I'd been around another one. Weird, off-putting couples had been commonplace in college.

What did these two truly admire in each other? It

might have simply been their mutual preference for chaos. Hugo had always been attracted to volatile women. And now he was a fugive from Federal law enforcement. Life might have been easier for him if he just preferred big tits like rest of us.

Loyalty was his great gift, though. Much to my decades-long delight and chagrin, he was true to the people who were true to him. He would never throw Francine under the bus, though that was what I wanted him more than anything to do. Her crime was his, I was sure he would insist, as true as that might or might not actually be.

"You know what the problem with basketball is?" Hugo asked, turning to the sports section of the two day-old newspaper on the floor beside him. "Too many points. Every game ends with scores like nine million to twelve, so who cares if one team scores a basket?"

"Guess I never thought much about it," I said.

"That's your problem, Ivan. You don't think as much as you think you do."

"Sometimes, it seems like I don't do anything else," I said.

"Yeah, well."

"You're like a basketball fan waiting for three hours for a final score that's only going to have a one-point differential. History is worthwhile, but what have you spent the last ten years doing?"

"Not running from the law, at least," I said.

"Anyone can do that," he laughed. "How many of us can say that we *are* fugitives from the FBI? That's an accomplishment, my friend."

"Are you enjoying sleeping on my basement floor, then?"

"I feel like Zeus waking up on the top of Mount Olympus every morning."

"You always did have delusions of grandeur."

"Don't get pissy," he sighed. "What I'm trying to say is, make sure you don't let another ten years slide by."

Francine yawned and kicked at the newspaper, crumpling it.

"Mind if I tip-toe up and take a shower?" she asked.

I nodded at her and turned back to Hugo after she'd creaked up the stairs.

"I don't have any regrets," I told him, though I had nothing but.

"Okay," Hugo said, shrugging.

I waited for the caveat, but there wasn't one.

"So what do you think of Francine?" he asked. "Really."

"What do you mean?"

"What do you *think*?" he pushed. "I'm asking you to *think*."

"She's okay," I said. "What do you want me to say?"

"I only ever want anyone to say what they're thinking. No one ever does."

"I do. You know that."

"We both know that's bullshit."

"Do you mean Karen?" I asked. "Don't be a dick." Reaching for the newspaper, I smoothed its wrinkles out against the concrete floor with the palm of my hand.

"So what do you *think*?"

"I think I'd like the two of you to get out of my basement, so I can patch things up with my wife and stop worrying about FBI agents kicking my door in."

"That doesn't have anything to do with Francine," he said.

"How long a shower is she going to take?" I asked.

"She likes to be clean, I wouldn't hold your

breath."

"Well, I guess I'd prefer her clean, too."

I stood up and stretched.

"What I really think, Hugo, is that you either need to ditch her and give yourself up or don't ditch her and give yourselves up, straighten this shit out, whatever it takes, or just get on and get out. This has to be the worst possible hiding spot you could come up with, and I really don't want to be an accessory to any of this crap. Can you imagine me in jail?"

"You're not pretty enough to worry about that," he laughed. His face was red, though, and I could see that he was bottling something up that might manifest into a punch in the face.

I gathered up the newspaper and made for the stairs.

"I wasn't done with that," Hugo complained.

"I was," I said and walked upstairs.

Hugo followed me up, despite the wide-open kitchen shades and bright daylight, and apparently despite his injured ankle. He wasn't even pretending any longer.

"If you want to get caught, that's your problem," I said, nodding toward the windows as he emerged from the basement stairs behind me.

"Not just mine," he said, leaning against the back door and gazing out into the yard. "I think we've established that."

"Get out of the window, Hugo," I growled.

He stayed put, watching the first reasonable snowfall of the year covering the lawn. A crow hopped across the sugared surface, leaving Y-shaped tracks like little arrows pointing the FBI directly at Hugo.

"God, I feel like a vampire looking at the sun for the first time in a hundred years," he said.

I inserted my arm between his face and the glass and tugged the shade down so violently that it ripped from its roller and clattered to the floor.

"Hey, easy!" Hugo shouted, jumping back.

"God damn it ..." I mumbled, staring at the shade on the floor. For some reason, the sight of it lying there made me overwhelmingly sad. The shade was yellowing slightly now, but Karen and I had bought them together, when we'd first moved in. I remembered hanging it, Karen leaning on the counter across the room barking unnecessary instructions at me.

"No problem. You can fix that with some masking tape," he said, sidling away now from the open window and nudging the shade with the toe of his boot.

"Whatever."

I rolled the shade back up and leaned it against the wall.

"I'm sorry," he said, slumping against the wall.

He pondered his feet like a rock star posing for a 1980s album cover. For the first time in weeks, I noticed how much better he looked than he had when he'd first appeared at the back door. Color had returned to his face, and he'd regained a little weight. He'd fed well on the former contents of my refrigerator.

"I'm just going a little loopy in that basement," he said. "Don't know if I can take much more of it."

"I believe it," I said.

"You'd think it'd be no big deal, right? I mean, it's not like I ever settled down before anyway. I was always drifting from place to place, and now I just have to be a little more discreet about it. What's the difference?"

"There's a difference," I said.

"Damn straight there is. I know there is. It's all psychological, but that's the worst kind. If you've got peace of mind, you can do anything. You can't have peace in this kind of situation. Not even for a second."

"I'm experiencing that."

"Do you know what?" he asked, lifting his head.

"What?"

"I started praying the other night. Can you believe that? Me. I never did that before. I wasn't even raised with any kind of religion, so it's not even like I'm falling back on old habits in a time of stress. I was just laying on that sleeping bag down there, with Francine's arm wrapped around my waist, and I could see a little bit of light coming in through that little, fogged window on the far end of the room. I suddenly remembered a time when I was a kid, and my dad took me camping up north near Torch Lake. I got up out of the tent in the night to pee, and I looked up in the sky to see the biggest, brightest, whitest moon I'd ever seen. Before or since. It was huge, the sort of moon that would have a happy face on it in children's book. I thought it might wink at me, even. Everything was coated in silver—the trees, the ground, the tents, the water of the lake. While I stood there looking, a pack of deer walked out of the woods. There must have been about twenty of them—bucks with huge racks, does, little ones with spots. What do you call them? Fawns. They looked like chrome statues in that light. I stood perfectly still and watched them pass. It was so amazing that I completely forgot to pee, and I crawled back into the tent totally gob-smacked. I wondered if that was what it was like to believe in some god."

"Cool, but that doesn't seem like something a kid would think. You're superimposing your adult thought process onto your memory."

"No, really—I did wonder about that even back then," he insisted. "All the other kids went to church every Sunday and I knew that they did, but, when I asked my dad about it, all he'd say was that he didn't feel like having to get dressed up on Sunday mornings. I was happy I could just watch cartoons on Sunday when my friends had to get up and go, but, that night, I thought I'd gotten a taste of why they bothered. The real stuff. I didn't think much about it the next day, or ever again, really, not until the other night in the basement. The light coming through the window reminded me of that moonlight, and I wanted to feel that way again. I wanted to feel like something else had power over my situation. I wanted to feel that it wasn't completely in my hands, that I didn't have to make my own decisions. I could just trust and have faith, and something good would come of it. You ever wish that?"

"Sure," I said. "Every single day."

"Me, too," he agreed. "At least, now I do."

"There's a reason why guys turn to Jesus in prison," I pointed out.

"I don't want to go to prison!" he yelled, looking up at me with suddenly red eyes. I felt sorrier for him than ever before. His hands shook, pressed against his kneecaps, and he slumped further down into a fetal crouch on the floor.

"I don't want to go to jail," he said.

"You might have to, Hugo. Unless—and what do I know about it?—there could be some kind of deal in it for turning yourself in? For testifying about Francine?"

"Not going to happen," he said.

He leaned his forehead against his arms, maybe crying, maybe not.

Later that evening, with the damaged shade repaired, I took pity on Hugo and Francine and allowed them both upstairs for dinner. We sat around the dining room table passing plates of frozen chicken patties,

Kraft macaroni and cheese, and the other dregs of my cupboards to each other like it was Thanksgiving dinner. They tore through the chicken patties with gusto, and we traded old high-school gems for a while.

"Remember Charlie Farley?" Hugo asked.

"The guy who hated his name?"

"Right. In tenth grade, he started insisting everyone call him Charles, but no one would?"

"He got so pissed about it that no one would talk to him after a while—"

"—so he bought that motorcycle to try to pick up girls with …"

"But then he was just Charlie Farley with the Harley, and it was even worse!"

"How about Connie Hammer? You remember her?"

"The first girl in school to dye her hair green."

"And the last. She meant to bleach it blonde."

It felt like a friendly reunion, a nice and warm illusion to wrap up in for a little while. Hugo dropped his attitude, and Francine at least feigned an interest in our old stories. She cleared the dishes from the table when we were finished eating and then retreated to the living-room sofa. I followed to make sure that all of the blinds were drawn.

"This couch isn't very comfortable," she said, occupying it anyway.

"Too bad," I said. "You won't have to deal with it for much longer."

"I think we both look forward to that," she said.

I went back into the kitchen to wash the dishes, and, when I returned, Hugo and Francine were snuggled up on the sofa as Karen and I once had. She leaned against the arm, facing the closed window, her legs stretched out over his lap. He lounged with one hand resting on her thigh, squeezing gently. The sight of them together that way brought home underlined Karen's absence, as if I were watching a made-for-television movie of our life together—badly miscast—with all of our melodrama boiled down into one obvious, clumsy plotline.

"Make room," she commanded, and Hugo edged over to the end of the sofa.

Francine patted the cushion beside her, and I sat down.

We watched television for the better part of the evening, Hugo chortling and ridiculing every commercial and news brief thrown before him, while Francine and I stayed quiet. She leaned against him, but our thighs met at the hip, and I found myself, more than once, glancing down at the point of contact, at the curve of her leg in tight jeans. When Hugo allowed his hand to stray to her abdomen and rest there, his fingertips half-tucked under the hem of her t-shirt, she caught me looking and grinned.

"Careful, Hugo," she purred.

"Huh?" Hugo said, unaware.

"She means me," I said, standing. "I'm going to bed. You two need to go back downstairs."

"One more hour," Francine said. "Go call your wife. I know you miss her."

"That's right," I said. "I do."

"It's obvious."

"Francine is a student of body language," Hugo said.

Dumb asshole, I thought. He had never seemed so naïve to me before, but I kept my mouth shut and retreated upstairs. When a total nut-bag was turning me on, it was time to retreat. Still, I considered her suggestion and picked the phone up from the desk in the study and carried it into the bedroom. Locking myself in, I sat down and auto-dialed Karen, staring at the room as I waited for an answer. It was a nice room, large and airy, and, even on overcast days, bright and cheerful. Though the house had been built in the 1920s and the rooms were smaller than you tended to find in newer construction, our bedroom would, if it had an *en suite* bathroom, have easily fit the "master bedroom" designation that television interior designers on television liked to throw around. The bed was old, though, and most of the furniture was scuffed or marred in some way, but that only reinforced the sense of home to me. The house was slowly filling with the essence of *eau de* Hugo and Francine, alas, and I wondered if there was still time to arrest the devolution. I needed Karen. The house needed here, too. Even if only to sit and read together, or to watch television or argue, I wanted to be surrounded by my own battered, psychological furniture again and not Hugo's or anyone else's.

"What's up?" Karen answered, startling me out of my musing at what must have been the final ring before my call would have shunted to voicemail.

"Hi, there," I said.

She waited a moment before saying anything else, and the sound of her breathing on the other end of the phone felt like the tide rolling in.

20.

    Karen pressed her knees together beside on the bar stool, her skirt riding up to mid-thigh as she balanced. Her kneecaps looked to me like two of halves of a single, young grapefruit, and my interest grew as I glanced down at them, both for lack of Karen and for lack of groceries. I wanted to sling my arm around her shoulders, even just in a platonic, friendly way, just to contact that familiar outline in some way. She leaned away slightly, though, ordering a cocktail from the bartender before really acknowledging that I was there in any way.
    "You look good," I said, interrupting her order.
    "Bullshit," she laughed, finally turning to look at me. "You've turned me into a whale in only a couple of weeks!"
    "Me? The only thing I've turned you into is a memory."
    "Oh, brother!"
    The bartender brought her martini, and she fidg-

eted with the olive in the bottom of the glass, prodding it back and forth with the end of the plastic sabre skewering it.

"Do you mind if I tell you that you look like shit?" she asked.

"Not at all. I know it," I said.

"What have you been eating?"

Whatever they leave me, I wanted to answer. Instead, I answered that I'd been eating only sandwiches and not getting much sleep. She nodded and said she'd expected as much.

I ordered a second drink, having finished the first one off waiting for Karen to arrive. When the bartender slid it over, we drank in silence. The bar was crowded, and it was easy to pretend that we had nothing special to say to one another beneath the low hum of the other patrons. We could have been two new co-workers awkwardly breaking the ice for all anyone knew. Or a tired married couple searching for a practical synonym to the word "divorce." One or the other, really. I looked around the room and saw others like ourselves. A heavy man in a disheveled suit challenged me with a glare as our eyes accidentally met, and I returned my attention to Karen.

"I'm glad you decided to come," I told her.

"Well, it was nice to hear from you last night," she said.

"Was it?"

"Of course. Why wouldn't it have been?"

"Well, you'd hear from me much more often if were living in the same house."

"Probably true," she said. "But maybe not."

"Right-o. I guess we don't have much of a track-record there."

"Not lately," she agreed. "Not in a long while."

"So what do we do about that?"

"What do *you* do about it, you mean?"

She laughed, but it was forced. She wasn't kidding.

"What do you mean by that?" I asked. "I think we were both pretty at fault in that regard."

"I don't feel like I want to agree with that," she said.

"You sound like a lawyer now."

"Well, that's what I am. You've never really liked that about me, have you?"

She was right, but how could I complain? It allowed me to read and to hide away in the sort of secluded garret that very few people ever enjoyed. It was a stroke of luck on my part and a stroke of good will on hers.

"You don't have to answer that," she offered, when I didn't.

"I'm sorry," I said. "I do know better, you know."

"I didn't, actually. It's nice to hear."

"Everything you've done for me, Karen, I guarantee you it hasn't gone unnoticed. It's just that I thought, after all of these years, you'd appreciate the fact that I was at least keeping house, June Cleaver-style. Would you really work less if I worked more? You love your job, and you even love the hours it takes. I'm a bit dumbfounded by this antagonism of yours. Or what I feel is antagonism. I could be wrong about that, but I feel like it rests on principle of some sort. On principle, you think I ought to be doing something all day long while you work besides what I am doing, I mean. Am I wrong?"

She stirred her drink again and drummed her fingertips across the bar. In profile, she was someone I never anticipated meeting. Worried, angry, frustrated. The suggestion of the girl I'd fallen in love with remained discernable around her eyes and in the curve of her earlobe and in the angle of her nose. Without a doubt, though, this was the person I was in love with now, still, and would be forever, no matter what happened. Did she see in me now any remnant of College Ivan? Why would she? Who really was I now, after all? Did it matter?

I wasn't sure. Hugo was the only one who still walked around with everyone's first impressions still stickered across the back of his leather jacket. I laid my hand across Karen's and squeezed it. She broke her gaze away from the olive and looked up, unfolding a little more of herself for me.

"That's nice," she said. "I don't want to argue."

"Strange characteristic in a lawyer," I laughed.

"I prefer to be paid for it. Arguing with you only costs me."

"So let's not. Let's just discuss. Can we do that?"

"If you can, I can."

"Deal."

We dipped our toes into the pool and started out with the trivial. This even proved to be difficult for me, however, given that absolutely nothing trivial had occurred in my life since she'd left, whereas, as far as she was concerned, it consisted of nothing but the trivial. She complained about her mother's lard-laden 1970s cooking and the blow to her weight it had dealt her over the very brief time she'd been back under her roof, and I probed for pointless details about her mother's health and the antics of her three cats. I did my best to shrug off any of her requests for updates on what the hell I'd been doing with myself, but I was clumsy about it, and I could see that, although she wasn't pushing me when I turned the subject back to her mother's cats each time, she was making mental notes of my informational lapses. After two drinks and nearly an hour, we waded deeper.

"Why are you so unhappy?" she asked me.

"Me? I thought you were …"

"Oh, I am," she agreed, "but I'm not morose. Not like you've been."

"I don't think I've been morose," I said. "At least, I wasn't until you left."

"Yes, you were. You were definitely morose. For years, I would look at you walking through the living-room and just think, 'How very morose!'"

"I don't see why. I was perfectly content."

"I don't think you were," she said, waving the bartender over. "Not even close."

"It wasn't you that I was discontented with," I admitted.

"No?"

"No. It was everything else." I heard myself deliver this answer and understood it to be true for the first time.

"What everything?"

What everything? It was her, and it wasn't her. It was the life she gave me, the life I wanted, and all of the space in between. It had nothing to do with her and everything to do with her.

"Everything," I said again, at a loss. "I'm sorry I can't explain it better."

"Well, try," she said, sipping her drink.

I didn't know how to answer that, so I said nothing. I looked into my own glass. The ice cubes had nearly melted, from the inside out, and were nothing more than hollow frames. Tipping the glass back and forth, I knocked them against each other until they cracked and fell apart completely.

"No ideas?" Karen asked.

She leaned on her hand, and her left eye nearly vanished into the folds of her expanded face. It was an odd look for her, but endearing. I loved her eyes.

"Not particularly," I said. "However I touch it will

miss the mark."

"Give it a go."

"Okay, then. If you say so."

"I do."

"As you wish," I said, thinking hard.

She ordered another round of drinks and settled back on her stool to listen. Her eyes were wide, and a slight smile illuminated her pretty features. She was prodding me a little and enjoying it.

"Do you remember our second year together, in college?" I asked her.

"Mm-hmm," she said. "Vaguely."

"Do you remember that guy Phil, who lived down the hall from me in the dormitory? The guy with the glasses and the crew-cut? The one who kept playing the same damn Steve Winwood CD all day long?"

"Sure," she said.

"Well, the moment I met that guy, I knew what I didn't want to be. Something about the way he shook my hand as though we were meeting for a business luncheon when we were eighteen fucking years old, or the way he smiled, with all of his perfect teeth screaming right in my face."

"He was a bit much," Karen agreed.

"Not only that," I said. "He was finished. Complete. Most people weren't, back then. I wasn't. You certainly weren't. Almost nobody was. We were just getting started. But Phil was already what he would always be. I had this terrible sense, whenever I hung out with him, that I was standing in the presence of death—if death can be interpreted as a complete and permanent lack of momentum. He smelled like plastic."

"You're being overly literary, aren't you?" Karen laughed, accepting our drinks from the bartender.

"No," I said. "I don't think so. Phil was a walking

British Museum. He was on a straight path to his MBA, already had the car of his dreams, that silver thing out in the dorm parking-lot, and he dreamt about nothing but having that car and taking very good care of it. He wore the sorts of clothes that were so standard they would never go out of style, particularly. His hair wouldn't muss under hurricane force winds. He got up and went to church on Sunday like clockwork. He was already engaged to a girl he'd known in his hometown who was studying to be a paralegal or a dental assistant or something. He had a face like a cornfield, that guy. Just a wide expanse of the American Dream from end to end."

"Now you're being literary," Karen said, pushing my drink at me.

I picked it up and sipped it.

"It suits my point," I said. "Phil was completely empty. He didn't read anything but his schoolbooks and *The Wall Street Journal*, and he could only carry on lengthy conversations about sports or the stock market. Even those Winwood albums were just Christmas gifts from his brother, I think. The kid was done. Cooked on both sides."

"So what?" she said.

"So I felt like I was dead when I was with him. I couldn't imagine what it must have been like to actually *be* him."

"That isn't very nice."

"So what, yourself?" I said. "It's the truth. I felt it very strongly. After a while, I couldn't stand to be around him. It was as though I were being attacked by Astroturf. His handshake was even loose and clammy and totally condescending. He confirmed something I'd known about myself since I was a kid: that I wasn't like him. Or, rather, like people like him. There's this entire lifestyle, this entire way of thinking and perceiving the world around you that is so pervasive in America. It's rammed down our throats day and night, seven days a week. We watch TV and there it is. We read a newspaper, and there it is. We open our front doors, and, suddenly, we find that we're up to our ears in it. It's in the advertising, in the marketing, in the vacuousness and shallowness of the political opinions people with business degrees are able to express. We're a nation of Phils. It's nothing new, but I never wanted to be one."

"So you think I've made you a Phil?" Karen asked. "You sound like Hugo, you know."

"Not quite," I said, "but something like that. But I didn't realize it myself until I started talking just now. I really haven't been very eloquent about things, even with myself. I never meant to be … nothing, though. I never meant to just sit around and depend on you. I just … After the library axed me, I just couldn't anymore. And you expected me to, so much …"

That was the gist of it. I was a prehistoric bug in amber. I hadn't even noticed until Hugo reappeared, although I would never tell him that in a million years as he was not really the cause of any deep change, just an inadvertent trigger, the mild temblor that shakes the picture frames off of the shelf.

"It was pretty obvious that you resented me, Ivan," Karen said. "It couldn't have been more obvious. You practically slapped me in the face every morning for daring to become a lawyer. But it makes sense now: you think I'm a Phil."

"That isn't what I meant," I said. "I was only talking about myself, not you."

"I don't think so."

She closed her eyes and shook her head.

"You're the most self-involved person I've ever met," she continued. "You say things like you just did about poor Phil, who, really—and take it from the girl upstairs that he tried to hit on repeatedly, was just compensating for something pretty messed up back home—but you've lived for a long, long time without doing anything different than Phil maybe is doing right now. On the macro-level, that is. I mean, what do you do? How are you different? Or better? You had support, you had options. You stayed home. You mowed the lawn. That's great, I appreciate it, but you did have options. I gave you those options, and you didn't do anything with them."

I thought about that, sipping my drink, listening to the basketball game on the giant TV on the wall behind Karen.

"I can start now, can't?" I said after ingesting this truth. "Maybe I can change all of that. But can you? You walked out rather than having this discussion earlier, didn't you?"

She stirred her drink and nodded.

"I suppose I did," she said, "but that's because I love you and it felt like the sort of conversation that could end up being our last."

"I love you, too," I said. "With everything I've got. I don't know what to say, though. Is it really something you want to end our marriage over? I can tell you flat-out that I don't. But—you're not wrong. About me."

She didn't answer, at first. I reached out to touch her hand, half-expecting her to pull it away, but she didn't.

"I want to say yes," she said after a hard few seconds. "But I don't know if I can."

"Only one way to find out," I told her. "Come home."

"Are you sure?" she asked. "If nothing is any different, that will be that, I think."

I nodded, gripping her hand. She pulled her hand free only to wrap it around mine.

"Mom will be disappointed to lose her Scrabble partner," she laughed.

Her hand was damp from the perspiration of her glass, and I was reminded of a winter evening in college, when she and I had walked across campus in a snowstorm, the only human beings anywhere in sight. Neither of us had worn gloves, and we held hands to keep warm as we passed through the increasingly ice-covered ghost-town of a campus, our fingers digging into each other's palms.

"We can go play Scrabble with your mom every Friday if you like," I said.

"You sure you want to commit to that?"

"Just give me until tomorrow to straighten out the house," I said, leaning in close. "I've let things go a bit."

"So what?" she said. "Why not tonight?"

"Tomorrow," I said. "Just give me the benefit of the doubt."

She pursed her lips, not believing for a second that I deserved it.

Leonard walked over to my car from his porch as I pulled into my driveway and parked. His little kid face was red from the cold, and his nostrils glistened. One of his eyes was blackened and swollen.

"Hey, there—what happened to you?" I said, climbing out of the car.

"Nothing," he said. "I got into a fight."

"I hope the other guy looks even worse."

He kicked at the ground, stirring up snow and leaves.

"Guess not, huh?"

"No."

"I'm sorry."

"It's not that, it's—"

"What?"

"Forget it," he said. "My mom told me come over and ask you something."

"So ask already," I said, jamming my hands into my coat pockets.

"My grades stink," he said, looking down at his feet, his frozen breath curling back up around his cheeks like mutton-chops.

"Yeah?"

"You sure don't rake your yard much," he said, dodging his own subject.

"I've been busy," I said. "What about your grades now?"

"Well, I just haven't studied. Or didn't do it right, I guess."

"Why didn't you study?"

"I didn't see the point."

"The point is to get good grades," I said. "I guess you've figured that part out now, though?"

"My mom has. That's for sure. She asked me if I would ask you to give me some hints about how to study."

"Oh," I said, nodding. "Sure. I'd be glad to. It's been a while, but I managed to get through college."

"Cool," he said, his puffy eye leaking in the wind. "Thanks."

"You bet. Maybe next week sometime? I'm a bit log-jammed for the next couple of days here."

"Cool." He said again but then leaned to the side to look at something behind me.

"Here it comes again!" he shouted.

Across the street, a ragged-looking German Shepherd settled its haunches and defecated in the leaves covering Jim's lawn there. It looked at us barked once, its whip crack voice echoing down the street and back.

"Shit," I said. "Where did that come from?"

"That dog?" shrugged Leonard. "He's been around here for about a week. Don't you see him when you look out the window all the time? He's crazy."

"Why?"

"He doesn't know which way to go. He runs back and forth around the neighborhood, then sits and watches you, and then just gets up and leaves."

"Maybe he's just indecisive," I suggested.

"I don't know," Leonard said. "I think he's bonkers."

We receded back from the curb, giving the dog more space than just the width of the street and watched it for a little while, until it, stood, ran a quick, tight circle around Fred's lawn, and then approached the curb, sniffing the ground. It began to cross the street but then froze still when it seemed to remember that we were standing there. It barked and then bolted suddenly to the left, toward Leonard's house, and then suddenly again back in the other direction until it founded the corner of another house, several plots up, and disappeared.

"See what I mean?" Leonard whispered, awed as if he'd glimpsed the Loch Ness Monster.

"I'd better call animal control, maybe," I said.

"No!" Leonard yelled, suddenly alive. "Let him be. They'll put him down!"

I wondered if Leonard himself was somehow the source of the dog's presence on the street. I didn't recall ever seeing Ellen come home with a new puppy or anything, but I assured him that I wouldn't make the call.

Hugo and Francine waited for me in the kitchen, the door and windows latched and shuttered. They sat together on one side of the table, staring at the door as I entered as if they were two angry parents awaiting the return of a teenager breaking curfew.

"What's up?" I asked.

"You were gone a long time," Hugo said. "Good news?"

"I think so, yeah."

"Oh, good," Francine droned, not meaning it.

She laid both her hands flat in front of her. Her fingernails were painted bright pink.

"Hope you don't mind," Hugo said, noticing the drift of my attention. "It's Karen's. Francine needed a change."

"Karen's nail polish?"

"Yeah. Is that alright?"

He smiled up at me with his old means-no-harm moon face.

"Please don't rummage through my house."

"Geez, I'm sorry," he said. "Didn't think you'd care. It's my fault, really. I told her it'd be okay."

"Well, it isn't."

He slid his chair back and threw his hands in the air.

"Well, pardon my fat Aunt Bessie," he said.

"You don't have an Aunt Bessie."

"Try telling her that."

Francine played a rim-shot on the tabletop with her painted fingertips, not smiling.

"This is all getting to be a bit much, you know," I said. "I can't do it anymore."

"I know it, mate," Hugo said. "You're not built for loyalty, I get it."

"What the hell does that mean?"

"What do you think it means? You think this is easy for me?"

I felt a sort of rage coming on that I hadn't felt in a long time, a bubbling, rising heat. My belly ached. I wanted to just say something that might put me back on equal footing with him, but my mind was blank. Instead, I stepped forward and pushed him. Francine jumped to catch him, but too late. His chair toppled backwards, and he spilled out and crashed into the wall. In almost the same movement, he sprang to his feet and grabbed me by the shirt. He pressed me back against the edge of the sink, his face redder than Leonard's.

I didn't know what to do next and couldn't meet his eyes as he stared me down. I knew if I looked up from his chest, all I'd see was that he was willing to go a step or two further than I was.

"You have to go," I said instead, looking off at Francine instead of him. "Both of you. Once and for all."

"When?" he growled.

"Tonight."

Francine grabbed Hugo by the shoulders and peeled him off of me. She picked up his chair for him and sat him back down. I tried to apologize for shoving him, but I couldn't quite get the words out. I stammered, and he refused to look at me. Francine then likewise took me by the arms. I allowed her to guide me toward the back door, as if I were an unwanted guest in *their* house.

"I'm sorry about the nail polish," she said, "but this has all been very hard. He really loves you."

"I know," I said, "but none of this is my problem. Not really."

Hugo stiffened when I said that, and Francine backed away from both of us. She didn't look confident that she could pry him off of me a second time.

"How can you say that?" she asked me. "He's your best friend."

Hugo snorted and turned around.

"Ivan doesn't need friends," he said. "Ivan has his little life and his lawyer wife. He's got an electric stove and cable T.V. and a computer. He's got two cars. He's got a lawn. The past means nothing for people like him, Francie, and we're the past haunting him, reminding him that everything he has is meaningless."

"Hugo, shut up" Francine said.

She wrapped her arms around his waist and leaned back as if she were about to sing an aria.

"You mock my life," I said to him, "but this is the first place you came when you needed someplace to go. You ridicule me and my house—but you won't leave."

"Ivan, man …" he started to say, but I cut him off with a wave.

"I think the trick to you, Hugo, is that this is what you wanted all along. Guess what? It's all yours."

21.

  I passed Ellen's house and then ran on for another five blocks until my unconditioned lungs heaved, forcing me to stop, panting, to lean first on my knees and then on someone's lawn. Where was I? I looked around and didn't recognize anything, but the street looked just like mine, with very few differences. There were more pine trees here, and the air tasted as it did up north, in the Upper Peninsula. The front door on the house across the street was painted bright pink. A bulldog behind a chain-link fence at the mouth of the driveway in which I crouched stared at me with the pink tip of its tongue dangling from its open, slack jaws.
  "Hey, buddy," I said to it when something moved at great speed in the corner of my eye. I tried to catch my breath and get to my feet fast as the crazy German Shephard careened toward me, growling and barking. The bulldog followed suit. I froze, unsure how or where to retreat, and the big dog barreled straight at me with teeth bared, and I crumpled, ducking the dog's open jaws,

or hoping to, bracing myself for some sort of puncture and tearing—but the contact never came.

Instead, the animal stopped two feet from me, planted its feet, and lowered its head. At the dangerous level of my groin, it bowed and whined and did not move forward. I sidled to the side, then backwards and away, one careful step at a time. It barked once but came no further. It too backed up a step, and then another. When I took my next step, the Shepherd skittered, scrambling around me, its nails scratching the sidewalk. The bulldog stopped its own barking behind the fence. With a cock of its long face, the German Shepherd took off, flying back the way it had come, back toward home.

Dumbly, I followed, trailing it at a distance, and it soon disappeared up the block. I found myself in front of Ellen's house. From his front window, Leonard watched me, his eyes wide. I waved at him, blushing.

Ellen brought me a cup of coffee while Leonard leaned back on his sofa with a motocross magazine. His shiner had receded somewhat and now presented as a simple bruise. Ellen cleared a spot for herself on an easychair cluttered with newspapers and muted the volume of the television with a remote control.

"He loves that motocross," she said, sitting down beside her son.

"I didn't know that," I said. "What's the thrill, Leonard?"

He shrugged.

"I dunno. I rode a bike once with my cousin, and I always wanted one."

"Typical man," Ellen said.

I yawned. "That sort of thing never held my interest much."

"Why not?" Leonard asked.

"I don't know, either," I answered. "I just prefer to sit still, I guess."

"The eye is looking better," I noted.

Leonard glanced at his mother, and she looked away from him.

"What's the matter?" I asked.

"Nothing," Ellen said.

She took his magazine out of his hands.

"Don't you think it's time you did some homework?" she said to him.

He threw his magazine on the couch, and exited the room. A moment later, we could hear him creaking around upstairs in his bedroom, very shortly followed by the unmistakable sound of video game gunfire. Ellen busied herself around the living-room, picking things up and moving them to shelves and drawers. She seemed to not want to look at me, either.

"I'm sorry," I said to Ellen. "I didn't mean to bring anything sour up—"

"Don't worry about it," she interrupted. "I didn't hit him, if that's what you're thinking."

"God, no!" I said. "Why would I think that?"

She continued cleaning. I stood up and touched her arm.

"Ellen?"

Her eyes were red when she looked up, on the verge of tearing up.

"I'm sorry," she whispered. "It's my fault."

"What are you talking about?"

She sat down, and I sat beside her. She leaned in and started to cry, and I recalled how many times lately I'd felt like doing that myself.

"My boyfriend," she managed, and that was it.

This guy she was seeing—Jim ... They were a bad mix, she said. I kept my mouth shut and listened, trying hard to squeeze a lid over my reaction, especially when she confessed that she hadn't immediately told him to hit the road when it had happened. He was still around, showing up at odd hours, taking her to dinners and movies, spending the night. She hadn't put a stop to any of it, and she was afraid that it would happen again. Leonard was withdrawing further and acting up at school. More calls from the principal, more bad grades, no help around the house.

I kept quiet. I wanted to tell her to call the cops, to press charges, but, again, the fact of Hugo in basement prevented me from urging her in the right direction. Why hadn't she just done that? I was disgusted. She would have a conversation over dinner with a man who had struck her child?

The doorbell rang, and we both jumped.

"Oh, geez," Ellen said, "That's him."

I didn't say anything but got up and answered the door. Ellen was saying something like "be cool" behind me, but I wasn't listening to her. I opened the door to find a man standing there with a pizza box in one hand. He was a good eight inches taller than I was, nearly twice as broad at the chest, with a buzz cut and a black goatee. His stance was stiff and military, as if he'd just been given permission to stand at attention, and there was a supercilious smirk on his face that I wanted to wipe off right away. He looked like a cop but the sort who offered to let women get away with traffic tickets in exchange for blow-jobs.

"Who's this?" he said over my shoulder to Ellen.

She started to answer him, but I didn't give her the chance. My stomach churned again.

"You like punching kids in the face?" I snarled at him.

"Hey, who the fuck is this?" he asked Ellen again,

ignoring me entirely.

"Jim, he's just the neighbor, don't—"

He tossed the pizza box onto the floor of the porch and reached past Ellen to grab my collar.

I cocked my arm back and punched him in the face. It was the first time I'd hit anyone since I was maybe thirteen years old. He stumbled back, nearly falling down the porch stairs onto the sidewalk, but caught his balance and lurched back at me with startling speed. A thin trickle of blood oozed out of his nostril that, for a millisecond, I felt pretty good about.

I'd only pissed him off, though. His eyes narrowed and his nostrils flared as he grabbed me by my shirt and nearly lifted me off of my feet. He yanked me forward and dragged me out of the house, throwing me headfirst off of the porch and onto the sidewalk. I hit the pavement on my knees and elbows and felt my jeans tear as I skidded off of the sidewalk and tumbled into the leaves piled on the adjacent lawn. "Was that it?" I wondered, hoping—but it wasn't. Jim pounded down the steps toward me, his eyes black and focused as he reached me, and it was all I could do to get to my feet before he cannon-balled a punch of his own at the bullseye in the middle of my face.

When it landed, I remembered every story I'd ever heard about bar-fights and what happened in them. I remembered an intern at Karen's law-firm, a young girl who'd come to Michigan to work while her boyfriend was treated at the University of Michigan hospital for brain-damage inflicted by a single punch in a bar-fight. I remembered hearing about a guy who'd had three fingers chewed off. A biker I worked as a fry cook with in college had bragged about stabbing a guy in the stomach with the splintered end of a broken pool cue. These things happened. This was how grown-up fights ended.

Jim's fist drove into my face, and it felt as though my brain bounced against the back of my head. Sparks shot up through my spinal cord to the base of my skull. I staggered, and he kept at it, pounding his fists into my stomach, pummeling me over and over again until I fell backwards onto the grass, a few inches closer but a few thousand effective miles from my own front porch.

I waited to feel the toe of his boot in my stomach, but it didn't happen. I rasped away on the ground, squeezing my eyes shut, bracing myself, when Jim grunted and crashed to the ground beside me.

"Try me out, motherfucker!" someone shouted.

I opened my eyes to see Jim rising from the ground where Hugo had shoved him. Hugo circled between the two of us, his fists clenched. Hugo wasn't much bigger than I was, but he wasn't cowed. Without speaking or skipping a beat, Jim charged, and I scrambled out of the way as Hugo stepped aside, dodging him. Jim took another swing, but Hugo swept it aside and stuck his own fist in the bigger man's throat. Jim fell backwards, coughing, and Hugo jumped on him, raining blows down upon his face. He broke Jim's nose with one punch and cracked something with the next. He stomped on Jim's bent kneecap and didn't stop hitting him until he was curled into a fetal position tighter than mine had been.

"Uncle! Uncle!" Jim warbled.

"You think this is a fucking playground?" Hugo shouted.

Across the yard, Ellen and Leonard stood on their porch watching. Leonard's mouth hung open as he gripped the porch-rail, and Ellen held her hands clamped over her ears, as if drowning it out would eradicate the entire, awful spectacle.

Hugo was an enraged terror. This was nothing like the scuffles he'd fought in high school. He kicked the man even while he pleaded for him to stop and tore at his clothing like an animal. I did everything I could to keep myself from vomiting but failed. I crouched over the hibernating bushes along the house and retched, my entire digestive system rejecting what was happening. I gagged on the acid taste. When I recovered, I managed to pull Hugo off of his victim and led him out into the middle of the yard, out of arm or leg's reach from Jim. He looked over and saw my neighbors and realized how wide-open my yard really was.

"Get the fuck out of here!" I yelled at him, and he nodded.

I pushed him toward the sidewalk, and he took off, running as fast he could, his hands still curled into bruised fists at his sides.

22.

Piroshev and Millar wrote that Anosov fell to his knees on the grimy bank of the Moskva near the Krutitski Barracks, within sight of the powder magazines he'd hoped to ignite. The Novo Spaski Monastery was beyond it, he knew, though he could hardly make out the onion-shaped minarets of the Cathedral of the Transfiguration inside through the pre-dawn haze. He would have met Lyudmila not far from there, a little further toward the Krasnoholm Bridge. Ah, these were just names he'd memorized. What did he know about Moscow? Nothing. Clearly: nothing. This was not his first visit, but it would be his last, no doubt about it now. Either way, visit was all he'd ever done, and he had always departed as quickly as possible. That had in fact been the plan this time as well. Enter the city, rally a little support, borrow as much money as possible, and then get the hell out to whatever remained of his men, out in the countryside. So much for that thought. Now, here he was.

What a shitty river was the Moskva. Even in the

half-light, he could see that it was impure, running thick with the waste of the Bolsheviks. Shouting, firm and almost jubilant, explode somewhere behind him in the dark. If they hadn't seen him, they knew where to find him. The builders of Moscow had not left many bushes or trees standing for one to hide behind. Cornered against the Moskva, without his sabre, without a gun, no way to go out fighting, for whatever that would have been worth. No way to take a few of them with him. He hoped that they would not simply murder him and throw him in the river, leaving him to float away and lodge against some stone-hewn bank with the rest of the city's refuse. He had earned some sort of honorific, hadn't he? Some kind of noble death? He almost thought "military death" but then remember Piorotkin and so many others, butchered and just left to rot where they'd fallen. That was the reality of military death. No salute or folding of the flag for them. What made him think he deserved any better? The air here was foul, acrid. This river again. Piorotkin lay beneath branches, on rich although frozen soil. The soil of Russia was good earth. It would be a good thing to lay upon it like his friend before stepping forward onto the ladder to Heaven, if that destination awaited him.

Come what may. Anosov had made the decision he had made, and he reminded himself as he caught his breath and stood back up not to feel sorry for himself. He hoped that Lyudmila would not wait for him long. She was a girl of good sense, always had been. She would know when it was time to give up hope that he was coming as planned. Of that, Anosov was sure. Lyudmila would not hesitate to keep her senses and think to her own well-being. Even as an almost-child in her village, when he'd met her, she'd had full command of her faculties and understood what she needed to do to move forward with things. It was the only reason she'd chased after him, following him back into the woods where Piorotkin lay. It was the reason she'd insisted on coming into Moscow with him—so that she could slide away from him as needed. He knew that, and he hoped that she would now do it. It was nothing personal. This was a dangerous world, and a woman needed to make some hard decisions from time to time, much more often than a man ever did.

Now, footsteps in front of him, and there they were. The reds in full uniform, a little groggy and bleary-eyed, maybe, but ready for him. No one had been sleeping in the barracks. They had known he was coming, and, now, they had him.

"Pardon me, sirs, but I seem to be a little lost. Is this the road to Yaroslavl?" he asked them, grinning.

"It's the road to the dungeon for you, saboteur," the foremost of them growled, aiming his rifle at Anosov's chest. "Arms in the air."

So it wasn't to be murder here on the spot, then. Anosov felt some relief about that as he complied with the man's order. He would not be thrown into the Moskva. Interrogation, then? Maybe the firing squad? That would work. Even if blindfolded, his death would not be anonymous. Perhaps he would make a brave final statement and be remembered for his eloquence or somesuch.

Or perhaps he would simply shit his pants.

Anything was possible.

23.

After Hugo was gone, Jim collected himself and fled as well, hobbling away on one good leg. I coughed out an apology to Ellen and Leonard, but they were too stunned to hear it.

"Who the hell was that?" Ellen asked, and, still hurting and disoriented, I instinctively muttered that I'd never seen him before. She didn't buy it, but she didn't have time to think it through, either. That would come later, probably. Clearly, Hugo and Francine needed to be gone for good when it happened, along with all of their clothes and nail polish and dirty dishes and backpacks.

I waved and staggered back into my house to tell Francine to pack and go. She was nowhere in sight, though. I stood in the living room and listened for her; there wasn't a sound to be heard other than the creaking of the pipes beneath the floor and the wind outside. Francine was being as deathly quiet as I would've liked her to have been earlier on. Any FBI agents visiting at that moment would have left none the wiser, but I didn't believe that it meant she was gone. Still, the silence was beautiful. A quiet house, my old and dear friend. I needed it. Just for five minutes as I washed my pulped face. I took it. And then sat down. And didn't move.

When I did venture downstairs some time later, when I'd gathered myself, I found Francine nursing Hugo's hands in the corner. She stopped me at the base of the stairs with a sour look.

"Happy?" she said.

"You came back again?" I sighed, shaking my head at my now too often used hurricane doors. "How did you even double back so fast?"

Hugo turned around, giving his back to Francine. She rubbed his shoulders and said something soft to him that I couldn't hear.

"I'm sorry, Hugo," I said, sitting down on the stair. "But it's time."

"He needs to sleep," Francine said. "He needs a doctor."

"Are you nuts? You know the jig is up," I said. "My neighbors won't forget that spectacle for years to come. It'll be a shock if I don't have to move myself. You need to get *out* of here."

"Do I?"

"You were *seen*, Hugo! I know you're not that stupid!"

"No?" he said. "I could be. I mean, *look* at me."

"You said it, not me."

He tucked the blanket in tighter around his shoulders. His knuckles were scraped raw.

"Karen is coming back. Like, any second now. I meant to tell you today."

He stopped fussing with his blankets and just stared off. Something about him had changed over the course of the day. I'd never been the focus of his hostility before, not in any serious way. The air in the room thickened, and I backed up the stairs a bit. His silence was an intimidation tactic, a threat of more violence. I could see that he meant it that way the way he was tensed. Threats were all he had left.

"You knew the score, Hugo," I said. "This only worked as long as it did because Karen wasn't here."

"So it's time to throw out the trash, eh?"

"You promised you would go. Long ago," I said.

"And you'd hold me to that? After I just saved your ass? Who the fuck was that guy?"

He stood and turned around, and his eyes were sharp coals, pinpoints burrowing through me.

"My neighbor's boyfriend, apparently, but what does it matter? Thank you! I mean, fuck: thank you! God knows what would have happened, but you've got to go. You know I wish you weren't in this mess, but you didn't expect that this could go on indefinitely? I can't share this with you, Hugo."

"I'll tell you what," he said. "I didn't expect you would turn out to be the sort of guy who'd throw a woman in need out in the middle of the winter. Francie can't take much more of this, Ivan. Can't you see that?"

True enough, she really didn't look like she could stand much more. Her hair was stringy, and her cheeks were hollow. She didn't look like a software engineer now so much as a late-stage meth addict.

"I didn't put her into this position," I said. "She did it herself. And thanks to your brilliant idea. If you turned yourself in, you'd reach some terminal point on all of this and at least get some clean clothes and a meal."

"Seriously? You must be joking. What did those Feds say to you, Ivan?"

He walked to the bottom of the stairs and glared up at me. I held my ground, though, and resisted the instinct that told me to keep backing up.

"We're not leaving," he said.

"You are."

"Or what?"

"I'm not giving you an ultimatum," I said. "Don't look for one. Just be as good a friend as I've been and go while you can. Before you screw things up for me worse than I've screwed them up for myself."

"But Francine is sick," he insisted.

"Oh, she is not!"

"Well, she will be, if we keep this up."

She didn't answer. He walked back to her side and held her hand, petting it like a kitten.

"You'll have to go tonight," I said. "After dark. That is, if the police don't come to arrest us all by then."

Neither of them responded in any way, and I was glad for it.

24.

  For the next few hours, we maintained no contact. They were as silent as death in the basement, and I tip-toed around the house, afraid to rock them into action. If they ventured up to eat in the kitchen or use the bathroom, I never saw them. When night fell, I ventured down to rouse them. Naturally, Hugo was nowhere in sight when I hit the bottom of the stairs. Francine sat alone beside my workbench.
  "Okay, then," I said.
  "Okay," she replied.
  "Where's Hugo?"
  "Out," she sighed.
  "Where?"
  She gave me a hang-dog look and said nothing. I returned her silence and sat down on the stairs. Her feet were bare, and she rubbed her toes together on the rough floor.
  "He went to get supplies," she said, finally. "For our trip."

"Ah. I see. That's a bit dangerous, isn't it?"

"What choice do we have?"

I didn't bother with that one.

"I've lost my shoes," she said.

I pointed her shoes out to her in the corner, and, she thanked me and crawled, half-staggering and swaying, toward them. Was she high? I didn't smell anything. She pulled the shoes over beside Hugo's denim hen backpack, against the wall, and then reached into the pack to retract a pack of gum. Unwrapping a strip, she folded it into her mouth and tossed the balled foil onto the floor.

"Hey, don't leave evidence," I said.

"We won't even leave ourselves," she said.

She chomped on the gum, smacking her lips, and then she picked up the ball of foil between thumb and forefinger and popped it into her mouth, swallowing it whole, along with the gum.

The display successfully unsettled me, but I decided not to acknowledge it at all. Before I'd formulated a further comment, the hurricane doors creaked open slightly and Hugo slanted in.

"I got everything we need, Francie," he said.

He strode across the room and dropped a plastic shopping bag into Francine's lap. She dug through the bag, nodding and shaking her head at intervals as she inspected the items he'd retrieved.

"No good," she muttered. "Great! No, no …"

Hugo ignored her negative reviews and beamed at the positive ones. He clapped his hands and rubbed the redness from his hands. All the while, he pretended not to see me.

"Damn, it's cold out there," he said.

"That's not good," she said.

"No, you've got to look at it positively," he said. "At least we'll be well preserved till spring if we croak."

He rubbed her shoulder.

"Waiting to lock the door behind us, Ivan?" he asked, without looking at me.

"Maybe," I answered, but he was already whispering something in Francine's tilted ear.

I got up and walked up the stairs but then stopped short of opening the door when I heard someone enter the house through the front door.

"Ivan?" Karen called, her voice dampened and worried through the floorboards. "Hello?"

I motioned for Hugo and Francine to keep quiet and still, but they knew the routine without my input. They held the shopping bag still between them, one hand each grasping the wrinkled plastic. Karen covered quick ground through the house, stomping through the dining room toward the kitchen. I lurched up through the door to head her off before she could peek down the stairs.

"Hey, there!" I said, trying my best not to look shocked. "What are you doing here?"

She smiled, propping the kitchen door open with her foot.

"Recon," she said. "Wanted to make sure you'd cleared all of your girlfriends out."

"Girlfriends?"

"I'm kidding. Obviously."

She strode through the kitchen and looked around at the countertops and walls as if it had been thirty years since she'd seen them last.

"This place feels so weird now," she said.

"How so?" I asked.

I leaned against the basement door.

"It's different," she said, running her fingers along the edge of the sink. "It all feels brand new, like some place I've never been before. But I know I have, so it all really feels askew."

"That's natural, I suppose."

"Is it? I wonder. I didn't think it would be any big deal coming back, but it was, right away. It hasn't even been that long, has it? I might have been on vacation somewhere, but, as soon as I walked through the front door and didn't see you sitting right there in the living-room, it was a big deal."

"Oh."

She toured the kitchen inch by inch until she ended up in front of the basement door with me. She stood close, and I could feel her breath on my cheek. Through the window in the back door, I could see that it was snowing again, much harder. This could be the first snow that really accumulates, I thought. Not good for people who didn't prefer to leave tracks. It fell over the yard, sticking to the fence, the grass, coating the bare branches of the enormous tree. Two young kids, packed into snowsuits, ambled down the alley like mummies. Cold air seeped into the kitchen around the door, and Karen, buttoned into her coat, wrapped her arms around me and held me close.

"This doesn't feel much different," she said.

"No?"

"No," she said.

I kissed her, and she tasted sweet, like the sticky cheek of a baby. She pressed her hands into the small of my back, and I unbuttoned her coat and slid mine inside. We kissed again and left the kitchen. In the dining-room, we stopped beside the large cherry wood table that, built for dinner parties of ten or twelve, had almost never accommodated more than two. She let go of me to look around, pacing the room as she had the kitchen, touching objects on shelves, rubbing at the surface of the table with her thumb, then returning. She took my hand and pulled me into the living-room, where she repeated the process, stopping particularly at the photographs on the mantel. We traveled in and out of the foyer, back through dining-room, up the stairs, past the study, and into the dark bedroom in this way, half-tumbling, wrapped together, exorcising something neither of us wanted to put a real name to. Beside our bed, she untucked my shirt.

"Not now!" I gasped.

"Why not?"

I couldn't tell her.

She waved me off and continued, and I went with it, unable to come up with any believable protest. We undressed each other piece by piece, a shirt here, a shoe there, the way we had in college, beside ourselves with anxiousness. Her bare body looked like an ice sculpture as I lay down beside her on the mattress. My hand on her stomach was a shadow. I covered her and tasted her and pulled myself onto and inside of her with the greatest need I'd felt since I was eighteen. She wrapped her thighs around me and sighed, her entire respiratory system working to catch up to my own exhalation.

I got out of bed and dressed again, worrying that Karen would wake and ask me why I was bothering, but I finished anyway and crept downstairs to find Hugo and Francine sitting together against the water heater like two nesting chickens. Francine's feet were still bare, and the shopping bags Hugo had returned with sat unmolested where they had dropped them. They didn't look at all ready to depart.

"Good for you," Hugo whispered, his face betraying no evidence of his actually being happy for me. He was wearing his fight-face, the hard, empty stare he'd worn ever since we'd faced off in the kitchen.

"You about ready?" I asked.

Hugo and I both looked at Francine for any answer for some reason, but she didn't respond. She'd given up pretending. Her fight-face was permanent, tattooed on.

"Is Karen leaving soon?" Hugo asked.

"No," I said. "She isn't. Hopefully, not ever. See what I mean?"

"You want us to leave now," Francine said.

"Yes, goddammit!"

We stared at each other for an awkward few minutes, and I realized how tired I was of looking at both of them. Everything about them was worn out and contrived.

"You think she'll make you happy this time?" Hugo asked.

I couldn't tell if he was mocking me or serious.

"I don't know," I said. "Who can tell?"

"Why bother then?"

"What else is there?"

He didn't seem to have an answer, and I turned to leave.

"You won't make her happy," he said, when I was halfway up the stairs.

"That's for her to decide."

I thought I heard Francine laugh when I shut the door behind me, but the optimistic shadow buried beneath my ribcage didn't want to believe that the rasping, cawing sound I heard scratching at the darkness behind me was anyone's expression of amusement. No. I pressed my ear against the door and listened again. She was crying.

I don't know why I thought Hugo and Francine would really be gone when I made my way back down to the basement in the morning, but my full and genuine expectation was to find the place devoid of all life, as featureless and empty as it had always been. This thought buoyed me, as much as the thought of Karen waiting for me upstairs did. By the time I reached the bottom of the stairs, though, I already knew what I would see. I heard the rustling and the whispering. Hugo and Francine lay pressed together on their sleeping bag, pretending to be asleep.

"Oh, come on!" I spat.

They groaned and mumbled as if only just wakening from deep sleep.

Hugo shielded his eyes with his hand as if the sun had followed me down the stairs and was hovering behind me.

"It's time," I said. "Past time, even. You'll have to go in broad daylight now."

Francine pulled herself free of Hugo and sat up, Indian-style. She wore only a t-shirt and a pair of nearly transparent, flowered panties through which her dark pubic triangle was visible.

"Well, about that," Hugo said.

"Yeah?"

"I don't think we can do it."

"You don't have a choice," I said, resolved.

"You'd call the cops?" he said.

"You'd make me do that?"

He looked at Francine. She nodded and rubbed her thighs as if they'd fallen asleep. He sighed and leaned his forehead on her shoulder, and she whispered something to him, stroking his hair back from his ears and holding his hand against her leg.

"I don't know what to do," Hugo said, holding her. "I don't know where to go. I don't know what to do."

"You can turn yourself in," I suggested.

He was at the end of his rope, able to feign mental and physical health only as long as he was stabilized in my basement, a fixed and certain point. He turned the idea over.

"I can't do that," he said, looking at Francine.

"He can't do that," she agreed.

"Well, what then?" I said. "What *can* you do, Hugo? This is it. This is the end of the line."

"I can keep going."

"Where? How? You don't know. You said so yourself."

I sat down on the sleeping bag with them and looked him in the eye.

"I can do it," he said, believing it. "Those Sixties radicals did it. You know, the ones who blew up ROTC buildings and stuff. They only stopped when they wanted to."

"You said yourself that they got tired, that there was only so far they could go with that. And they had friends, Hugo. You only have me. And I can't do that for you."

The water running through the pipes in the ceiling stopped as Karen finished her shower. The boards in the walls creaked as she walked through the upstairs hallway.

"I have to go back up there," I said. "You have to go or let me call the cops for you. I'll be with you all the way, man. And so will Karen. You wouldn't have to worry about legal representation."

"That's not the point," he said.

Francine crawled out of his grasp and leaned over me to pull his backpack toward her.

"What is the point?" I whispered.

"I'm afraid," he said after a hard pause. "The details don't matter because I'm too scared to do it."

He looked at me with wide, hollow eyes, and the color he'd regained over the past weeks leaked away. His hungry pallor returned, and he wrung his hands together, scrubbing at his bruised knuckles like an obsessive compulsive, frowning with a quivering lip like a little kid.

"You have to get past it," I said. "I'm sure I'd be terrified, too, but it won't get any better any other way."

"The legal system sucks," he said.

"I know it," I agreed. "But you're in good hands with us, Hugo. You have been all these weeks. Take advantage of it. You're not some cast-off depending on court-appointed lawyers to avoid the noose."

Francine opened up the backpack and began pulling things out of it. She removed several t-shirts and the science fiction paperback that Hugo had complained about, some shaving cream, and a razor without a blade in it.

"What are you looking for, baby?" he said, but she ignored him and kept digging.

"I don't know, man," he said, returning his attention to me.

"Well, you have to do something," I said. "You can't stay here. If you can't think where else to go, that doesn't leave many options, does it?"

"I guess not."

I kept at him.

"You didn't do anything that awful, Hugo," I said. "You didn't kill anybody. You don't need to be running like this."

He looked at Francine again and shook his head.

"No," he said. "No, she can't make it without me. She wouldn't know what to do. All we can do is stay low and keep our heads down. If I'm with her—if she's with me—we can work this out. We just need some time and some safe place to spend it in. And I don't know any other place. And neither does Francie. Do you, honey?"

"No," she said, over her shoulder.

She then lifted something I was already too familiar with from movies and TV shows, that ominous and metal thing that I knew had been in Hugo's backpack all of this time. The gun. A hand-gun, a revolver, whatever they called it. It was now pointed at me.

"Everything you say is shit," she said, clicking the safety off. "You're only thinking of yourself."

She stood and backed away from me, allowing herself ample area to cover me if I moved. She stood like a cop, arm straight but not tense, her other arm folded over to block the recoil of a shot, her knees cocked. In her underwear, she made for a strange sight, but the gun scared away any scent of the comical. A gun was pointed at me. It didn't seem real. My neck was cold. Was this how Anosov had felt?

"Put that thing down, Francie," Hugo hissed, moving away from both of us.

"Cops are corrupt," she said.

"You watch too much T.V.," I said.

"That cop tried to kill us," she said, "with this gun. It's ours now."

"She's got a point," Hugo said. "You know about that kid in Ferguson, Missouri? It's vicious. Especially if they think no one is going to worry about you afterward."

"That isn't true in your case."

"Close enough."

"Close enough for what?"

The sound of the door opening at the top of the stairs shut us all up.

"Ivan?" Karen called from above.

She marched suddenly down the stairs without waiting for my answer, slowing and stopping to duck under the overhanging ceiling, stopping cold halfway down when she spotted the three of us frozen in our tense formation below. Francine sucked her breath in.

"Karen, get out!" I shouted, and my volume startled everybody.

Francine swiveled and trained the gun on Karen, and both Hugo and I both jumped at her. He reached for her arm while I tripped on one of the plastic bags. Francine ducked, dodging both of us. Her foot caught me in the chest, flinging me backward with the momentum of my own in-progress stumble. I crashed into the concrete wall, skull first. Then: a shot, a real gunshot, a splitting reverberation that rattled the water heater and furnace and knocked me fully down onto my side. As the echo died off, something crashed to the floor.

I uncurled and saw Karen lying at the bottom of the stairs, clutching at her abdomen, where a dark stain was spreading over her ruined shirt. She gritted her teeth, groaning, and then wailing. Hugo sat beside her, his eyes wide and mouth pronouncing some word over and over again.

"Holy shit!" he gasped.

Francine stood rooted, staring hard and cold at my wife, unsurprised. She held the gun poised, half-cocked at the end of her bent arm, apparently ready to fire again.

"Karen!" I shouted.

I rushed to her side and tried to hold her, but she shoved me away.

"Hurts..."

"You freak!" I screamed at Francine. "What the fuck?"

Francine lowered the gun and then dropped it, swiveling around toward the hurricane doors, her now empty hand thrust out as if she expected any of us—Hugo included—to attack. She rounded the furnace and then bolted up the short stairs, unlatching the big doors and diving up and out. A rush of cold wind blew into the basement, and Karen coughed, shivering. She clamped her hand around my wrist and tugged my hand to her belly. I laid my palm flat over her wound, and the blood seeped up between my fingers. My stomach turned, and, choking on my own breath, I turned to Hugo.

"Oh, my god," he whispered. "My god."

"You did this!" I said. "You did this!"

"I'm sorry!"

He leaned over us to inspect Karen's leg. He pressed a single, long finger to the back of my hand and allowed Karen's blood to coat his fingertip.

"Oh, fuck …," he said. "I'm so sorry!"

The wind blew through again, and Hugo pushed away from us, teetering into the middle of the room where he grabbed his jacket and backpack.

"I'm sorry!" he shouted.

He ran up and out the way Francine had gone. Leaning back in, down through the hurricane doors, he took one last, stricken look at us, lying there, and then slammed the doors shut.

"Hugo!" I shouted after him, not for a minute hoping that he would stop or come back.

I rested Karen gently against the stairs and ran upstairs for my cell phone. I found it and dialed 911 as I tripped back down the stairs to her.

26.

Agent Khurram offered me a paper cup of coffee from the waiting room vending machine.

"Gonna be a long night," he said, his perfect teeth shining.

I thanked him and took the cup. The coffee was terrible, like hot water with a brown crayon melted in it, but better than nothing. He watched me drink with what appeared to be genuine concern. I swallowed it in a few gulps and crushed the cup in one hand, disregarding the dregs that dripped out of its wreckage into my palm. Nurses and residents in sea-green surgical shirts hurried by without paying me any attention, but I felt as though they were all talking, fixing me in the center of some plotless gossip.

"That's the guy," I swore I could hear from around every corner, behind the information counter, under the tables. "The one the Feds are grilling!"

In fact, I was not being grilled in any way. Not now. It had already happened, or it would happen again.

Carl and Khurram had arrived with the cops, along with the ambulance, leading an impressive, charging array of law enforcement and safety vehicles into my drowsy neighborhood. They'd burst into the living-room at the head of a platoon of deadly serious men and women in black Kevlar vests, baseball hats, and protective goggles. They hadn't waited for me to show them to the basement but plowed through the house like bison until they located Karen, still lying on the basement stairs. Khurram reappeared to take me aside and inform me that I would be coming with them. Carl remained downstairs to ensure that the never pristine basement was left unscathed by the paramedics who, like Hugo and Francine, found the basement easier accessed through the hurricane doors in the back.

    I watched, from so far away, as they hoisted my wife out through the doors on a stretcher and roared her off into the night in a screaming ambulance in which I was not allowed to join her. I was handcuffed and stuffed into the back of Khurram and Carl's car. Ellen and Leonard and the rest of the neighbors gawked, milling, whispering god-knows-what to one another. As Carl revved the engine and backed away from the ring of police cruisers surrounding it, Khurram began to ask me questions, probing in a voice as silken smooth as a midnight DJ spinning Al Green records. I answered everything as well as I could, my mind whirring, creaking to come up with a plausible story that wouldn't implicate either Karen or myself, but, in the end, by the time we pulled up to the hospital where the ambulance had taken her, I wasn't the least bit sure what I'd said other than that I managed never to say the name "Hugo."

    It was enough for now, apparently. Khurram was left to baby-sit me in the lobby while Carl kept an eye on my sleeping wife, once she was out of surgery and intensive care. I'd nearly burst into tears at the news that Karen would be okay, and Khurram kindly acknowledged my relief by leaving me alone for a little while. His coffee wound its way through my digestive system, and that was good enough. He hummed beside me, his DJ voice flattening into a resonant trilling so low that, as quiet as it was, still stood out amidst the general clatter of the emergency room. A baby in the next set of pre-molded, plastic chairs howled in his mother's arms.

"What's that you're humming?" I asked Khurram.
"An old song from home," he said.
"Pakistan?"
"Yes," he nodded.
"When did you leave there?"
"When I was very small," he said. "I don't really remember it."
"That's too bad."
"It is," he said. "But that's what the song is for."
"Am I in trouble?" I asked him.
He laughed a little, and I wasn't sure why. It either made me nervous or comforted me, and I couldn't tell which.
"I can't say," he said.
"You don't know or you're not allowed to tell me?"
"Both," he nodded. "Then again, what the hell. You're fucked, Mr. Tracy."
We stared at the floor until Carl reappeared, lumbering down the long corridor toward us.
"Here's the man," Khurram said, pointlessly.
His partner stepped up, and Khurram stood to greet him. I didn't feel as though I should do anything provocative in any way, so I stayed put, looking up at him.
"She's still out of it," Carl grumbled.
The crying baby quieted as its mother rocked it.
Khurram shook his head at him and said some-

thing under his breath that I couldn't understand. Carl nodded in response, and they took a few steps away from me and continued to speak. I picked up bits and pieces, despite their best efforts. Karen, it seemed, had awakened briefly, had not said much, only that she couldn't recall who had shot her, though it wasn't me, which I gathered from their respective head bobs in my direction at that moment was never a realistic consideration for them. I could shoot someone, couldn't I?

"Typical lawyer," Carl sighed.

I laughed, and they dampened their voices further.

After a while, Carl and Khurram sat down beside me again.

"Am I under arrest?" I asked them.

"Not at the moment," Carl said. "But someone shot your wife and someone attacked your neighbor's boyfriend, and we know it was the same guy. I think you know that, too. So no guarantees about jack until we get what we want."

I nodded and tried to bury a shiver.

"You okay?" Khurram asked

I forced a deep breath into my lungs and collected myself.

"Yeah," I said.

"I think the nurses will let you see your wife—if you want," Carl said.

"Why wouldn't I want to see her?" I asked.

The big man shrugged.

"Why would someone shoot her?" he said. "Your marriage hasn't been going too good, has it?"

I declined to respond.

I thanked them without feeling thankful but then didn't stay to watch them depart. Hurrying down the hall, I felt their eyes on the back of my neck the whole time.

I found Karen behind a flimsy curtain, half-asleep. Her skin was pale, and her arms lay stretched along her sides, with IV tubes inserted into both of them. Her breathing was shallow and quick, a sort of panting, like the German Shepherd's. She was conscious and followed my movement through slitted eyelids.

"Hey," I said, taking her limp hand in mine.

She mouthed "hey" in reply. I'd never seen her so weakened, even during her worst illnesses, and the emotion I'd held in check for the agents burst forth as she squeezed my hand with only the strength of a small child. I bent over her and tried to kiss her, but she managed to turn her head just enough to dodge me.

"I'm sorry," I said, thinking that it didn't sound any more convincing coming from me than it had from Hugo.

"Shh," she whispered, tugging her hand weakly from mine.

My hand felt strangely warmer without hers in it.

"What a mess," I said, chuckling lamely as if I'd just dropped a pudding on the floor.

She did not look as though she was about to laugh, however. Her eye-lids fell shut, but, then, opened again, wider. I guessed that they'd pumped her full of some sort of drug that she was fighting as best she could.

"I got shot," she slurred.

"I know. You're going to be okay, though. The bullet didn't hit anything good, apparently. Went straight through."

It was true, but I felt stupid saying it. Shot was shot, wasn't it?

"This is so weird," she said.

"Yeah," I said. "It is."

"Where is he?" she asked, dropping her voice further, and we both knew who she meant.

"I don't know."

"I'm glad."

"Me, too."

"Are you?"

Was I? Yes. But not completely. How he'd looked, gasping "I'm sorry!" over and over on his way out of the hurricane doors. I did want to know where he was. I still wanted him to be okay. Did he catch up with Francine or head off in a new direction? I wanted to believe that he'd made the latter decision, that he'd run for a while but then come to his senses and stopped. That he'd show up one morning at FBI headquarters in Spokane, Washington, or Tallahassee, Florida, with his hands and pockets empty, alone and ready to change things. Not likely, really. This time, I really had probably seen him for the last time. I told myself that I was happy about that, but the thought that kept creeping up over me was that we hadn't even really said goodbye. I told Karen what she needed to hear.

"Yes," I said.

"Good," she answered, squeezing my hand again. "They were supposed to be gone."

"They weren't supposed to have been there."

"I know. It was stupid."

I brushed a strand of her hair from her forehead, which she usually preferred free of stray bangs.

"Do you still want to come back?" I asked her.

She gazed out the window, but there was nothing to see. It was night-time and dark outside and only showed two hollow-eyed ghosts, not just one, the way the car window had on the way back from Saginaw. I'd transformed the both of us.

"I don't know …" she started.

"—I don't blame you," I agreed, interrupting her.

She turned from the window to face me, and there was some softness in her moist eyes.

"I *feel* like I shouldn't," she whispered, "but I do want to."

"You do?"

"Yeah," she said, "but wanting isn't everything."

She then drifted off, this time for the duration, and I was relieved to not have to ask her the next logical question: *Why?* I didn't want to know right now. I just wanted to know whether we shared some realization that nothing had ever really disappeared in the years we'd spent learning each other's bad habits and mood swings. That everything we'd once had was still there—excitement, laughter, passion, love, youthful ambitions both fulfilled and unfulfilled. That, in that single moment before she fell asleep, there were still bottles of Boone's Farm passed back and forth, impromptu car trips to apple orchards and the beach, roller-coaster rides, gin-rummy games, midnight movies, the Chicago Art Institute, fireworks, and everything else we'd ever enjoyed together and talked about doing again but never did. There, in that moment, I wanted the past and the future to coalesce and hang there without any fading or diminishing of its glow. I wanted that shared moment—just three glitter-coated seconds—to be simply us and ours. I wanted Karen to have agreed in that space of time that it wasn't possible for us to be happy without each other, despite our petty miseries, to agree that anything else would have meant piercing the fabric of time and stepping forth from the world of running water onto a barren moon-scape.

Karen just slept, though, and I sat and watched her breathe, something I hadn't done since the first nights we'd spent together in college, lying after our first fumbling attempts at sex in the undependable light from the flames of melting candles, so thrilled to be in bed beside this incredible girl, wanting to take in every second of the sight of her, until the last candle on her dorm-room desk shivered down to nothing. I caressed her freckled arm beneath the loose sleeve of her hospital gown and vowed that, in whatever direction our moment might veer once she awoke, I would leap into action, without tripping, without fumbling, and steer it back. I could still march in formation behind Anosov's charge, kick the lock off of my cell door, and take aim at the one thing that I had ever really aimed for.

Anything was possible.

ACKNOWLEDGEMENTS

It has taken me a while to get this thing into print, and some thanks are due to quite a few people who've lent either this book or myself personally an ear over the years.

After revising this page a couple of times, I've decided to leave out those who are no longer with me, in whatever respect, as I am dubious of both the existence of an afterlife and of the value of the forgiveness of personal slights.

That said, thank you first and foremost to Zeynep and Arya.

Further gratitude to: Dr. Michael F. "Mikey Fear" Verde, Kelly McGuire, Bart Bealmear, Ralph Heibutzki, J.D. & Barb House, Kiliç Arslantürk, Jessica Sahutoğlu, Andrew Fabbro, Don Hargraves, Kiri Salazar, Laura Salazar, Troy Christensen, and Keith Jon Nipper, Craig Bernier (wherever he is), and Robert Schneider (the other one) for feedback, guidance, inspiration, and example.

ABOUT THE AUTHOR

John Hilla is a writer, poet, and musician living in the foothills of Detroit with his wife, daughter, and two senile cats.

The former editor and publisher of *Rebel Route* Magazine ("Rock & Roll, Past & Present"), John has written numerous album and book reviews and 300 bad songs.

His poetry has most recently appeared in *The Cimarron Review*, *The Bosporus Review of Books*, and *The 3288 Review*.

CPSIA information can be obtained
at www.ICGtesting.com
Printed in the USA
FSHW010627140321
79436FS